Titles in the Needlewoman series
A Square of...
Cross Stitch

# Cross Stitch

# Cross Stitch

## Amanda James

**Sequel to A *Stitch in Time***

*Where heroes are like chocolate – irresistible!*

Published 2015 by Choc Lit Limited
Penrose House, Crawley Drive, Camberley, Surrey GU15 2AB, UK
www.choc-lit.com

A CIP catalogue record for this book is available
from the British Library

ISBN 978-1-78189-199-5

MIX
Paper from
responsible sources
FSC® C018072

Printed and bound by Clays Ltd

*For Esmé*

# Acknowledgements

I would like to thank my husband, daughter and immediate
family for their continued love and support, my wider
friends and fellow Choc Lit authors for their comradeship
and encouragement, the Choc Lit team and panel (Olivia,
Betty, Julie H, Sheri, Linda F, Janice, Vanessa, Caroline
and Margaret J) and my fantastic editor who was as usual
patience personified, has a great sense of humour, and
of course helped to make this book the best it can be.

Special thanks goes to those readers of the
prequel, *A Stitch in Time* who constantly
chivvied me until I produced this sequel!

# Chapter One

Sarah Yates, part-time teacher and time traveller extraordinaire, looked at her reflection in the bedroom mirror and felt her heart do a rumba against her ribs. Even if she did say so herself, she looked beautiful, serene and, yes, she had to admit it, a little bit radiant. The ivory silk gown clung in all the right places and rippled sumptuously to the floor. Sarah smiled as she noticed that with her slightest movement, the silk caught the light and poured material across her curves like cream over a spoon.

A single string of pearls adorned her neck and the matching teardrop earrings added lustre to her peaches-and-cream complexion. Her fingers traced the handmade lace decorating the neckline, until it tumbled to a halt, revealing just a hint of cleavage rising and falling in time with the rumba. And Sarah was happy to note that her long golden hair, twisted artistically into Botticelli style tendrils with some side tresses secured behind her head in a simple pearl clasp, looked absolutely perfect.

Pale blue eyes, bright with emotion, looked up from her appearance and locked onto her mum's, brimming with tears as she stood behind her. Sarah's lips trembled into a smile and her mum answered it, her pride and joy almost tangible. This was it. No going back. In an hour's time Sarah would walk down the aisle, join hands with John, forsake all others and change her name from Yates to Needler.

Gwen pulled a tissue out of her bag and dabbed at her eyes. 'Bloody Norah, look at me.' She fanned her hands at her face. 'I'm going already. I'll look like a panda on the photos!'

'Told you not to wear black and white.' Sarah chuckled.

'I meant the mascara—' Gwen began, and then grinned.

1

'Oh, har har … seriously, love, you look absolutely beautiful. That Karen couldn't hold a candle to you today, and if Neil could see you—'

'Please, Mum.' Sarah held up her hand and turned around. 'I don't want to hear their names mentioned, especially today of all days. This day is full of joy. Any hint of bitterness will spoil it.'

Gwen stepped forward and hugged her daughter. 'I'm sorry, love, of course you don't. You'll have a new husband soon, not that other rat! I'm just *so* pleased you have met John and are happy.' Gwen sniffed and dabbed at her eyes again. 'There was a time when I thought you might not be.'

Sarah pinched her mum's cheek and shot her a bright smile. 'Yes, well I thought that too, but those days are gone. Now, go downstairs and pour us both a glass of champers. We have a bit of a wait until the carriage gets here.'

Sarah turned back to the mirror, applied a little more lip gloss and tried to get her heart rate under control. Adrenalin raced through her blood stream like wildfire and if she didn't douse it with a splash of calm, she'd get her lines mucked up at the altar, or get her dress tangled round her legs and fall on her arse, or faint as John was slipping the ring on her finger. Perhaps it would be all three knowing her.

As she stepped away from the mirror to follow her mum downstairs, Neil's face surfaced in front of her eyes. He looked surprised, nervous, his Adam's apple bobbed up and down in his blotchy neck like a float on a lake. Sarah closed her eyes. She tried to dispel the memory of that day. That God awful day when she'd challenged her ex-husband outright about being the father of her best friend's baby. Why on earth had Mum brought him up? Those were the last thoughts she wanted in her head right now.

A heavy sigh escaped her lips. It wasn't all Mum's fault.

2

She had to admit that Neil had been hovering like a bad smell even before Gwen had mentioned him. Wedding days tended to do that, didn't they? Charged with more emotion than an angry bull, occasions such as these threw up all sorts of memories and feelings. Sarah thought of her first wedding day when she'd been younger, more naive, more trusting. It wasn't as if she were having doubts about John, or that she still had any vestiges of love for Neil, but she guessed the main reason he'd popped up was that she was still scared of being hurt again.

But that was only natural, wasn't it? It had been eighteen months since Neil had left her and set up home with her best friend and become a father, something he had never wanted to be with Sarah, even though he knew how much she had longed for a child. She'd promised herself that she'd never allow a man to wound her so deeply again, never give her heart away so foolishly again and certainly *never* get married again. But then she'd met John and everything had changed.

In her mind John's handsome face now quashed any thoughts of Neil. His deep green eyes twinkled and his wide sensuous mouth broke into a heart-stopping smile. That smile never failed to give Sarah goosebumps. She thanked her lucky stars for the umpteenth time that such a wonderful guy wanted to spend the rest of his life with her. And despite their 'less than normal' relationship, she was now the happiest woman in the world.

'Sa-rah, you coming down for a glass of champagne?' Ella, Sarah's sister, shouted up the stairs.

'Er, does the earth revolve around the sun?' Sarah shouted back and hurried out of the room.

The little village of Moorendsworth, on the outskirts of Sheffield, looked like something from a Dickensian novel as Sarah's horse-drawn carriage clattered through the cobbled streets. The breeze twirled a baton of crisp autumn leaves, blowing their red and gold hues high above the carriage. Some of them settled on Sarah's hair, confetti sprinkled by nature's hand. The breath of autumn filled her lungs and pinched her cheeks and the sky painted itself a forget-me-not blue. Just perfect.

Gwen sat beside her with a beaming smile, waving at people here and there as if she was the queen. She looked at her daughter. 'Isn't it a beautiful day?'

'It certainly is, Mum. The best.'

A cloud darkened Gwen's sunny visage. 'If only your dad were sitting here instead of me.'

Sarah squeezed her hand and swallowed a lump of emotion. 'I know ... but don't let's get upset; I know he's with us in spirit.' Sarah realised it would be eight years in December since her dad had died of cancer, though there wasn't a day that passed without something that reminded her of him.

The driver guided the horse up the driveway to the tiny eighteenth-century church flanked by chestnut trees, and the photographer knelt to get the first shots for the album.

Ella, standing at the door, blew Sarah a kiss before entering the church to let everyone know the bride had arrived. She popped out again a few minutes later with Angelica, her daughter, who waved her hand shyly at the bride. Six year old Angelica was Sarah's only bridesmaid and dressed in Sarah's favourite colour – turquoise. Turquoise might not have worked on everyone, but with Angelica's sandy curls and freckles, she looked like the personification of a summer's day at the beach.

The driver's hand felt warm and dependable as Sarah took it. Thank goodness he was there to help her down from the carriage. Her legs trembled like jelly on a plate and she couldn't stop them as she placed her foot on the first step.

4

'Watch where you're putting your feet, Sarah. We wouldn't want you falling in a puddle, would we?' he said with a smile.

'That would be just like me to do something like tha—' Sarah's voice caught in her throat as she watched a woman walking up the path towards the church, a tall raven-haired beauty dressed in crimson, wearing the most ridiculously high heels in the world. The red slash of her mouth matched the dress perfectly, and as she got nearer to Sarah, the slash curled into a triumphant smile.

*Oh my word ... shit, it's Josephina.*

'What's wrong, love?' Gwen frowned at the expression of disbelief on her daughter's face.

The woman waved an expensive looking bit of camera kit at Jack, the photographer, and called, 'Hey there, everyone. I'm Hazel, Jack's assistant. Sorry I'm late. I forgot the other lens.'

Sarah put her hand over her mouth and then laughed out loud with relief. 'Oh my God, Mum. For a moment there I thought it was Josephina, John's ex.'

'You silly sod girl, just nerves getting the better of you,' Gwen said, grabbing Sarah's arm and leading her to the church door. 'Now, my love, take deep breaths ... Angelica, get behind your auntie here and hold your bouquet upright!'

If Sarah's heart was doing a rumba before, it was doing the quickstep now. Slipping her arm through her mum's she stepped through the door and walked down the aisle to *The First Time Ever I Saw Your Face*. She and John had chosen that song because they realised after a few interesting hiccups, that they had probably fallen in love at first sight. Had it only been a year ago since she'd opened the door, grumpy and irritable after a hard day at school, to find John smiling at her on the doorstep? Now Sarah felt like she'd known him forever. And although every face was turned to her as she walked down the aisle, the only one she saw was his.

Looking divine in a dark grey suit and green shirt, John shot her a smile that rivalled the bright sunlight streaming through the stained glass window. Though he was obviously delighted to see her, Sarah could tell by the way he ran his fingers quickly through his dark curly hair and then straightened his tie that he was as nervous as she was. Harry, John's dad and today doubling as best man, patted his son reassuringly on his shoulder and winked his approval at Sarah.

The song ended, a hush fell over the congregation and Sarah's eyes met John's. The depth of emotion within them swelled her heart until it felt as big as the sky. She thought it might burst with happiness. Gwen and Harry stepped to the side, and suddenly it seemed as if they were the only two people there – save the vicar, of course.

Sarah heard his words, repeated them, thankfully not stumbling once, but all the while the events of the last year raced through her mind at light speed. The same evening she'd found John on the doorstep he'd told her things that had changed her world irreversibly. And although she would give her life for John – at that moment was pledging her life to him for richer, poorer, better or worse – she had found their unique relationship a little difficult to grasp from time to time.

That evening, John had explained that Sarah was in fact a Stitch. Furthermore, the old saying, 'a stitch in time saves nine', actually meant, a person – a time traveller, aka a Stitch, aka Sarah – needed to travel to the past to sew up holes that had opened up in time. And why must she do this? To ensure that nine people didn't die. John apparently was a Time-Needle – a person who found willing Stitches ready to complete their mission. He came from a long line of Time-Needles and it was something he accepted, though it could often be dangerous and unpredictable work.

Needless to say, she had thought the whole thing was impossible and completely bonkers. But it beat the hell out of her why was she thinking about all that again now when she was in the process of getting married!

Sarah fixed her eyes on John's sensuous mouth and listened to him repeat the wedding vows, but her mind refused to concentrate. She shook her head slightly to try and push the memory of that evening away. The congregation came back into focus and her mum waved a soggy hanky at her from the front pew. Two rows behind her mum, a small child –Sarah's second cousin, Jake – poked his nose and held the result up to his mother for inspection. Sarah had to pretend to clear her throat to avoid laughing out loud. *Get a grip and concentrate.* What was happening to her?

'For better, for worse,' John said. A small frown crept across his brow as he looked at Sarah's anxious expression. 'In sickness and in health ...'

Sarah had to stifle another giggle of hysteria at those words. Once more, unwanted thoughts elbowed their way to the forefront of her consciousness. After John had dropped all that information on her that evening, she had certainly thought she *was* sick. In fact she had been convinced that she'd been having a breakdown. At first she believed she'd imagined John and the whole kit and caboodle. Then John had explained that it was perfectly normal to feel like this and she'd agreed to his crazy plan just to get rid of him.

Trouble was, reality had jumped up and slapped her in the face the very next day when she'd walked out of her classroom and found herself whisked back to the Sheffield Blitz of 1940!

'Sarah?' John said and squeezed her hand. 'Are you all right, love? You look a little pale.'

Sarah stared at John and then at the vicar. Their faces wore identical expressions of worry and concern. She nodded, but didn't feel all right, didn't feel all right at all.

Her stomach twisted and she felt a flush start at her feet and spread up her body like a fever. What the hell was happening? Beads of sweat popped all along her top lip and her stomach twisted again, sending waves of nausea up into her throat. *Please God, don't let me be sick right here in front of everyone!*

The nausea abated a little and she distantly heard the vicar ask if John would take her to be his wife. John's 'I do' sounded as if he was speaking from somewhere up in the rafters and then the nausea returned with a vengeance. Jelly legs accompanied the nausea seconds later, and she squeezed John's arm to steady herself.

'Sarah. I give you this ring as a sign of our marriage. With my body I thee …' John's words faded in and out as if someone was turning the dial on a radio, and then John and the vicar's face receded along her tunnel vision as though she was looking at them down the wrong end of a telescope.

The ring felt like a lead weight as John slipped it on her finger and as if in a dream she heard snatches of vows said, repeated, said, and repeated. Then, after two attempts she slipped John's ring onto his finger and with all her resolve whispered from numbed lips, 'John … I give you this ring …' and a few seconds later heard the vicar say something about the giving and receiving of rings … proclaiming them … husband and wife … then her legs buckled.

Just as the floor floated up to meet her, John's strong arms hooked under hers, saving her from falling flat on her face. On her knees, slumped against him, she heard her mum yell, 'Oh, no, what's wrong. Sarah!'

She also heard the distant peal of a bell and another voice shout, 'Right, line up class five and get inside, you've a board of sums to copy out!'

Shaking with trepidation, Sarah looked in the direction of the voice and reeled at the scene before her eyes. The church had disappeared and been replaced by an old-fashioned school playground complete with old-fashioned children. By the door of the school stood a tall, thin, angular woman dressed in 1930s clothes. Her bony white hand clasped a bell which she shook at the children as if it were a weapon.

Sarah didn't see or hear anything else. Her world turned dark ... and she fell.

9

# Chapter Two

A cold narrow bed, a yellowing cracked ceiling, a smell of chalk mingling with strong disinfectant and a drumming of ... rain on a window? Sarah lifted her head off the bed slightly and rubbed her eyes. Was she in the hotel that John had booked for their honeymoon in New York? Because if she was there would be hell to pay ... A harrumph and a snort of exasperation snapped her view from the ceiling to a face that would have suited a horse much better than the woman wearing it.

'Ah, at last you are with us. Now, who on earth are you and what are you doing wandering into our school?'

Horse Face stepped closer and peered imperiously down her nose at Sarah. Two beady black eyes, neither helpful nor friendly, bored into Sarah's from a long, thin, milk-white face, and chopping this Munchian creation to a sudden stop was a jaw you could slice bacon on. *What the hell?* Sarah, to no avail, tried to pull her eyes from the woman's almost non-existent top lip, above which a single hair sprouted from a huge dark mole.

A tiny fist of adrenaline prodded low in Sarah's belly and then gathered momentum, quickly punching shock into her heart rate. The mole loomed larger, so Sarah closed her eyes against it and took a deep breath. This must be a dream, or a bloody nightmare. She pinched her arm with some force. Ouch! That would be a negative then. This was real! What the hell had happened? One minute she had been marrying John, the next ... no ... PLEASE NO! Don't let this be another time trip ... not now ... not on the happiest day of her life when—

'Excuse me,' Horse Face snapped and poked Sarah on the shoulder. 'Open your eyes. I don't want you going off again!'

'Um …' Sarah began, opening her eyes and trying to force her frazzled thoughts into some kind of coherent logical order. But her brain wasn't having any of it. All she could manage to do was to stare at the woman in a fuzzy state of panic. The drumming that Sarah had heard she now discovered wasn't rain on a window at all, but the woman's skeletal fingers tapping against a book clasped to her chest. Raising her eyes from the book to the woman's face again Sarah felt, to her horror, a giggle caper up from her depths when she noticed the hairstyle. A half-hearted attempt had been made to tease a tawny haystack into some kind of Marcel Wave bob, but had failed miserably. The old scarecrow, Worzel Gummidge's locks looked more refined.

But this was no laughing matter. Sarah looked round the spartan little room which appeared to be an offshoot from a school corridor. Nope. If she had gone back in time on today of all days, this was no bloody laughing matter at all. She swallowed hard. Okay, attack is the best form of defence, and she felt like she *had* to defend herself from Horse Face. Looking the woman square in the eye she said in her best teacher's voice, 'I have no recollection of what happened. Now, please, tell me where I am.'

'Don't you get all hoighty-toighty with me!' Horse Face glowered. 'You were the one crawling around on the floor in the yard and then upped and fainted. Not a good example to the children at all.'

Not a good example? Sarah sat up on the bed and put a hand to her swimming head. Was the woman bloody crackers? 'If I fainted I hardly think that I had a choice in the matter … Miss?' Sarah put her head on one side, glared at the woman and tried to muster a confident expression.

'Miss Ratchet. And what do you mean, "if you fainted"? Of course you did, or why else would I have summoned the caretaker to carry you into the medical room here? Or are you in the habit of walking onto school premises and pretending to faint, Miss?'

Ratchet, yeah that'd be right. She looked about as human as a screwdriver. Sarah paused and wondered if she was actually married. Oh to hell with it, what did it matter? 'Mrs Needler. And no, of course not, what a ridiculous thing to say.'

'I will remind you that you said "if" not "when" you fainted, Mrs Needler. That led me to suppose that—'

'Okay, cut the prattle.' Sarah eased her feet – no longer wearing cream satin sling-backs but encased in sensible brown lace-ups – to the floor and sighed. 'Where are we, and what year is it?' She really couldn't be faffed going over the whole, 'I must have bumped my head so can't remember anything' scenario she'd used the first time she'd travelled to the past. And judging by the clothes she and the woman were wearing, the surroundings and the scene she'd first glimpsed before she'd fainted, there really wasn't very much doubt that she had indeed left Kansas, Toto.

Miss Ratchet put her hand to her mouth, shook her head and said less fiercely, 'You must have bumped your head in the yard.' Sarah wanted to laugh again and say, *No, that's my line*, but of course she didn't.

'I suppose I must have. So … the year is?'

'1939, and you are in Southampton.'

'Southampton?'

'Southampton, yes. Where did you think you were?' Ratchet furrowed her brow and folded her arms, slicing the air with sharp elbow joints.

*Ratchet Scissorhands* surreally floated across Sarah's mind and she leaned against the bed to try and ground her thoughts. Well, this was just marvellous, wasn't it? Here she was dumped in the past again. A momentous year, the war about to start, or perhaps it had already, in a town she'd never visited before and with no clue who she was supposed to save.

As a reward for her exemplary stitching, the 'powers that be' – the name she'd given to the guardians of time – had allowed Sarah to know something about her latter missions before she'd gone. Looks like they were chucking her back in at the deep end just as they had in her first two trips … but why? What the hell had she done wrong?

'Do you think you want to be sick because you look pale and I have no stomach for sick people.' Ratchet backed quickly away towards the door, the bell hanging from her belt clanging weakly against her hip.

'No, I think I'm okay, just had a bit of a shock, that's all.' She sighed. That was the understatement of the year. Sarah felt her eyes grow moist as she thought of John and a church full of people back home. They were all probably gathered around John looking at the empty spot beside him, worried to death. How the hell would they explain her vanishing to the whole congregation when she got back? Dear God, why did this have to happen now?

Ratchet waved a bony hand vaguely in Sarah's direction. 'I'm no good with weeping either … Look, just sit here quietly and have a cup of water. I have to teach my class, but it is the last lesson of the day and I'll be back in a short while. I'm sure you will be right as rain by then.'

'Yes, I'm sure I will. Thanks,' Sarah said, and then muttered under her breath, 'As right as any time traveller *can* bloody be.'

Almost through the door Ratchet's head snapped round and she hurried back over to Sarah, thrusting her mole inches from her face. 'What did you say?'

Sarah recoiled. 'I said I'm sure I will be all right—'

'No, no, after that,' Ratchet hissed, her eyes glowing like two hot coals.

'Er … nothing.'

'Yes, yes, you did ... I *heard* you.' The word 'heard' was accompanied by a hard squeeze of Ratchet's talons around Sarah's wrist.

Bloody hell was this woman a 'wanna be' witch from *The Wizard of Oz* or something? Sarah half expected her to turn green, throw back her head and cackle manically. 'Oi, get off,' she snapped, pulling her wrist free.

'You said something about time travel. I heard you, you did, didn't you?' Ratchet's voice rose higher with every word until she was practically shrieking. The look on her face really did match the anguish of Munch's famous artwork now.

'Veronica! I really need you to attend to your class. I've been teaching mine as well as yours for the last twenty minutes and enough is enough.' A stout short woman looking very much like Dawn French stomped in and placed her hands on her hips. She gave Sarah the briefest glance, accepted a nod from Ratchet and then stomped out again.

'Right.' Ratchet turned to Sarah, her voice quavering. 'You stay there until I get back, do you hear me?'

Gawd, she made Sarah feel like a naughty schoolgirl. 'Yes, well I can't think where else I would go to be honest,' Sarah said, blinking back fresh tears. *I mean, it's not as if I have a wedding reception to go to or anything, is it?*

John had to shout to make himself heard over the hubbub. 'I said stand back for God's sake! Give her some air!' The anxiety and volume of his voice forced the knot of anxious wedding guests to step back as one, and a space was cleared around Sarah and John, apart from his dad and Sarah's mum. John laid Sarah on her back, slipped his hand under her neck and tapped her cheek gently with the other.

'By 'eck, lad, I think she's fainted,' Harry said.

'Oh really? I would never have bloody guessed!' John snapped and then immediately regretted it as he noted the crestfallen look on his dad's face. 'Sorry, yeah I know, Dad, but why is she still out?'

Gwen tried to hitch up her tight dress and then knock-kneed, lowered herself to the floor next to her daughter. 'Sarah love, can you hear me?' She gave Sarah's shoulders a little shake. John's heart lurched as Gwen grabbed his arm and wailed, 'John, do something, she's not waking up!'

The vicar rushed forward and knelt then. 'Mrs Mason, please don't get hysterical, we need calm. And we also need to get your wife into the recovery position, John.'

For a split second the word *wife* sent an indescribable glow of happiness through John's heart, and then the sight of Sarah's ashen face highlighted by two pink flushes of colour on her cheekbones brought anxiety rolling back into his belly. The vicar shot him a 'don't just sit there do something' look. So putting his hands carefully against Sarah's side, he pushed, as the vicar bent her leg and rolled her over.

'Tip her head back a bit now,' Harry said, biting his nails. 'I remember that bit from *Casualty*.'

John tipped her head back, noting that her skin was very hot and clammy to his touch. Lowering his ear to her mouth he listened for a breath and was rewarded by a little puff of hot air to his cheek, then another few in quick succession. He didn't like the sound of that. He shot an anxious look at the vicar. 'Her breathing seems a bit too shallow and rapid to me.'

'Yes, and I don't like her colour,' the vicar said getting to his feet. 'Right, I'm phoning an ambulance.'

'And while we wait I'll pop across to see if Doctor Stewart is at home,' the vicar's wife called from the back of the crowd.

Five minutes later as Dr Stewart assessed Sarah, still unconscious but now on a sofa in the vestry, John paced up and down across the parquet floor, his heart beating louder than his footsteps. What the hell was wrong with her? Was it just nerves getting the better of her as Gwen had suggested a few minutes ago? He doubted it. Sarah had always been a tough cookie, even tougher now after all the missions through time she'd been on over the past year. John could tell that Gwen had probably just said that to try and calm him, though her face was nearly as pale and pinched as her daughter's. Still, the doctor had cancelled the ambulance so it couldn't be that bad.

Gwen's face suddenly lit up and she flapped a hand at him from where she stood just behind the doctor. 'I think she's stirring, John,' she gasped.

Taking his wife's limp hand, John watched her eyes roll and twitch under her eyelids and her mouth trying to form words. She still didn't look like she was coming round any time soon. Stroking a damp curl away from Sarah's cheek he felt the contrast in temperature between her face and hand. Summer and winter.

Doctor Stewart put his stethoscope away and snapped his bag shut. He glanced at John and gave a brief smile of reassurance.

'Have you found out what's wrong with her, doctor?'

The doctor's practised voice of calm treacled into his ears as if from a long way off. 'I think she will be all right in a while, John. It seems she fainted but then fell into a deep sleep. My examinations show a regular heartbeat, but she does have a fever.'

'A fever? She has a virus or something?'

'I'd say it was a very bad case of flu. She needs to go home to bed immediately, I'm afraid. No wedding reception for this young lady.'

Sarah's eyes opened briefly and she whispered, 'Horse face ... bell ... no way, Rachet.'

'"Horse face, bell, no way, Rachet?" What is she on about?' Harry muttered.

'She is delirious, Mr Needler. That is normal for severe cases of flu.'

'But how could it happen so quickly?' John said, turning to Gwen. 'She was fine this morning, wasn't she?'

She shook her head, no. 'She did complain of a headache and feeling shaky last night and this morning, but we thought it was just nerves. She had paracetamol and felt a bit better.'

'And that's what she must do now,' the doctor said, making as if to leave. 'Bed rest, plenty of fluids, paracetamol and ibuprofen. Call your own doctor if she's not improving by tomorrow.'

'But what if it's pneumonia? Her breathing was weird earlier and she looks really ill,' John countered. He wasn't happy with that flu diagnosis; something didn't feel right in his gut.

'Her breathing is fine now. Flu cases can look much worse than they are, but there's a chance it could turn to pneumonia, so as I said, call your doctor if she gets worse.'

An hour later, John kissed Sarah on the head and tucked the duvet around her. She definitely seemed a bit better now she was warm and comfy at home. The delirium had stopped and she seemed to be sleeping normally without the twitches and rolling of the eyes. John stroked a finger along her cheek and neck and thought selfishly about his missed wedding night.

The other day when Sarah had been in the shower, he'd peeped in the carrier bag she'd shoved in a drawer when he'd come into the room. In it was a selection of sexy underwear and a red silk basque. The thought of it was even now causing a familiar stirring and he had to tell himself off. *For God's sake, stop it. Here's Sarah, ill, missing out on the celebrations and all you can think of is jumping her bones.* John kissed her hand and smiled. Even when she was ill she was still the most beautiful woman in the world.

But hell, why did all this have to happen today? After everything that had happened with her last husband she deserved a day to remember. He smiled humourlessly. This would certainly be a day to remember, but for all the wrong damned reasons. If Sarah's illness wasn't enough, another bombshell had been sent blasting through his heavy heart just before they left the church too. The vicar had pulled him to one side and said that although he and Sarah were married in the eyes of God; until they had both signed the register the marriage wasn't legal. Obviously Sarah was in no fit state to put pen to paper at the moment, but as soon as she was able, they must get it done.

One thing was for sure, if or when they went to New York next week, he would make sure they had the best time of their lives. He sighed and crept backwards out of the bedroom. Gently closing the door, he turned slap bang into his dad on the landing.

'Bloody hell, Dad, what are you doing creeping about here?' he hissed. 'I thought you were holding it together for me at the reception.'

'I am, but I just popped back to bring you a bottle of champagne. You might not feel like drinking it but have one glass at least to mark your day,' Harry said, searching John's face with perceptive blue eyes.

John knew that was his dad's excuse to check that he was all right and felt a sudden rush of affection for him. 'It wouldn't feel right without, Sarah, Dad. But thanks.'

'How is she?' Harry asked, leading the way downstairs.

'Better now, I think. At least she's stopped talking gibberish.'

Harry reached his hand to the handle of the back door and then turned to face John, a dark cloud passing over his normally sunny expression. 'I wasn't going to say anything ... but I can't see how I can keep it quiet really ... I think it might be a bit more than gibberish, lad.'

A cold finger of anxiety poked John in the chest. 'What do you mean?'

'Well, on the way back here in the car, I heard her say a few things about 1939 and not today of all days ... that kind of thing.'

'So? That was just part of the delirium.' John shrugged.

'Well, that's what I assumed at first, but it felt a bit familiar. And then I remembered something from years ago. Something your mum told me about another Stitch ... a really weird time trip this woman had had ... it started with fainting and a fever, and Sarah did mention 1939 ...' Harry left off and sighed.

'Eh? But Sarah's still upstairs in bed if you hadn't noticed, Dad.' John began to wonder if his dad had been drinking too much champagne. He also sometimes wondered if Harry was a little jealous, or felt redundant now that he had retired from needling, and assumed that everything was to do with 'the business', as they often called the task of needling and stitching. It clearly wasn't this time because how the hell could Sarah have gone on a time trip and still be here? Besides, they would have been warned, consulted with beforehand wouldn't they – now that Sarah had proved herself to be more than good at her job? And the powers that be certainly wouldn't have just whisked her away the minute after they were married ... would they?

Harry tutted. 'Yes, of course I had noticed, but that's another thing that's similar. This other Stitch stayed here the whole time too, well her body did *and* she had a fever. Perhaps it was something to do with her mind or spirit being back in the past somewhere. Anyway, when she got back she was right as rain.'

John frowned and shook his head in bewilderment.

'I know it doesn't seem possible,' Harry continued. 'But

you see there are special conditions that can send the whole thing haywire ... and, well, Sarah could have this special condition. I could be wrong though and it could just be flu like the doc said.'

'What special condition?' John's frown deepened. He was beginning to get fed up with all this hinting and hedging. Harry always was one for melodrama. Now he was looking at the floor and not answering! 'For goodness sake, Dad. What special bloody condition?'

His dad looked up. 'Since the time disaster with Norman that persuaded the powers that be to only use female Stitches, it's the kind of special condition *only* Stitches can get ... if you take my meaning,' Harry said, his eyes twinkling.

John sighed and glared at his father. But then a second later, from somewhere deep in his brain, a penny poised itself over a slot and threatened to drop.

# Chapter Three

Sarah picked tea leaves from her tongue and gagged at the ones that she had inadvertently swallowed. It was 1939, they didn't have teabags, she knew that, so why had she just gulped it down without a thought? *Oh, I don't know, Sarah. Perhaps it has something to do with the fact that one minute you were marrying the love of your life, the next you wake up in a medical room faced with someone who looks like they have escaped from* The Nightmare Before Christmas.

And now the nightmare continued. She had been taken back to Ratchet's cold little cottage by the sea, and there she'd discovered that the war was only a few months in, that she felt light-headed and dizzy if she turned her head too quickly and that oddly she was hungry ... ravenous, in fact. Upon asking for sustenance she had been given tea and cheese *again*. What was it with people from the past and bloody cheese? At least three of her trips back in time had resulted in cheese on crackers or cheese on toast, but the worst of her discoveries had been that Ratchet was obsessed with the fact that Sarah had let slip in her mutterings about being a time traveller.

Upon her return from the classroom at the end of the school day, Rachet had quizzed her again and even though Sarah had used the tried and tested 'I can't remember saying that' and waffling about a bump on the head, Ratchet wasn't convinced. She insisted that Sarah come home with her, and having no real option, dumped in 1939 in an unfamiliar town with no clue as to who she was there to save, she had gone with her.

Throughout the consummation of the ritual tea and cheese, Rachet just wouldn't let the whole thing drop. And now after a vigorous wipe of the kitchen table and a clatter of dishes in the sink, it looked as if she was limbering up for interrogation. Seconds out, round three.

'Right, Sarah,' Ratchet said, scraping the legs of her wooden chair across the tiles with a squeak that set Sarah's teeth on edge. She sat down opposite at the table. 'I know what I heard and I won't shut up until you tell me who you really are.' The coals of her eyes glowed hotter than the meagre little fire that she'd lit in the grate earlier.

Trying to buy time, Sarah noticed a beautiful diamante brooch in the shape of a conch shell on Ratchet's jumper. It was the only beautiful and frivolous thing about her, in fact in the whole house. 'Do you know, I have never seen such an unusual brooch – quite exquisite,' Sarah said.

Ratchet's mouth curled up at the corners but the heat of her words quickly ironed the smile flat again as she realised Sarah was using flattery to catch her off guard. 'Glad you think so. Now what *is* your name, madam?'

'I told you. My name is Sarah Yat ... I mean Needler and I have amnesia.' Sarah buried a smirk. She felt like she was in a meeting for Amnesiacs Anonymous.

'If you have lost your memory, how come you know your name?' Apparently happy to have scored some kind of a point, Ratchet leaned forward and grinned like a maniac, the skin of her cheeks stretched to full capacity to accommodate this rare occurrence and the hair on the mole danced like a fishing rod over a muddy pool.

'Deuce it all, I would hazard a guess it's just one of those things, Sherlock.' Sarah sighed and closed her eyes. This was all getting too much.

'Eh? Don't get smart with me, madam.'

'It would be difficult to do otherwise.'

'How rude! I take you under my wing, bring you to my home—'

'Interrogate me,' Sarah said, still with her eyes closed.

'*What do you expect?*' Ratchet banged her fist on the table snapping Sarah's eyes open and onto hers. 'I need to find out what you know about this here time travel. You say nothing, but your name is Needler too and I have heard that one before and quite recently. So you see, I *know* that you are lying. I'd hazard a guess that you haven't lost your memory at all, Sherlock!'

Sarah's mind went into overdrive. Why was the name Needler significant? Had John been back here for some reason? No, that was doubtful unless he had been given permission by the powers that be, or the Spindly Ones as Sarah preferred to call them. And if he had, why had he?

Trying to keep her voice neutral she said, 'What has my surname to do with anything?'

Ratchet sat back in her chair and nodded knowingly. 'You know something, I'm right. And we will sit here until you talk some more.'

Sarah tossed her head. 'Oh, please, the "we have ways of making you talk" phrase belongs to nasty little German men in smart uniforms wearing jackboots. Mind you ... you do have a look of—' Tempting as it was to ridicule, seeing the puzzlement on Ratchet's face, Sarah buttoned it before she said too much. It would do to remember that one of her remits as a Stitch was not to divulge anything from the future to folk in the past. The last thing she wanted now as punishment for such a slip was to get a bout of the giggles, or flatulence like she had on past trips.

'German men ... are you saying I look like a Nazi?'

Sarah looked at the table. *Funny she didn't question the gender, but looking like that ... okay get a grip.* 'No, of course not, I'm sorry. I am a bit confused I think,' she muttered looking back up at Ratchet.

'Hmm, well cut to the chase. How are you related to Josiah Needler?'

That really did confuse Sarah. Who the hell was that? 'I don't know a Josiah, I'm afraid.'

'So you don't know anything about a man who came here knocking on my door just as I was preparing a bit of cheese on toast on Sunday evening, said his name was Needler and told me I was a … a …' Ratchet shook her head and swallowed hard.

Sarah watched Ratchet's lips trying to form words but to no avail. She began to get a very unsettling ripple of anxiety in her tummy. This woman couldn't be, could she?

'Just spit it out, woman!' Sarah snapped.

Ratchet blinked rapidly and cleared her throat, then words shot from her mouth running into each other and as rapid as machine gun fire. 'He said I was a Stitch, like the old saying "a stitch in time saves nine" and there were holes in time that I had to mend by stitching them up and if I *didn't* stitch them up …' Ratchet took a shallow breath '… in other words take three trips back in time to save the lives of three important people and then their children, or perhaps grandchildren, would go on to make the nine, like the saying …' Ratchet took a deeper breath '… then people would die or never be born and horrible things would happen and it would be all my fault!' She finished with a shriek and put her hands over her face.

Sarah's unsettled ripple grew into a wave as her previous thought was answered. So yes, this woman could be, no, *was* in fact a Stitch. So what had gone wrong? Why the bloody hell had she been whisked away from her John if Ratchet-face was a Stitch anyway? And who was she supposed to save? Sarah sighed and leaned back in her seat as Ratchet took her hands away from her face and wrapped her arachnid arms around her body. She then began to rock slowly back and forth.

*Right, judging by Ratchet's wild eyes and body language she's teetering on the brink. Slowly does it Sarah.*

'Okay, Miss Ratchet. Calm down. I can see that you are a little distraught—'

Ratchet continued as if Sarah hadn't spoken. 'And he said that a Stitch was a job, but it was also an acronym for the task of a time traveller.' Ratchet rolled her eyes up to the left. 'Now what was it ... ah yes:

S-ave

T-hree

I-mportant

T-errestrials

C-ome

H-ome.'

'No, you got the last two wrong, it's C-lose H-ole,' Sarah said, figuring there was no point trying to keep up the pretence any longer.

'So you *do* know about it!' Ratchet yelled triumphantly, her eyes gleaming like polished beads.

'Oh, so that was a trick was it? Spare me the theatrics.'

'Oh, thank God! I thought I was going stark staring crazy!'

'Yes, been there, done that, bought the sodding T-shirt.'

'Eh?'

'Never mind. Right, so why did you let this strange man into your house?' Sarah thought she already knew the answer to that one.

'I didn't! I shut and locked the door on him, came back here into the kitchen and you'll never guess what?'

'There he was, standing in front of you?'

'Yes! How did you know?'

'They do time tricks, you know, reverse time a few seconds to just before you shut the door, stop time and dodge past you and then start it again. They are only allowed to do it for a few seconds, because otherwise it would muck the dimensions right up apparently.'

Ratchet nodded respectfully. 'Yes, that's exactly what Josiah said.'

'Same thing happened to me. I'm a Stitch, too. Not with this Josiah, of course, but with John ... who right at this minute is probably standing at the altar most put out by my impromptu disappearing act.'

'You married a Time Needle?'

'Yes, well, at least I hope we were married before I was shunted off to this hell hole!'

Ratchet bridled. 'How dare you call my lovely home a hell hole?'

'No, I didn't mean your house in particular,' – although Sarah thought that it couldn't be called a lovely home by any stretch of the imagination – 'I mean that my bloody wedding is ruined!'

After another, and this time carefully sipped cup of tea, no cheese and a full recount of what had happened to Ratchet, Sarah felt less worried that she herself was on a stitching mission, but still worried about why she was here and what the hell she was supposed to do.

Ratchet, it seemed, had refused to go back in time to save someone in 1879 and thrown Josiah out. She 'couldn't cope with things out of the ordinary' apparently, it 'threw her constitution out of the window and made her really queer in the head'. Sarah would quite like to throw Rachet out of the window if the theory buzzing around her brain had any credence.

'You seem unable to cope with a lot of things, don't you, Miss Ratchet?' Sarah said coldly. 'In school you said you couldn't deal with sickness or tears. It's a wonder that you survive as a primary school teacher, to be quite frank.'

Rachet's long face grew longer and her top lip settled into a snarl. 'I'll have you know I am one of the most feared teacher's in Southampton! It's just that bodily fluids and emotions make me shudder.'

'Oh really? Well, I'll have you know that inciting fear is

not a good basis for the imparting of knowledge and good learning skills to children, madam,' Sarah retorted, gratified to find that the formal and old-fashioned tone of her words had made an impact. Ratchet screwed up her face in distaste and became immediately on the offensive.

'I fail to see why you are getting so angry, Mrs Needler. I have made a rational choice not to hurtle off to goodness knows where on a foolhardy mission through time. There will be others to do my stitching job, I'm sure.'

'Yes, and I have a horrible theory that I have been sent back here to do just that, on my sodding wedding day of all days! God, why did you have to pass the time, you bloody coward.'

'Me, a coward? How dare you! And please refrain from using language of the gutter in my house.'

'Language of the gutter, ha! You ain't seen nothing yet, babe!'

Sarah stood up and began to pace, breathing in through her nose and out through her mouth to try and calm herself. From time to time she glanced at the silent Ratchet, her skeletal fingers picking crumbs individually from her tablecloth and putting them into the palm of her other hand. A mask of bewilderment clung to her face and Sarah did feel a small pang of sympathy for her.

Even though the woman was infuriating, 'Miss I can't cope with this, that, and the bloody other', Sarah realised that it *was* a shock after all being confronted with something beyond human experience. God, she herself had been there not so long ago. And Sarah also felt a pull on her heart strings to make things right, but the strings weren't tugged to the extent that she would take on Ratchet's job in 1879. She had done enough lately ... above and beyond. Someone else would just have to take this one for the team.

Eventually Ratchet looked up from her crumbs and said quietly, 'Why did you say that I passed the time? I don't understand.'

'Oh, there are lots of ordinary everyday phrases that have time travel meanings, but have been corrupted over the ages. I found that out, and you would have too if you had decided to run with the baton instead of chickening out.'

Sarah received a black look, but Ratchet kept her thin lips pressed together.

'Okay, "passing the time" actually means that a Stitch, in this case, you, has decided to back out of a time trip to save someone.' Sarah glared at Ratchet. 'Which means someone else, another Stitch, in this case, me, has to do the damned job. So you have effectively "passed the time" to me.'

'But don't you get a choice in whether you want to take a "passing the time"?' Ratchet sniffed.

'Yes, normally. But for some reason I have been just dumped here. And we all have choices, don't we, Rachet? Norman had a choice and like you, he couldn't be arsed!'

Ratchet recoiled. 'Your language really is outrageous. And who is this Norman you speak of?'

Sarah sighed and sat back down. 'Time waits for no man. That's a bastardisation of another old phrase. It was originally, "Time waits for Norman," but like you, he couldn't be bothered to go and save someone. And that meant that someone truly evil was born when they shouldn't have been.'

'Oh my goodness.' Ratchet gulped and put her hand to her mouth. 'Who was that?'

'Adolf Hitler.'

'Crikey!' Ratchet took a breath, then wrinkled her nose. 'We know he's a power- hungry maniac, but is he truly evil?'

'Oh, yes and then some. But you will find that out shortly.' Sarah shook her head to stop herself from divulging more. 'Right. I hope that what I have told you has changed your mind, but if it hasn't, I have selfishly for once decided that I am not going to put myself out. Are you noting this, Spindly Ones?' she said to the ceiling.

'Spindly Ones?' Ratchet's mole twitched and she cast her fearful eyes skyward.

'Yep. That's what I call the powers that be that control the whole shebang. I imagine them to be tall and spindly wearing long medieval-type robes with those asymmetric sleeves which they shake in triumph at our mistakes and laugh like drains,' Sarah said, a giggle of hysteria in her voice. 'Alternatively they might not have any form at all or look like Humpty frigging Dumpty. To be quite honest, I don't give a shit. All I want to do is get back to my wedding day.'

Ratchet's mouth fell open in shock and a beetroot flush shot into her cheeks. 'My goodness, you say the vilest words.'

Sarah folded her arms and huffed. 'So are you going to do this 1879 job or what?'

'I ... I ... don't know.'

Relief woke from the bottom of Sarah's dark pit and climbed a little way up the rescue rope. *Okay, Sarah, gently does it.* 'Hey, that's a start, Veronica. Can I call you Veronica?'

Ratchet frowned, then nodded, eyeing Sarah carefully.

'Just think of all the people's lives you will change for the better if you save this one.'

'But I don't even know who I have to save. Josiah didn't tell me.'

'No. That's normal at first. It will be fine, just go with it and trust your instincts.'

'What do you mean, at first? Do you know where you are being sent later?'

'It depends. I did after the first few missions, but only because I was greatly tested by the Spindly Ones, and thank God I passed. Nowadays I get a date, time, and a vague idea of who the people are ... but that's all.'

'Hmm. I'm still not sure I'm cut out for a life of—'

'You're getting ahead of yourself now, Veronica. You only have to do three missions ... you could even just do the one.' Sarah crossed her fingers behind her back. She wasn't sure about that at all, but if it changed Ratchet's mind ... 'I made the choice to keep doing more. Crazy I know.'

'Really? We-ll, I suppose I could do just the one—'

'Yes, of course! Wow that's fantastic, Veronica!' Sarah said, scraping her chair back and clapping the other woman on the shoulder. A bubble of excitement popped in her heart and pins and needles began in her feet and hands. Oh, yes, now that was a sure sign that any time now she'd be back standing next to John at the altar. Thank God, she'd managed to change Veronica's mind without having to take a 'passing the time'. *Re-sult!*

Veronica grabbed Sarah's hand that was still on her shoulder and clasped it hard. 'But will it be all right? Will I ... will I succeed?'

'You'll be fine. As I said, just trust your instincts.'

Veronica's face began to fade and Sarah felt a heavy tug in the centre of her body and her right arm, then a floating sensation as if she were coming up from the bottom of a deep pool. *Yep, soon be back home, thank the Lord!* Then cool fingers cupped her cheek and she felt a warm mouth graze her lips.

'Sarah, are you back with us at last, my darling?'

Opening her heavy lids, John's green eyes full of anxiety and love swam into focus and she cried out with happiness and relief. 'John! Yes, I think I am, my love!'

# Chapter Four

John looked at his wife's face glowing with happiness instead of the fever she'd had for the last few hours and laughed with relief. 'Oh, Sarah, I am so glad you are back with me and looking more like yourself.' He kissed her again and dabbed at her brow with a damp cloth.

'You and me both. I've had such an awful time.' Sarah shook her head.

'The fall must have woken you, good job.'

Sarah frowned. 'Fall?'

'Yes, I was downstairs a few minutes ago and heard a bump, then you walking about. I assumed you'd fallen out of bed.'

'Did I? I ... don't remember ... and why am I here in bed?' Sarah put a trembling hand to his face, her eyes anxious.

'Don't worry about it. It doesn't matter, we just need to get you well now,' John soothed. The last thing he wanted was for her to get stressed given the fact she'd just woken from the ruins of her wedding day.

'What do you mean, well? Am I ill? What happened, John? What happened at the church when I disappeared ... how did you explain it to everyone?' Sarah's voice shook and she tried to sit up.

John felt his heart sink. She was obviously not out of the woods yet. 'Hey, relax, lie down, sweetheart,' he said, placing his hands on her shoulders. The heat of her body through the thin night shirt told him that she probably did still have a fever, and now she was rabbiting about disappearing ... still delirious ... unless ... His dad's words from earlier gave him a quick kick in the gut. He looked into Sarah's worried blue eyes almost turquoise in the lamp light, her damp golden hair clinging to her hot cheeks, and he wondered how to broach the possibility that she had been on a time trip without alarming her if she hadn't. But then she solved that problem for him.

'John? For goodness sake, say something. How *did* you explain my disappearance, and how long was I in 1939?'

Bloody hell! His dad had been right then. 'You were in 1939? What ... on a mission?' The thumping of his heart in his ears threatened to drown out Sarah's answer as he wondered about the explanation as to *why* it had happened ... the 'penny dropping' part of his dad's story.

'Well, not exactly, as it turned out.' Sarah sat up then, ignoring his protests. 'But I definitely went back in time.' She shoved her damp hair impatiently from her face and frowned at him. 'Where else did you think I'd gone when I suddenly disappeared at the altar, John?'

There was no dodging round this one. She'd be shocked, but hey ho. John released a sigh, took her hand and said, 'You didn't disappear, sweetheart. You fainted with a fever.'

A few hours later John watched the dawn light tease pale fingers through the curtain and traced his own across Sarah's cheek, her breath on his bare chest deep and regular in sleep. He shut eyes that felt like someone had been sandpapering them and shifted his position slightly. What a bloody night. He'd only managed a few winks and not for the right reasons. It should have been champagne, celebration and passionate lovemaking, but what it had been was worry, fever, tales of Ratchet and 1939, all finished off with tears from Sarah when she realised they weren't legally married. Great.

Still, Sarah was definitely less feverish and had calmed down when John had explained that it had happened to some other Stitch in the past according to his dad. He had just shrugged his shoulders when she'd asked him why though. It wasn't his place to pass on wild theories that might be just a load of bunkum anyway. Besides, she'd had enough shocks for one day. Tomorrow was Sunday. He checked himself, no ... it was tomorrow already. They would have a nice day recovering, just the two of them. If Sarah felt up to it, they might even see the basque put in an appearance. *Don't get ahead of yourself, John. She's just getting over this flu or whatever the hell it is.* He smiled to himself and tried to push away the feeling that Sarah's hot body – in every sense of the word – pressed against him was giving him. As soon as she woke up he'd make her a lovely breakfast and then they'd hare down to the church and sign the marriage certificate. By Tuesday afternoon they would be on a plane to New York.

The thought that some of their plans could be salvaged and the rhythmic sound of Sarah's breathing began to relax him. Perhaps sleep might come at last. Just as he was slipping into oblivion, Sarah's snoring grew louder and seemed to echo around the room like thunder. Funny, she never usually snored at that volume. Forcing his weary eyes open again he looked down at her and realised that she was still breathing deeply and sleeping soundly, but she wasn't snoring. Then who the bloody hell was? The snoring grew louder and louder and seemed to be coming from the built-in wardrobes along the far wall.

With a certain amount of trepidation and a thumping heart, John gently rolled Sarah onto her side and slipped out of bed. Tiptoeing nearer to the wardrobe he hoped that his ears were deceiving him and the noise would turn out to be a rattling floorboard or something. It had been really windy lately and perhaps with the wind coming down the chimney and ... yeah right. *You have a screw loose if you think that noise is a floorboard, John.* There was no mistaking it. A snore was a snore and this one was loud enough to shatter the windows.

*Right, a weapon of some description.* Some old tramp

33

had probably sneaked in while they were at the church. He had seen a few lately walking the country lanes around the house and his market garden. The chancer must have scampered in here when they came back. John had rarely been out of the room since, so there had been no time for him to make his escape. He swallowed his nerves and took a deep breath. He wouldn't really need a weapon, would he? The guy was probably harmless. *Ah, yes, John, but he might try and attack when he's rudely awakened.*

The heavy wooden tea tray that he'd brought Sarah's water jug and glass upstairs on, sat on the floor just next to the wardrobe. John felt more prepared as his fingers closed around the handle and felt the solid weight as he lifted it above his head. *Right, let's see who the devil's in there.*

John hooked his fingers into the groove of the sliding door and pulled hard. The door wheeled smoothly open and then stuck as it met a barrier. The barrier, huddled in the corner with its bony knee against the wardrobe door, stopped snoring opened its eyes which were on a level with John's naked lower half, travelled up to the raised tea tray in his hand and let out a blood-curdling scream.

John nearly did the same as he scanned the dishevelled creature in front of him. The angular limbs – which at the moment were flailing like a spider cut from its silken thread – the haystack hair, the mole on its top lip ... oh, no. His gut did a somersault. It couldn't be, could it?

'Ratchet?' The creature stopped flailing and stared fixedly at his groin with something akin to curiosity and wonder.

John hurriedly covered himself with the tea tray and flushed the colour of beetroot. *Damn, how could he have neglected to put on his pants?*

A sleepy and mumbled, 'John, I thought I heard screaming ... or was I dreaming,' came from the bed behind him. Sarah then yawned long and loud. 'John?'

When he didn't answer he heard her pad across the

floor to stand behind him. She slipped her arms around his shoulders and kissed his neck. 'John, what are you doing standing looking in the ward—' She had peeped over his shoulder and he felt her body tense against his. '*Oh my God. Veronica Ratchet!*'

# Chapter Five

Veronica Ratchet, large as life, sat on the edge of Sarah and John's bed, her arms wrapped protectively around her body, rocking to and fro, her eyes round with shock. Sarah collapsed into her rocking chair and followed suit, her brain struggling, but failing, to comprehend the fact that Veronica had somehow left 1939 and had ended up snoring in her wardrobe.

John started to back out of the room, the tea tray covering his modesty. 'Now, just try to calm yourselves,' he muttered, scooping up his clothes and looking far from calm himself. 'Take a few deep breaths and I'll be back as soon as I have got dressed ... okay?' He shot them a weak smile and closed the bathroom door behind him.

Sarah rolled her eyes. *Keep calm? How the hell was she supposed to do that?*

Veronica took a few deep breaths and then some more. Her face grew pink and Sarah feared she was about to hyperventilate.

'Right, that's enough, Veronica. Just breath normally now.'

'Normally? How can I?' she wailed. 'Not only do I find myself caught up in this time travel nightmare, but I have just been rudely awakened to find a man's ... p-privates, inches from my face!'

If the situation wasn't so awful, Sarah would have laughed out loud at the horrified expression on Ratchet's face. A fleeting thought danced across her frazzled mind. Perhaps the poor woman hadn't seen a man's privates before. She had to have, surely. She must be at least forty ... *God, get a grip and calm the woman.*

'I know that must have been a shock, but please try.'

Sarah stopped rocking, it was making her feel seasick. 'And tell me how the hell you ended up here.'

'Your guess is as good as mine,' Veronica moaned. She stopped rocking too and raked her fingers through her haystack. 'You started to fade away when you were sitting ... right there at my kitchen table. And that really scared me. I realised I couldn't go through with this damned stitching lark, so I lunged out to grab you by the arm to tell you I'd changed my mind, but then I landed with a thud here on your bedroom floor. You were in bed just rousing from sleep and me ... I was in this strange house.' Veronica looked wide-eyed around the room as if she expected the walls to close in.

Sarah sighed. That's what the heavy feeling in her right arm had been. Bloody Ratchet hitching a ride through time. And the bump John heard, and assumed Sarah had fallen out of bed, was Ratchet landing. 'Okay, but why did you go to sleep in my damned wardrobe? Not the logical thing to do, was it?'

Veronica shot her a look that could have felled a bull elephant, her eyes beading to black. 'Logical, she says. How in the name of all that is holy *do* you behave logically in these situations?' She snorted. 'I pulled myself up from the floor but then a man – who I later realised was your husband – ran up here a few minutes later calling your name. I was so scared I hid in the wardrobe!'

'Okay, calm down, I realise this must be very strange for you –'

'Strange ... my God, that doesn't even begin to describe what I am ... what I am ... *bloody* feeling! See, I have been driven to curse and I never do that.' A flush of shame crept up her neck.

'Hey, sometimes a curse is the only way forward. It stops your head exploding.' Sarah tried a bright smile and then realised by Ratchet's saucer eyes and open mouth that she thought she was serious. 'That was a joke. We don't have

people with exploding heads in the twenty-first century ...
well, not as far as I know.'

'Twenty-first ...' Veronica's hand fluttered to her mouth
and she fell silent.

'Yes, but don't think about that for the moment or your
head might ...' Sarah began and then giggled nervously.
'Sorry. So you were in the wardrobe, John came in, I woke
up and then what, you went to sleep?'

'Not right away. I heard you talking about going back in
time and what happened to your wedding and everything. I
stuck my fingers in my ears, just squeezed my eyes shut and
told myself this was some awful nightmare. I suppose the
shock of it all sent me to sleep.'

Sarah thought that was probably it. Veronica's brain
must have shut down as a defence mechanism. Poor woman
must have been in a terrible state. And Sarah right at this
minute wasn't far behind. How on earth was Veronica able
to travel to the future? As far as Sarah knew Stitches only
went to the past. Perhaps John would know. And thinking
of John ... he had been in the bathroom an awful long time.

On cue in he came. He was dressed and looking less
alarmed. Sarah noticed he avoided eye contact, though in
fact he was wearing his special evasive Needler face, or ENF
as she called it. She remembered this face very well from
the early days in their relationship when she'd tried to prise
more information out of him about the way time travel
and the stitching and needling worked. The powers that
be were very secretive and only shared a certain amount of
information at a time.

'So, what do you think has happened, John? Why has
everything gone haywire?'

John's emerald green eyes danced over Veronica's hair
and he murmured, 'Eh, what do you mean, everything gone
haystack?'

Veronica patted her hair and blushed.

'I said haywire.'

John rubbed his knuckles over his dark stubble and sat down on the other side of the bed apparently lost in thought. Presently he sighed and said, 'Not entirely sure but I had an email to my phone just now in the bathroom. Seems like Veronica held on to you for grim death, so she arrived back here with you.'

'The Spindly Ones sent you an email to tell us something that we already knew?' Sarah felt her temper turn up from flickering flame to blowtorch mode. John was deffo hiding something. 'They *must* have said more than that!'

John nodded and held up both of his hands. 'Okay, no need to get angry. They said we had to try to stay calm … and that this kind of thing has happened once or twice before. They suggested that if Veronica just sits quietly for a few hours and goes to sleep she will find herself back at home in no time,' John finished, flashing her a too bright smile and a manic stare.

'Okay, what exactly is "this kind of thing"? As far as I know Stitches only go back in time, not forward.' Sarah noted that Veronica was beginning to hyperventilate again. 'Veronica, just stay calm, we'll get to the bottom of this email in a minute if John just tells the truth.' She looked pointedly at her husband.

Veronica shook her head and gave a shuddering sigh. 'What is this email thing? I don't know what you are both talking about. I just want to go home like John said.'

Of course she didn't know what a bloody email was. Sarah glanced at her poor bewildered face and her heart went out to her. 'Sorry, Veronica. It is like a jazzed up version of a telegram which is sent to a phone or a compu—' Sarah rolled her eyes internally. 'The Spindly Ones communicate to us, well to John, by it.' She could see that her words were making no sense and why would they? 'But never mind all that, I am sure you will be home very shortly.'

'I am telling the truth.' John pouted his sensuous lips and knitted his dark eyebrows together making Sarah want to kiss him, despite the situation. Why did he always have to look so damned sexy?

'But not all of it. What actually happened today ... yesterday or whenever it was?'

John stood up and went to the window and turned his back giving both women a nice view of his firm bum and long legs in his tight blue jeans and the contours of his muscular back visible through the thin white T-shirt. 'It is called Cross Stitch, apparently. Two or more Stitches get thrown together, sometimes because one of them needs to pass the time, sometimes ... well, nobody really knows.'

Not this old chestnut again, Sarah thought. Back to, we don't know, or it is not known. She looked at Veronica's disgruntled expression and thought about how she'd behaved back in 1939. Cross Stitch was an apt description for her.

'Well, in the end, Veronica didn't pass the time, did she? She decided she'd go through with it.' Sarah gave Veronica a withering look. 'Well, at first anyway. And have you ever known Stitches travelling to the future?'

John turned around and shrugged. 'Not me personally, but I have heard of it.' He looked at the floor to avoid Sarah's eye. 'Look, like I said, it was a mix-up. A Cross Stitch and what happens now is that Veronica goes back in the wardrobe, goes to sleep and then she should wake up back in her own time.'

'What, just like that?'

'Yep. That's what the email said.'

'Why do I have to go in the wardrobe to sleep?' Veronica asked pouting, but unlike John not looking in the least bit sexy. 'I want to go home as soon as I can, but I need to stretch my legs a bit ... I don't really feel tired at the moment—'

'That's exactly why we want you in the wardrobe. If you go wandering around the house seeing what we have here in the present it might weird you out.'

'Weird me out ... what do you mean?'

'It might scare you, or make you uneasy,' Sarah said. 'You have had a shock and if you see some of the gadgets we have in the present day it will make you even worse.'

John nodded and slid the wardrobe door open. 'And then we can all get on with our lives. You can go back to the war, we can get back to our wedding celebrations, sign the register, go on honeymoon ...'

Veronica heaved a heavy sigh but showed no sign of moving to the wardrobe. Sarah glared at John. Why did he have to juxtapose their lives like that? He could be so insensitive sometimes. Going back to the war ... hmm, bet Veronica could hardly wait. Still, she couldn't deny that her heart had started to thump with excitement at the thought of resuming their celebrations. The wedding had been pretty grim so far after all. A thought occurred to her then. 'But what about 1879? Who is going to take that mission?'

'Done and dusted apparently,' John said, pushing the wardrobe open to its fullest extent and gesturing at Veronica to climb in.

'So the job was done by someone else?'

'Yup. Now we really must get you home, Veronica.' John had his no nonsense voice on but Veronica just folded her arms and looked at the floor.

Sarah jumped up, grabbed a pillow and blanket and made the space as comfy as possible. She held out her hand to Veronica and felt her heart strings twang. Poor cow probably was worried about where she'd end up with everything going haystack. Like John when faced with Veronica's hair, haystack seemed the appropriate word. 'You'll be fine, love. Soon have you home if you can drift off.'

'Hmm. Like I said ... I do want to go home ... just hope I have a home soon. You both know what happens in the war. We obviously won or you would be talking German, but what happens to me? Do I survive ... or ... or what?'

John took her gently by the elbow and guided her to the wardrobe. 'We don't know, but chances are very good that you did. Now stop worrying and try to sleep. We mustn't say any more. The powers that be don't like it.'

Veronica reluctantly stepped inside and lay down. Sarah put the blanket over her and held her hand. 'Well, I can't say I have enjoyed meeting you because the whole experience has ruined my wedding, but that wasn't your fault.' She glanced up at John. 'Seems it was just one of those things and that nobody knows why it happened, eh?'

He nodded, coloured up and looked away.

*He knows something for sure.* 'But I do wish you well and I am sure everything will be fine.' Sarah wasn't sure at all, but what else could she say?

Veronica, her face pale and drawn bit her bottom lip and nodded. 'Yes, best foot forward an' all. I will be fine I expect. Thank you for being so kind when I ruined your wedding ... and goodbye.' Veronica withdrew her hand and settled her head down in the pillow.

John shut the door, took Sarah's hand and whispered, 'Right, let's go downstairs and have breakfast. We'll pop back up in an hour and see if she's gone.'

Once in the kitchen and out of earshot Sarah turned on John. 'Right, matey, what aren't you telling me?'

'Eh? Nothing ... now would you like a cooked breakfast or just toast?'

'Don't, "eh nothing me", and cooked, I'm starved.'

'That's a good sign. You look back to normal now. Have you any aches or pains?'

Sarah realised she was back to normal. All of her flu

symptoms had miraculously disappeared. Weird. 'Nope, nothing. So what aren't you telling me? You went as red as a strawberry upstairs just now. *And* you had the ENF on earlier.'

John had his head in the fridge so she couldn't see his face. 'I'm sure I didn't and if you must know I wanted to make sure I didn't worry Veronica, but I am a bit worried about her to be honest.' He shut the fridge door placed bacon and eggs on the counter and fiddled with the grill pan.

Sarah pulled her dressing gown tighter as she felt a sudden chill. The woman was obnoxious and definitely unlikeable, but she did have a vulnerable side and Sarah didn't want to think that something horrible happened to her back then. 'Why? What happened to her?'

John sighed and took her in his arms. She leaned her head against his chest and was comforted by the steady beat of his heart. 'I don't know for sure, hon, but Southampton was hit hard in the blitz. My great aunt lived there at the time and I remember her telling me and my sister Lucy about it when we were young.'

'Oh, no, poor Veronica.' Sarah lifted her head and searched John's face. 'Do you think she died?'

'I honestly don't know. I just hated saying that she would be fine, but I couldn't say anything else, could I?'

John broke their embrace and busied himself with the breakfast. Sarah looked around their bright and airy kitchen. Although the cottage was ancient it was kitted out with every modern appliance, but tastefully done and in keeping with the surroundings. The lemon and white of the walls complimented the original stone flags and the light wood cupboards. A tall sash window overlooked the fields and the morning sun angled in, painting everything in warm gold.

Sarah loved it here, had done from the very first time

she'd set foot in it before she and John were even together romantically, and now it was hers too. How lucky was she sat in this comfort with her new husband, safe, protected? While poor Veronica … Being a history teacher, Sarah knew a good bit about the war, plus she had real experience of it having visited 1940 on her first time trip. The air raid sirens had sent chills through her blood but she had only been there for a few hours. What must it have been like to hear it on a day-to-day basis? How on earth people managed to carry on in wartime, never knowing if they or their loved ones would wake up the next day, beat the hell out of her.

Sarah stirred her coffee and thought again about poor Veronica upstairs, now on her way back to 1939. She wouldn't experience bombs falling until the year after, but there would have been drills and preparations. Veronica would be watching the skies and listening for the sirens every night in that cold little house by the sea … all alone. No wonder she had been scared to take a time job. She had enough on her plate already; her nerves must be stretched to breaking point, hidden under that grouchy exterior. And Sarah had been less than sympathetic about the whole thing. Sarah, who had never had to worry about war, who had the most wonderful man in the world by her side, and even though her wedding day had been ruined, had many happy days stretching out in front of her.

Aware that the general sounds of cooking had stopped, Sarah looked up from her coffee to see John staring intently at her.

'Penny for them?'

Sarah gave him more than a penny, unburdening herself of the worries and sadness she felt for old Horse Face upstairs.

John placed breakfast in front of her and drew up a chair. 'Look, sweetheart, there's nothing we can do about it. The whole thing is out of our hands. The mix-up happened, buggered up our wedding and now it's over. I know I might sound selfish, but the main thing is that you are back safe and now we need to make the best of a bad situation and try to enjoy our honeymoon.' He tucked a strand of hair behind her ear. 'Okay, beautiful?'

Sarah sighed. 'Okay, but what about Veronica? Don't you care what happens to her?'

'Of course, but as I said, what can we do?' John lifted her hand and placed a kiss on her new wedding band. He smiled and looked thoughtful. 'I guess we could look up what happened to her in the records, or perhaps the Spindly Ones could tell us if we asked nicely. Will that make you feel better?'

It would, even if it was bad news Sarah felt she had to know. 'Thanks, John. I can't bear just going on with my life and forgetting I ever met her. I know she was a royal pain in the arse but—'

'I know exactly what you mean. Now eat your breakfast before it goes cold and then we'll go and see if she's left us.'

Hand in hand John and Sarah tiptoed across the bedroom. Sarah's heart bumped in her chest and trepidation tickled in her tummy. No snoring met their ears and unconsciously holding her breath she watched John's hand slide back the wardrobe door. Releasing the breath in a huff of relief she hugged her husband tight. 'Looks like she's gone safely, then.'

'Yep ... looks like. And let's hope that the old Ratchet keeps herself safe for the duration of the war,' John said, leading Sarah back downstairs.

# Chapter Six

began es up our tie
sound which but the main thing is that you are back said
and now we need to make the best of a bad matter and
to enjoy our honeymoon.' He twisted a strand of hair

*This is definitely more like it.* John stretched languidly, relishing the feel of cool, silky sheets against his skin and propped himself up on one elbow. The dawn light crept through the vertical blinds and cast grey bars along the knee deep luxury carpet in their Manhattan apartment suite. John cast his eye over the clothes strewn on the floor and the red basque crumpled on the end of the bed and grinned. Boy had they had fun last night and in the early hours. It had damn well been worth waiting for.

His wife, for now she was legally his wife, sighed softly in her sleep and shifted position. The sheet slipped down her gorgeous body to reveal one of her full breasts and one smooth thigh. Though they had made love three times already, John felt his excitement grow and he traced his fingers gently along her leg. Sarah responded by giving him a lovely view of her back and firm bottom as she turned over.

John lay back down and closed his eyes for a few moments. Perhaps he should let her sleep; she had struggled with jet lag and there would be plenty of time to make love again later. A sigh of contentment escaped his lips. Thank God everything had worked out. Veronica had gone back to 1939, they had signed the register, had a few friends and family over on Monday for a belated celebration, and then flown out here yesterday afternoon. The apartment was just as wonderful as it had looked on the website and there had been champagne and chocolates waiting. Not that Sarah was drinking much lately; she said it gave her heartburn.

That thought brought a picture of his dad's frowny face to mind. On Monday when they'd had folks round, Harry had pulled his son to one side and from the corner of his mouth said, 'So, have you told her about the reason for this

Cross Stitch malarkey, or whatever the powers are calling it?' Harry jerked his head in the direction of Sarah chatting to her sister on the patio in the autumn sunshine.

'No, I haven't because there might be lots of reasons for it or no reason at all. The powers that be said it has happened before and—'

'Aye and I bet they said that one of the reasons might have been what I mentioned the night she had the fever, eh?'

John pursed his lips and glared at his dad. Harry always had this knack of making him say stuff that he wanted to keep hidden, so he tried the old Needler evasion tactic as Sarah called it. 'It was hardly the same, was it? A Stitch wasn't hauled back from the past with the woman you told me about, now was she?'

'Not as far as I know. But the whole travelling but leaving the body here was very similar if you ask me. Now *did* they say the reason that I told you?'

As well as being good at wheedling things out of him, Harry was like a bloody dog with a bone too, so better toss him a morsel. 'It *was* mentioned in passing, but—'

Harry's eyes shone with excitement. 'I knew it, so why haven't you told—'

John had grabbed his dad's elbow and guided him into the kitchen out of Sarah's earshot. 'Shush, will you? I haven't told her because it might not be true and you know damn well how much she would want it to be.'

'But what else could it be?'

'Like I said, Dad, lots of things. Or maybe time just screwed up for no reason ... chucked Sarah back to 1939 by mistake.' John noted his dad's cynical smile and realised that his words were being taken with a huge pinch of salt. A flash of logic would wipe that off his face. 'And besides, don't you think Sarah would be the first to know?'

Harry held his finger up and grinned. 'Not necessarily, your mum once told me about this woman who—'

John held up his hands. 'I don't want to know about "this woman who", just keep your gob shut, right?'

Harry knitted his eyebrows together and shook his head. 'All right, don't get your knickers in a twist, lad. I guess whatever will be, will be.'

John opened his eyes and turned to face the contours of Sarah's naked back again. Whatever will be, will be, huh? He so hoped that it would be. But for now he would put all that out of his mind and concentrate on having the best time here in Manhattan. They only had a four day break as his market garden wouldn't run itself. Helen and Roy ran the shop part-time, but John did all the hard graft in the fields. One day he could hopefully afford a horticulturalist to assist him, but until that day it was down to him and Sarah, of course, lent a hand when she wasn't teaching.

Sarah's back was just itching to be kissed, as was the curve of her waist and the swell of her hip. It was no good, she could sleep later. John moved along the bed and put his lips on her shoulder, lifted her hair and nuzzled into the warmth of her neck. 'You awake, my love?' he whispered, running his hand along her thigh and over her tummy.

Sarah muttered something, yawned and then pressed her bum against him. 'I am now and it feels like you have been "up" for a while.' She chuckled.

'And would you like to go back to sleep?' He stroked her breast feeling the nipple grow erect between his fingers. 'I mean, I know how jet-lagged you are.'

Sarah turned around and looked sleepily into his eyes, though he noted a growing flame of passion igniting her baby blues to a deeper midnight. 'Oh, I think I can manage to keep my eyes open for little while.' Her fingers sent shivers through him as they ran along his chest, back and squeezed his bottom, and then he gasped as she pushed him onto his back and he felt the heat of her mouth.

'Wow, you are awake, aren't you?' he moaned as he

stroked her hair fanning out over his belly. As she continued, John wound his hands in her hair as every nerve ending sang with pleasure. If she kept that up there wouldn't be time to get inside her and he was desperate to do that.

Gently lifting her head he turned her over and heard her cry out as his mouth returned the favour and he slipped his fingers into the heat of her body. 'John, I need you inside ... now,' Sarah panted, moving her hips against his mouth.

John moved his kisses further up her body tasting the salt on her skin and then the sweetness of her mouth. Submerging his senses in the ocean of her eyes he groaned, 'I love you, my darling, my wife.' And then he felt her open to him and he thrust deep inside. Her arms and legs wrapped around him and he felt her hot breath on his cheek, his rhythm matching hers until he could no longer tell where she began and he ended as they soared towards shuddering climax.

Trying to catch their breath a few seconds later and still inside her, John stared into Sarah's eyes and felt his heart melt into hers. No words were needed. What they had was perfect ... like a hand in glove, bacon and eggs, horse and carriage, Wallace and Gromit ... John grinned. Where did that last one come from?

Sarah wrinkled her nose. 'What's funny?'

John told her.

'Charmin'. So which one am I?'

'Gromit, of course,' John said, settling beside her and pulling the duvet round them. 'You have the wet nose and floppy ears of the outfit after all.'

'Why, you cheeky article!' Sarah pulled the pillow from under his head and walloped him.

'Ow! Right, you've started something now,' John roared, taking her pillow and kneeling up on the bed. 'Pillow fight, seconds out, round o—'

Sarah whacked him across the head and for the next few minutes they abandoned themselves to sillydom.

John debated whether to tell Sarah she had cappuccino froth on her top lip and decided against it. She looked so damned cute and he'd sneak a photo in a minute. The wind at the top of the Empire State Building a few minutes ago had put roses in her cheeks, and made rats tails of her honey-blonde hair. Her blue eyes, accentuated by the turquoise scarf around her neck, sparkled with excitement.

Now warming up in The New York Bagel, they sipped coffee, munched on toasted raisin bagels and planned the last jaunt of their trip. Tomorrow they'd be UK bound and John felt his heart sink a little at that thought. They had had the best time and though he loved his job, right now he wanted to stay in the moment, in New York, on honeymoon forever.

'Right, we have done the Empire State, Central Park, open top bus tour, so ... do you want to do the Statue of Liberty boat trip, or something else?' Sarah asked, the frothy moustache wiggling as she talked.

Trying to keep his face straight, John said, 'Something else.'

Sarah looked at his twinkly eyed expression and sighed. 'No. We have plenty of time for bed when we get back to England.'

John frowned. 'No, I didn't mean that actually ... though come to think of it.' He put his head on one side and winked suggestively, but received a withering look for his trouble. 'No, I actually meant that ...' he looked at his watch and back at her '... we have exactly one hour to get down to the Heliport at Pier 6. They like you to arrive early because—'

'Eh? Heliport ... my God, you mean—' Sarah began, her moustache jiggling crazily as her excitement mounted.

'Yes, I do indeed my little cappuccino features. I have

booked a surprise helicopter flight over Manhattan. We get to see the Statue of Liberty, Ellis Island, the Empire State from another angle —'

He was cut off by a squeal and chuckled to himself as he watched her clap her hands together like a kid at Christmas. 'Let's mark the moment, eh?' He pulled his phone out of his pocket and took a photo.

'Oh, John. You are such a wonderful husband! What a fantastic end to our time here.' Sarah grinned taking his hand across the table.

'Well, I wanted to do something special given the way our wedding day and celebrations were so rudely interrupted.'

'You certainly did that, my love. And *you* are so special.'

'And you look *so* special.'

'I can't do, I must look a right mess after being out in the wind.' Sarah sighed patting her hair.

John quelled a torrent of laughter building in his throat. 'No, it's true. You *do* look *really* special.' He held up the photo.

Sarah froze in horror and then scrubbed at her mouth with a napkin. 'You swine, John. How could you let me sit here with a cappuccino moustache?' Though her voice sounded fierce he could hear laughter under the surface.

'Easy, it's just what wonderful husbands do.'

# Chapter Seven

The dip and rise had her belly on a string, and exhilaration pulsed through her veins as the helicopter buzzed past the Statue of Liberty in a blue sky swept of cloud. A gravy-brown Hudson crawled towards the sea beneath, while John held her hand and told her he loved her more than life …

Oh, to be back there instead of here. Sarah sighed, zipped up her school trousers and groaned. What a difference a few days made. Monday morning, and a quick glance through the bedroom curtains told her the sky was cloudy, swept of blue … in fact it looked like rain. As if on cue a patter of raindrops tattooed the pane. Yep, back to reality big-time.

Buttoning up her shirt she wondered if the day would be kind to her. Her timetable floated briefly into her mind … that would be a no then. Double Year 9, break, double Year 8, lunch … and oh, thank goodness for Year 10 in the afternoon. Even though she had no free lessons now that she had gone part-time, Year 10 would be a joy to teach. And if she wasn't mistaken it was a lesson on how the homesteaders had made use of the wind pump and red turkey wheat to survive the harsh climate in nineteenth-century Kansas.

Bitter sweet memories of Kansas in 1874 flooded in as she brushed her teeth. She often thought of her time-travelling mission there and could hardly believe how she'd coped with that awful heat, filth and back breaking work. And though it had been hard, she had *so* loved being someone's mother for a time. Sarah tried to quell a lump as big as a tennis ball rising in her throat: the sadness at leaving behind the 1870s Sarah's son, Artie, had played heavily on her mind. It wasn't as if she'd failed, in fact she had been fantastically successful, having saved the person she was supposed to and more besides. It was the awful thought that the lovely blond-haired little tyke she'd been a mother too for such a short time and had fallen in love with, had grown up, grown old, and was now long dead.

John had talked her through the times when she'd been maudlin and tried to lighten the heavy feeling in her heart. Just a few weeks ago she had been having a wobble and he had taken her in his arms and said, 'Look, Sarah, I know how you feel but just be satisfied that you did your job and made that whole family happy. Artie wasn't abandoned because his real mother never left, did she? And as you know, he grew up to be a senator responsible for the civil rights bills and made a huge difference to the world.'

Listening to the steady thump of his heart as she rested her head on his chest she had felt calmer, but still couldn't help blurting, 'But he's dead now, along with Martha and little Elspeth and—'

'You mustn't do this, Sarah. It helps nobody. And I know that this is all tied up with what that bastard Neil did to you.' He had lifted her head to look into her eyes. 'One day in the not too distant future, hopefully you will be a mum again, my darling. And when you are, it will be for keeps.'

John always knew exactly the right thing to say. She spat the toothpaste into the sink and sighed. Nothing happening so far though, was there? They hadn't been using contraception for a few months now and, while not exactly 'trying' for a baby regarding ovulation charts and stuff, they were spending a lot of time between the sheets. She regarded her downcast reflection and mentally gave herself a talking to. For goodness sake a few months is nothing and you know it, Sarah. Now get your teacher's head on and get going.

In a flap, unable to find the keys to her car, Sarah had taken John's truck and as she bumped and hurtled down the country roads on her way to the school on the outskirts of Sheffield, she hoped there was nothing important he needed for the market garden under the tarpaulin. Didn't he say he'd bought a new hose pipe irrigator or something just before they'd got married? Damn it, she'd have to check and ring him if it was in the back. He could come and collect it in her car – if he could find the keys – and if he could fit it in her boot. Bloody hell, why couldn't they have stayed in New York?

Slamming the door and grabbing her school bag, Sarah pulled her hood up against the rain, dragged back the corner of the tarpaulin and peered inside. Veronica Ratchet's pale and worried face peered back.

Sarah's legs turned to string and she had to grab the side of the truck. Her brain had a gag on her mouth. This was impossible! 'Jeez! What are you doing here?' she blurted eventually.

'I hid in this lorry thing not thinking that you would drive it away. It has been one of many necessary hiding places over the past while that I—'

'The past while? How long have you been back from 1939?'

Veronica smiled triumphantly. 'I never went back.'

Sarah's heart raced faster than Mo Farah heading for gold. '*You never went back?*' she yelled, blowing a raindrop off the end of her nose. But that was, she reckoned in her head, what, over a week ago?

'I'd thank you not to shout, Sarah. And no, I didn't go back. I thought I'd be safer here, to be honest. Can we get inside the lorry; we're both getting soaked.' Sarah opened her mouth and then shut it again. The bloody cheek of the woman!

Steaming like a couple of racehorses they sat in the cab staring at the wet bedraggled kids filing into school like animals into an Ark.

'They look awfully big some of those children. Why aren't they at work?' Veronica asked absently, pulling at the hair on her mole.

'The school leaving age is a lot higher than it was back in— Hang about.' Sarah twisted in her seat and poked Veronica in the arm. 'This is neither the time nor the place for idle prattle. What the *hell* are you still doing here, how did you manage to hide, and how have you survived while we were in America!'

'It wasn't hard, and refrain from poking me, please.' Veronica narrowed her jet beads and rubbed at her arm. 'I crept out of the wardrobe that day I was supposed to be dispatched home and hid in the spare room in that huge walk in wardrobe. While you were still in the house, I stayed there mostly and in the shed sometimes. It was pretty comfy in both places as I found some pillows and blankets in the airing cupboard. At night I would eat very well from your bountiful cupboards. You never missed anything, not even fresh bread.' Veronica shook her head in bewilderment.

Sarah rolled her eyes. She had noticed the bread disappearing faster than normal but she just assumed it was John being a pig. 'But what did you eat when we were away?'

Veronica tapped a finger at the side of her nose. 'I am very clever, Sarah. I spied on you once when your husband was in the shower. I noticed that you took frozen things out of the tall cooler and put it on a plate overnight. The next day it was thawed and you cooked it. The things you do have in the twenty-first century.' Veronica waggled her head in admiration. 'The flat box, which I have learned is a television, is phenomenal – once I got it working, of course. *Coronation Street* is my favourite, though the language is a little coarse, and the music when the break is on and people are trying to sell us things is so loud.'

'You've been watching telly? My God.' Sarah put her

hand to her mouth. What must this woman have seen of the future? Could she ever go back to her time now and be normal?

'Hmm, though I'm not sure what's happening most of the time and the news is so shocking. Even the selling bit is unreal, or perhaps a comedy, because why would people believe that you had to spend a month's wages on fried chicken in some kind of a bucket?'

Sarah's brain creaked into action. She needed to get Veronica back to her house and ask John what to do, because *she* certainly had no clue. But how could she do that when she was due in school any minute? It would be too late to organise supply at this short notice and besides, she'd already waved cheerily through the window at the head teacher as she'd driven into the car park. Damn it, what should she do!

The electronic buzzer sounded out for the start of tutor period. Her Year 7s would be taking the place apart if she didn't get there in a minute.

Veronica leaned forward and doubled up in her seat clamping her hands over her ears. What the hell was she doing now?

'Veronica, what are you doing that for?'

'That noise. I watched a film the other night where they had a nuclear war and that noise sounds like the warning siren that they had before they dropped the bomb!' she shrieked.

Bloody Norah, Veronica shouldn't even know about those things. Damn it all, Hiroshima hadn't happened in her time yet. Sarah put her head in her hands. *What a terrible mess*. Peeping through her fingers she noticed that Veronica was still trembling in her seat even though the buzzer had stopped.

'It's okay, Veronica, it isn't a nuclear war, just a new fangled version of that damned bell you wore dangling from your belt the day I first met you.'

'It is?' Veronica looked up and attempted a smile. 'How marvellous. Shall we go in then? I expect you'll be late if we don't go soon.'

'We?' Sarah looked at Veronica in disbelief. 'I don't think so, lady. You stay right here until break time and then I'll make some excuse and we'll go home and see John.'

'And I don't think so, lady,' Veronica mimicked. 'He'll make me go back to 1939.'

'But that's where you belong!' Sarah threw her hands up in exasperation and got out of the truck. 'Right, I'll come back in an hour or so before second lesson to check on you. Don't touch anything; in fact do *not* move, okay?'

Veronica did a half-shrug and looked away.

Damn it, damn it all to hell, Sarah cursed as she hurried through the rain soaked car park.

Tutor period safely executed, Sarah ran across the playground to the history block. Thankfully it had stopped raining and a rainbow arc promised a sunny spell or two. She shrugged off her damp jacket. Year 9 arrived in dribs and drabs and looked about as ready to start a written assessment on 'Why did Hitler Rise to Power?' as fly to the moon.

The only real insect in the ointment this year was Wesley Baker. There was always at least one hideous child who could disrupt a class. He wasn't as awful as Danny Jakes had been last year, but he could really try Sarah's patience. And by the look on his nasty little face as he slouched into the classroom, Sarah guessed that today was going to be one of those trying days.

While the class settled themselves, Sarah set up the Powerpoint and the title, 'Hitler's Rise to Power', along with the animated lesson objectives, bounced across the whiteboard. 'Right, you lot. Can we get our books out and jot these down first, please?'

There was general muttering, shuffling and sighing as each pupil prepared to do as she asked. Then on cue, Wesley stuck his hand up, a frown on his face deeper than the Grand Canyon.

'Yes, Wesley?'

'I ain't got me book.'

'So what happened to it this time? Dog chewed it again?' Sarah asked with a sigh, handing him some paper.

'No, it were me chameleon. He loves a bit of Nazi homework for his tea, miss.'

There were a few giggles but most of the class were ignoring him. Sarah decided to do the same and sorted through some notes, until a heavy sigh from Wesley grabbed her attention and she looked up to find his hand up again.

'What now, Wesley? Most of the class have written down the objectives for today and *you* haven't even started.'

'Well, duh, I can't start, can I?' Wesley's face darkened and he hawked in his throat most unattractively. Sarah thought that he was probably on about twenty a day judging from his yellow fingers and the stench of nicotine hanging over him like a yellow cloud.

'Why can't you start, Wesley?' she snapped.

'Because you ain't given me a pen, 'ave you?' he said with a smirk as if he'd scored some kind of point and then he leaned back in his seat.

'I think you'll find that it is your responsibility to bring a pen, a book, a ruler and any equipment you might need for the day. But here, have one for now and crack on with the objectives.' Sarah placed a pen by his hand. 'In fact you will have to copy them from someone else as I want to get to the first slide now.'

Wesley scrawled across his paper and said in a growly voice-over style, 'Objective one: To be able to understand and explain at least three reasons for Hitler's eyes to flower.' This got more of a laugh than last time.

'It doesn't say that, as you well know. Now, be quiet and—'

'Objective two: To decide which reason for Hitler's eyes was most important,' Wesley continued, grinning stupidly.

'Okay, you have a verbal warning. Next time you will have your name on the board.'

Sarah moved onto the first slide which was a picture of Hitler against a background of a huge swastika. 'Right, can anyone tell me one of the reasons for Hitler's rise to power that we learned last time?' Sarah looked at the class. Good, Wesley features seemed to be getting on with it at last.

There was a general air of bewilderment accompanied by nose picking, head scratching and out of the window gazing. Then Kylie Marsden put her hand up. Good, Kylie could always be relied upon to answer a question. Sarah nodded encouragingly.

'Treaty of Versailles, miss. That was a long-term cause, not a trigger, wasn't it?'

'Excellent, Kylie! It was indeed.'

Sarah clicked the remote control and the Treaty of Versailles in bold type bounced across Hitler's face and came to rest against a rather fetching star bullet point. 'Can anyone tell me a short term cause or a trigger?'

'I can, miss.' Wesley chuckled, tapping his pen against his table. Sarah doubted that very much but had to give him a shot.

'Okay, go ahead.'

'It was because he only had one ball. The other is in the Albert Hall apparently and—'

'That's enough, Wesley!' Sarah said above the guffaws. 'If you have nothing constructive to say, don't say anything.'

Wesley's face rearranged itself into a hard done by expression. 'But it's true, miss. There's a song about it and everything. He tried to get power 'cos he was well peed off about having a mono ball and—'

This time it was the head teacher who cut Wesley off. Mr Lockyear opened the door and glared at the gigglers and Wesley in particular. Wesley turned puce and shrank to the size of an ant under Lockyear's eagle eyes.

'Everything all right, Mrs Needler?'

'Fine thanks, Mr Lockyear. Apart from Wesley here who thinks he's a comedy act on stage at the moment.'

Sarah wanted the floor to open up. What a shitty morning she'd had so far. Back to reality with a bump from a wonderful time on honeymoon, late for school, getting soaked then finding bloody Veronica. And now to top it all, the head sees her struggling to control the class. It couldn't get much worse.

'Does he now?' Lockyear growled at Wesley. 'He can come and entertain me for an hour after school tomorrow if he carries on. Let me know if he doesn't improve, won't you?'

'Oh, you can count on it, Mr Lockyear,' Sarah said.

'And here's your lesson observer. She's sorry she's a bit late.'

Lesson observer? Sarah puzzled. She wasn't down to be observed.

'Hope I don't have to see you later, Wesley,' Lockyear continued. He nodded at Sarah and held open the door for someone to enter the classroom. Then Veronica Ratchet walked in and things just got a whole lot worse.

Thirty pairs of eyes followed Sarah's as she gaped like a fish out of water at Veronica. Her brain went into free-fall and she snapped the pencil she was holding in a death grip. How the hell did Ratchet get in the school and past reception with the Rottweiler receptionists snapping at the leash?

Veronica nodded a greeting. 'Hello class, my name is Miss Ratchet,' she boomed, and strode to the front of the class to join Sarah.

Every fibre of Sarah's being was shouting *No, stop! Turn around and get out* but her tongue clove to the roof of her mouth and immobile with shock, she felt as if in a dream, or nightmare more like.

From the front of the class, snatches of whispered conversation met her ears – the darlings of the class were concerned as to why miss looked so 'out of it'. And from two of the more fashion conscious girls, whispers and giggles about moles and the need for a good hair conditioner.

Veronica's eyes sparkled with mischief, her thin lips creased into a smile and she pushed the unruly mop of hair behind her ears. Sarah noticed that she had on a pair of her good earrings and bloody hell, yes, her blue flowery blouse under Ratchet's jumper and black trousers too – the cheek of her! The lovely conch brooch was still in pride of place though, seemed as if it was very special to the old trout. She'd not really taken much notice of what Veronica had been wearing in the truck, being preoccupied with picking her jaw up from the floor where it had dropped upon seeing the damned woman again. Still, Sarah guessed it was better than her turning up in her 1930s garb. That really would have set the kids' tongues wagging.

Talking of wagging tongues, at that moment hers thankfully became free. 'Miss Ratchet,' she began in a voice that sounded like a mouse on helium. 'I wasn't expecting you just now. I wonder if you could please wait in reception until the lesson has ended.'

'Oh, really? Judging by the subject matter of this lesson,' Ratchet nodded at the whiteboard, 'I think my expert help will be invaluable, don't you?'

A few of the kids nudged each other and pulled faces in response to Veronica's old-fashioned clipped BBC radio voice.

'Perhaps, but the students need to find things out for themselves, and because you are,' Sarah gritted her teeth and tried to smile, 'an expert they might be tempted to quiz you and—'

'I think you'll find I know how to answer inquisitive pupils, miss.' Veronica flashed a shark grin at Sarah and turned to the class. 'Right everyone, look at me and listen. Who can give me the correct answer for why this horrid man has risen to power?'

There were more giggles at her voice and patronising tone. Veronica held up a finger and looked sternly at the gigglers.

Sarah's heart sank and with it her confidence in being able to retrieve her class from a head on collision with Ratchet. She could see Wesley already warming up for a fight, rocking back on his chair, his piggy eyes narrowing, bottom lip stuck out.

Kylie's hand went up. 'I thought there was more than one reason, miss. That's what the assessment we're writing is all about.'

'No, child, there is only *one* reason and do *not* shout out before I select you to speak.'

Sarah swallowed and leaned against the desk. She must do something, but what?

'So what's the one reason then?' Wesley growled. 'I'm guessing it had to do with Hitler's trouser department.'

Veronica scowled and tutted loudly. 'Young man, please do not shout out and show your ignorance. Mr Hitler does not even own a trouser department.'

The whole class erupted in guffaws again and Wesley shouted above the din, 'Told you he only had one – seems like he had none now!'

As if by magic Sarah's training kicked in and she banged on the desk. 'Be quiet, right now or you all stay in at break!'

The din subsided and Kylie muttered to her friend loud enough for Sarah to hear. 'That's not fair, I never did anything wrong and that woman is talking about Hitler as if he's still alive.'

Veronica obviously heard too. She shot Sarah a guilty glance and went to look out of the window.

Ignoring Kylie's comment Sarah, still on auto-pilot, clicked the remote control and the other bullet points were revealed in full. 'Okay, I was going to test your understanding by having a Q&A session, but we're falling behind today because of our,' she glanced over at Veronica's ramrod straight back, 'interruptions. So jot down these reasons for Hitler's rise, order them in terms of importance and give explanations for your choices. Discuss quietly with a partner if you need to. Ten minutes – go!'

The class having the threat of break time detention hanging over them settled quickly to the task and Sarah went over to Veronica.

'How the hell did you get into the school?' she hissed.

'I said I was an observer from The Ridings School. I read your school diary while you were away and you had an observer booked for tomorrow. I just told the ladies on the desk that it had been moved forward.'

Bloody hell, she was smart. 'Did you, now? Well, you can just go and tell them that you have been urgently called away and let me get back to teaching this class. You have already made Kylie suspicious.'

Veronica looked from the window and down her nose at Sarah. 'Kylie ... what a ridiculous name. Whatever were her parents thinking?'

'Never mind that now, just go. Wait for me in the truck,' Sarah said, and made to move away. Then she felt Veronica's talons on her arm.

'Not quite yet. I think I'll have a chat to Madam Kylie first.'

Before Sarah could stop her, Veronica had hurried over to Kylie and was peering over her shoulder at her work. A few seconds later she straightened and snorted. 'Preposterous! Appeasement led by Mr Chamberlain was an important reason for Hitler's success?'

Kylie coloured up and looked to Sarah for support. 'But it was. Miss taught us about it last week.'

'Yes, I did, and I will thank you not to talk to my students in such a way, Miss Ratchet.' Sarah grabbed Veronica's arm and tried to guide her toward the door.

Veronica shook her off and went back to Kylie. 'I'll have you know that Mr Chamberlain was acting in the country's best interest. It's only just over twenty years since the first war which cost us the lives of millions. Why would we want to hurtle into another, hmm? Unfortunately that is exactly what we have had to do – but don't blame Mr Chamberlain, blame the warmongering nature of the Hun!' She finished her tirade by poking Kylie on the shoulder.

Kylie blinked back tears and shouted, 'You can't talk to me like that, or poke me! My dad will come up to this school!'

Sarah ran over and wrenched Veronica away. 'Okay, Kylie, don't worry, Miss Ratchet is just leaving.'

'Miss Ratchet is *not* leaving.' She wrenched herself free again. 'And since when can't a teacher poke a child?' Veronica snapped haughtily. 'Looks like this lot could do with a poke or perhaps a caning or two.' She marched over to Wesley and grimaced at his scruffy scrawl and doodles. 'My God, lad. You have more fat in you than a tub of lard and you are practically illiterate – that means dumb, if you aren't sure. A spell in the army would sort *you* out!' she yelled in his ear.

Wesley stood up, tipping the desk over in the process. 'You can't talk to me like that, you snotty bitch!' he shrieked, raising his hand. He was a good foot taller than Veronica and at least two stone heavier.

Veronica grabbed a ruler and went to whack him on the face.

Sarah's heart galloped in her chest as she stepped between them. 'Please, Wesley, sit down and keep calm. Miss was

64

very wrong to say those things, okay?' *God don't let him wallop her, or me come to that!*

Wesley, still fuming and panting like a raging bull, slowly lowered his hand and then his body back into the chair.

*Phew.* 'Come with me right now!' Sarah yelled in Veronica's brick red face, dug her nails into her arms and dragged her out of the room.

Outside the classroom, Sarah slammed the door on the uproar ensuing from the class and pushed Veronica down the corridor. 'Go to the truck and wait for me and God help you if you don't do as I say!'

Veronica looked as if she might argue, but then thought better of it and scuttled off.

Sarah swallowed hard and went back into the chaos of the classroom. She could *so* use a time trip right about now.

# Chapter Eight

An hour later John and Sarah faced Veronica across their kitchen table. John took his wife's hand and felt a grateful squeeze in return. The colour had returned to her cheeks and she'd stopped rambling that she wished she could have been whisked off on a time trip to the Alaskan wastes or somewhere equally remote.

Sarah had frightened the life out of him ten minutes ago as he'd opened the door to find her standing on the doorstep looking like an escaped crazy person, her hair rivalling Ratchet's on the unruly front. It had taken John a good few seconds to calm down her ramblings as he couldn't make head nor tail of it at first. Something about Veronica hiding in a cupboard and nearly coming to blows with a fourteen-year-old pupil? Puzzled, he'd told her gently that Veronica had gone back to 1939 and then Sarah had pointed over her shoulder at a tousled haired woman clambering down from the truck and a cold shiver of panic in his gut had organised her words into a frighteningly coherent pattern.

He'd sat dumbstruck as Sarah had explained how Veronica had come to still be here and outlined the mayhem she'd caused in school. It was impossible? How could the powers that be not have realised that she hadn't gone back? He had never heard of such a thing in all his years as a Needler and he was pretty sure his dad hadn't either or he would have told him about such an extraordinary event.

Sarah glanced at him now and laid her head on his shoulder. 'It took all my imagination to come up with an explanation to the kids and the head. I'm not sure he believed me, to be honest, as I kept going red.' She sighed.

'What did you tell them?' John asked.

'Well, I went back in the classroom and told them that Veronica was an imposter who'd sneaked in. I also said she was obviously a nut job and she'd been escorted from the premises. I told the head the shock of it made me feel sick and I had to go home.'

'A nut job?' Veronica frowned. 'I expect that means a nut case and how dare you say that about me?'

Sarah lifted her head from John's shoulder and stuck her neck out at Veronica. 'Well, it isn't far from the truth, is it? Waltzing in and calling Wesley dumb and a tub of lard!'

'I said he had more fat in him than a tub of lard, actually.' Veronica sniffed and studied her fingernails.

'Oh, that's all right then!' Sarah spat, her blue eyes steely. 'And I don't suppose you banged on about Chamberlain and Hitler like they were still alive and the First World War only just twenty years over, either? It was enough to scare the shit out of the kids let alone you verbally attacking Kylie and nearly whacking Wesley across the bloody face!'

'Okay, that's enough, Sarah,' John said, slipping his arm around her. 'We've just got you calm and this isn't helping the situation. What we need is to get Veronica home and I *mean* home this time, okay?' He glared at Veronica.

'I don't want to go. Who in their right mind would?' Veronica threw up her hands.

'Well, you aren't in your right mind, are you, so—'

'That isn't helping, as I just said, Sarah. Now you two sit here, drink your coffee and I'll try and contact the powers to see what to do next.' He stood and walked to the door. 'And don't let me find you rowing when I get back.'

When he returned a little while later, he listened at the kitchen door for any sign of raised voices. Good, nice and quiet. But upon entering he could see that the reason for it wasn't good at all. Veronica had her head on Sarah's shoulder, blubbing for England and Sarah looked at him with tears in her own eyes.

'What's up?' John asked, though the reason for Veronica's upset was obvious.

'She's terrified that she'll end up flattened in an air raid,' Sarah said, patting Veronica's arm. 'She's also very lonely. Edward, a widower who wants to marry her, gave her that beautiful brooch,' she said, nodding at the sparkly piece on Veronica's jumper. 'Then he joined the Home Guard and was sent to Lond—'

Veronica sat up and flapped her hands at Sarah. 'Shh, I told you that in confidence,' she hissed.

John drew up a chair and leaned his elbows on the table. It looked like he would have to allow Veronica some knowledge of what would happen to her in order to pacify her enough to comply. The powers had expected as much. When he'd contacted them by email just now, they had been mildly surprised that Veronica was still here, but it *had* in fact happened before and they weren't that perturbed about her having knowledge about the future. John rolled his eyes internally, and we all know why that is, don't we? Because soon she'd remember nothing at all as her memory would be wiped as soon as she returned home … God, sometimes he hated this job, but if she was allowed to keep her memories of the twenty-first century there'd be no telling what damage would be done.

'Okay, Veronica,' John said quietly, looking into her grief-stricken and blotchy face. 'I have just had a word with the powers and they said not to worry. You won't be flattened if you go back.'

'I won't?' Veronica's expression turned sceptical, but hopeful too.

'Nope. In fact you will marry Edward and survive the war. He will be invalided out of the Home Guard, but apart from a slight limp and a twitch in his cheek he will be as good as new.'

Veronica's hand fluttered to her mouth. 'My God, that's marvellous! And he's always had a twitch in his cheek ... but how did he get the limp?'

'I think he stepped on a shard of glass when he was helping to clear a bombed out house.'

'And when will we get married?'

'1941.'

Sarah beamed at him, then turned to Veronica. 'Now, that's a bit of good news for a change, isn't it?'

Veronica sighed and dabbed a tissue at her eyes. 'But how do I know you aren't just saying all that to make me go back? I thought you said that knowledge of one's future is very dangerous, not to say all the stuff I learned here about the twenty-first century. Won't I be affected by that?' A sly look crept across her face. 'I could let something slip ... not on purpose, of course.'

'I think you are far too sensible and clever to just let things slip, Veronica,' John said, noticing that Sarah was looking at him in disbelief. He attempted an encouraging smile. 'Right, now let's get you upstairs and into that wardrobe. Once you've dropped off, you will be home quicker than you can say mole.'

Veronica covered her top lip self-consciously. 'Mole?'

Shit, why had he said that? Just prattling because he was nervous he guessed. 'Yep it's a daft saying we have here in the twenty-first century.'

Upstairs, Sarah and John sat on the bed and watched Veronica walk towards the wardrobe. She turned and looked at them, a wistful look softening her long angular features. 'I suppose this is goodbye then.'

John saw Sarah's eyes fill up. She seemed to have a love hate relationship with the old trout. Must be a Stitch connection or something, or perhaps she was unduly emotional because ... he banished fanciful thoughts from his mind and nodded. 'Yes, this is goodbye. Still, you can look forward to a happy life after the war.'

Sarah stood and embraced Veronica. 'It will all be fine.' She helped her step into the wardrobe and get settled under a blanket. 'Just take deep breaths; think nice thoughts and you'll soon be asleep.'

John heard Veronica strangle a sob. 'Thank you, Sarah. You have been so kind and I haven't exactly been on my best behaviour. Goodbye and good luck.'

Sarah stepped back into the bedroom and joined John on the bed. They lay down, held each other tight and waited for telltale snores. There was no way they were going downstairs this time in case Veronica decided she'd do another disappearing act.

John felt his heart sink as Sarah whispered, 'All that stuff you told her about being clever and not slipping up, was it true?'

'Um ... not strictly.'

'Didn't think so. So how are you so sure she won't blab about her marriage in 1941 and what she's seen here?'

'Er ...'

'They are going for a memory wipe, aren't they?'

'Er ...'

'Damn it, John. It's just so unfair ... it's a violation really.'

Thankfully John was let off replying by the thunderous snores suddenly reverberating through the wooden doors of the wardrobe. He gave Sarah a squeeze. 'Thank goodness, give her a few minutes and then we'll take a look.'

Sarah slipped from the bed and tiptoed to the wardrobe. The snores petered out and then stopped. She glanced round at him, a smile playing over her lips. 'Sounds like she's gone,' she whispered.

John went to join her and they both peeped through the

gap in the door. Bloody hell, she was *still* there, asleep but just not snoring. Sarah rolled her eyes at him and whispered, 'She doesn't look very comfy, her head's not on the pillow right. I'll just adjust it and then she might relax more.' As she reached out her hand to touch the pillow, Veronica moaned in her sleep and slipped her fingers around Sarah's wrist. She yawned loudly and started to snore again.

John felt the hairs on the back of his neck prick up and an ill omen hammered a warning in his head. 'Sarah, pull your wrist away! I think she's going to—'

It was too late. John was left staring at an empty wardrobe.

Three at a time he charged down the stairs like an angry bull. Had the powers that be lost their powers for some bloody reason? Couldn't they control what was bloody happening any more? He jiggled the mouse at the computer and typed another email – his fingers furiously flying over the keys.

I did as you asked and Veronica Ratchet has successfully returned to 1939. The trouble is Sarah has been taken with her – AGAIN! What the hell is going on? Bring Sarah back right now!

He paced up and down the living room cursing at the top of his voice, raking his fingers through his hair as he waited for a reply. Eventually after ten long minutes he got it:

We can understand your frustration, John, but we would thank you to refrain from adopting such a rude and disrespectful manner. Veronica has been diverted from her quiet return home to 1939 as she's required for another mission. It appears that Sarah has gone with her. Most unfortunate, but there it is … the Cross Stitch hasn't run its course.

Most unfortunate? Is that all they could say? John felt his temper go from simmer to a rolling boil, and before he could stop himself he'd written:

What do you mean, most unfortunate? I know what you said about the fluke of the Cross Stitch thing, but isn't it up to you lot who goes on missions and where and when any more? Where is she? Have you lost your bloody powers, been taken over by a multi-universe time-travelling agency or something? I said bring her back, right now!

This time John had his reply much quicker.

Because you continue to be abusive we will have to end communication for today. Of course you are upset and we can understand that, but at present we don't appear to have full control of Sarah's actions. There are investigations into the possible cause of her ... erratic disappearances, and there are some theories, some of which you know, but for now there is no firm conclusion. We cannot speculate and, as you know, cannot tell you about your personal future in detail, suffice to say we are confident that Sarah will do her best and be back to you shortly.

'What!' John snorted aloud and went to reply, but the screen went dead and no amount of switching on and off would change it.

He stared at the screen and helplessness washed anger from his blood. *What have they done with my Sarah? My poor baby, stuck God knows where with that stupid bloody woman.* Nausea bubbled in his stomach and he ran to the kitchen door. Birds sang, fields rolled, clouds floated and the scent of new mown hay wafted in on the breeze. Just a normal autumn day in the country. But everything was far from normal, wasn't it? Even by the standards of a Needle and Stitch.

John took a deep breath or two and felt his sickness pass but his anxiety remained. A fine bloody husband he was. Not five minutes in the job and he'd failed to protect his beautiful wife twice now. What the hell was going on? He didn't know, and the powers had as good as admitted that they didn't know either. Maybe it was time to give in and pick his dad's brain on the outlandish theory he had cooking in it. It would probably do no good because the goal posts had been moved now. Last time, at the altar, Sarah's body was left behind just like the other Stitch that Harry had told him about. But this time she'd disappeared, gone back to the past as normal. Well, not as normal, as Veronica had dragged her off, but at least as she *usually* travelled on a mission.

Still, even the smallest detail his dad could remember about the other Stitch would be better than nothing. And, most importantly, at least John would feel like he was doing something.

Grabbing his coat from the hook he slammed the door, ran to the car and drove away like a bat out of hell. If Sarah had been in the passenger seat she would have gone bananas at him for reckless driving. She wasn't though, was she? In fact, he hadn't the slightest clue where in the world she was or even what time period she'd been dumped in. John swallowed a lump of emotion and floored the accelerator.

# Chapter Nine

Unsure if the high pitched screeching busting her eardrums was coming from a human or an animal, Sarah rubbed her eyes and shook her head. Then the darkness lifted, her senses focused and she realised that part of the screeching was indeed human. Veronica lay prone a few feet away, her mouth as wide as her eyes, but her efforts were also accompanied by the wail of an electric guitar.

She further discovered that instead of kneeling over Veronica in the wardrobe, she was on her knees in a damp, filthy bedroom. A tattered poster of a punk band, possibly the Sex Pistols, hung above a single bed, its dubiously stained sheets strewn with takeaway cartons, and a bucket in the corner caught a succession of drips escaping from a large damp patch on the ceiling.

The guitar screech coming up through the floorboards beneath her feet fell silent for a few seconds and then started up again even louder. Veronica screeched again at roughly the same volume as the guitar and shuffled crab-like across the floor to the far corner where she folded herself into a ball and whimpered.

Sarah grabbed the bed leg and struggled to her feet, anger fighting with anxiety in her gut. She glared at the pathetic bundle in the corner and felt like whacking her across the head. Bugger it all, the stupid mare had grabbed her wrist and now here she was, catapulted unceremoniously into the past *again*. But it sure as hell wasn't 1939.

The guitar strains faded and Veronica looked up at her, snot and tears mingling in dirty rivulets down her nostrils and chin. 'My God, what happened to you …' Veronica stared fixedly at Sarah. 'And where … where are we, Sarah? You *are* Sarah, aren't you?' she snuffled.

'Of course I'm Sarah. What a ridiculous question and how the hell should I know what happened to us and where we are?' Sarah flung her arms up. 'Obviously not back in cosy war-torn 1939, thanks to you!'

Veronica's face crumpled in despair. 'But I didn't do anything ... I just w-went to s-leep,' she said with a sob. And then the guitar starting up again sent her shrieking under the bed.

Sarah stomped over and peered at Veronica quaking amongst empty crisp and biscuit packets, withered apple cores and long abandoned coffee mugs inside of which grew what looked to be alien life. Once again pity for the poor woman flooded through her. It was true, Veronica had been asleep and had no idea that she'd grabbed Sarah's wrist. But for goodness sake, all this would try the patience of St Peter himself. She blew down her nostrils in exasperation. 'It's okay, Veronica, the noise is only a guitar.'

'A guitar? It can't be. It sounds like the hounds of hell!'

'It's an electric guitar. You probably wouldn't have heard one, and definitely not played in this punk rock style.'

'Punk what?' Veronica didn't look convinced or any less scared.

'Rock. In the 1950s there was a new kind of music called rock and ... oh, never mind. We need to find out when and where we are, why we are here ... and then get you back to your time and me back to mine.'

It sounded simple said out loud but Sarah had a sneaking suspicion it wouldn't be. 'Right, come out from under there before you get a disease. Whoever lives here is a perfect candidate for *How Clean is Your House?*'

Veronica crawled out and sat on the edge of the bed with her fingers in her ears. She averted her eyes from Sarah's as if she were afraid of her as well as the guitar and scanned her up and down, a look of distaste clear on her miserable face.

Sarah sighed and glanced down at herself. It was then that she realised that her clothes had changed. Drainpipe black jeans, winkle picker shoes, a crazily black and yellow patterned T-shirt with holes in it and, she patted her hair … oh my God, tall hairsprayed-stiff spikes? That's why Veronica had asked what had happened to her and if she was Sarah!

A grimy mirror by the wardrobe told the rest of the sorry tale. Blonde punk spiked hair, heavy black make-up on her eyes and lips, a safety pin hanging from her ear and white face powder. No wonder Ratchet was scared. *Great this is not happening*. On the other time trips the same thing had occurred. Sarah was definitely herself when she looked in the mirror, but her clothing and make-up became appropriate to the time period she found herself in. But she *wasn't* on a mission now, was she? Unless she'd been sent on one without her permission and Veronica bundled along too. Oh no, no, no. This was just unbearable.

She turned to Veronica. If they were both on a time trip, why hadn't *she* been changed? She was still wearing the school clothes that she'd nicked from Sarah. The 'music' stopped abruptly and then they heard footsteps thumping up carpetless stairs. The two women looked at each other with trepidation and then the door flew open and a tall skinny young woman looked at them in surprise. At the sight of her, Veronica's face drained of colour and she wrapped her bony arms protectively around her chest.

Like Sarah, the woman wore her hair in spikes, but pink, not blonde, drainpipe yellow trousers, black heavy boots draped with chains and a deep purple T-shirt – torn and with the blood spattered face of a gargoyle on it. Her make-up was identical to Sarah's and she had a piercing through her lip and nostril. The nostril sported a silver skull, the lip a pointed stud.

'Didn't know you were home, Sarah. Thought you were

coming back at about three-ish,' the young woman said, eyeing Veronica curiously. She looked back to Sarah. 'You seen my new studded choker collar?'

Sarah's heart thudded to her winkle pickers. *Shit she knows my name and ... home?* That confirmed it. She *was* here on a sodding mission then. But why was Veronica here, and who did she have to save?

'Nope. I haven't seen it.' Sarah sighed, bewildered and flopped down next to Veronica.

The young woman harrumphed. 'Yes, that's what you said last time about my shoes and then you were wearing them at the gig last week.'

Sarah rolled her eyes but said nothing.

'And seeing as you're not introducing me to your new friend, I'll do it myself,' the woman continued, striding up to a shell-shocked Ratchet and sticking her hand out. 'I'm Gerry, short for Geraldine, and you are?'

Veronica stared at her long black painted talons and gingerly shook hands. 'I am Veronica.'

'Ronnie for short?'

'No. I don't shorten names. I think it is a little common.' Veronica sniffed.

Gerry took a step back and looked at Sarah in disbelief. 'A little common?' She imitated Veronica's clipped tones perfectly. Then she tossed her spikes. 'Bloody hell, where'd you dig her up from, Sarah?'

Despite the situation Sarah felt a smile tug at her lips. 'Er ... Veronica is a little old-fashioned, I guess.'

'You're not kidding. Her clothes are way straight, but her hair is ... "out there", a bit Debbie Harry on speed.'

Sarah had to bite the inside of her cheek to stop a giggle.

Veronica frowned, clearly affronted and flapped a hand at Gerry. 'I'd rather be old-fashioned than look like, like a demon from Hades! And what in God's name have you done to your nose and lip, young woman?'

77

Gerry took Sarah's arm and pulled her over to the window and from the corner of her mouth she said, 'She another of your "strays" you found down the docks? 'Cos anyone in their right mind can see she needs professional help.' Gerry glanced back at Veronica and then hissed in Sarah's ear. 'You can't just keep on bringing weirdos home.'

Unable to think of an adequate response, Sarah just shrugged. She needed to find out what year it was and then try to find out who she had to save. The sooner she got out of this nightmare and back to John, the better. And if Ratchet got stuck here, well, so be it. She was *so* over caring what happened to her. But where to start?

Gerry's keen blue eyes regarded her through the heavy make-up. 'So, what's she doing here? This squat is already bursting at the seams. Laz and Ollie will do their nut.'

Squat? Right, they were squatters. That would explain the condition of the house. Sarah said the first thing that came into her head. 'She had nowhere else to go … a bit lost.' At least the last bit was true.

Gerry sighed but said nothing.

And who were Laz and Ollie? Was it one of them playing the guitar downstairs? Sarah wandered back over to the bed and sat down. 'Was that you playing just now, Gerry?' She smiled.

Gerry rolled her eyes. 'No, it was the Pope.'

'The Pope?' Veronica said, putting her hand to her face. 'Really? Mind you, I shouldn't be shocked. It is the twenty-first century after all. Do you think I could meet him?'

Sarah cringed. She needed to get Veronica on her own pretty damn quick to tell her the ground rules about stitching.

Gerry's eyes grew round and she shook her head in bewilderment. 'It was a *joke*, Ronnie. I was playing the guitar. And we are in the twentieth century, love,' she said slowly and gently.

'But it can't be. That's *my* century! People dressed like you ... in *my* century? What year is it?' Veronica shrieked.

'Blimey, love. You on a bad trip? It's 1979.'

A faint bell rang in Sarah's head. *Of course ... the year I was born. Well done, Veronica, now shut up.*

'I think we should have a walk outside, Veronica, come on.' Sarah stood up and flashed a warning with her eyes at her.

'But that's only forty years in the future. Goodness, I hope I'm not alive to see it. And are we in Southampton?'

Sarah shook her head. *Great, that worked then.* 'Let's go, Veronica.'

'No, love. Bristol. And I think you should go for a walk with Sarah, like she says.'

Gerry looked at Sarah above Veronica's head and mouthed *What the hell?*

Veronica shot from the bed and pointed a trembling finger at Gerry. 'Not so fast! You said a bad trip. Do you mean a time trip?' She looked triumphantly at Sarah. 'I bet she's a Stitch too and trying to test us. You won't fool me. I'm trained for those kinds of shenanigans. There *is* a war on after all!'

Sarah grabbed Veronica's elbow and practically dragged her past an open-mouthed Gerry, through the door, down the rickety stairs and out into a steep narrow street. The bright sunshine took a bit of getting used to after such a dismal interior, but then Sarah could see they were standing on a hill overlooking the city. Opposite a cluster of brightly coloured Victorian houses hugged a hillside and in the distance, masts of tall ships bobbed on twinkly water. She turned to Veronica who stood blinking and shaking. 'Right, you mustn't say one more word to anyone until we can find a place to chat safely, okay?'

Veronica nodded mutely.

Ten minutes later they were sitting on a park bench next to a pond watching the ducks sail past quacking contentedly as if they hadn't a care in the world. Sarah wished she could join them. But at least she felt a little calmer now and she had to smile when she remembered Gerry's expression after Veronica's outburst.

Veronica knitted her bushy brows together. 'I fail to see the humour in our predicament, Sarah. Just what by all the saints are we doing here?'

When Gerry had said they were in 1979 a few bells had begun to ring, but because of Veronica's runaway mouth she hadn't had time to think straight. But now, she at last started to piece together what little information she had.

'Okay, Ronnie,' she began, until she received a glare that could curdle milk. 'Er ... I mean Veronica. I am scheduled to do a time trip to 1979 a month after my wedding. As well as saving a life, I thought it might be interesting to go back to the year of my birth to see what it was like back then. But as we know since the day I stood at the altar, my time travelling schedule has gone horribly tits up. Who knows what the Spindly Ones are thinking, if they are thinking at all. They can't be can they, sending you here too?'

'Tits up?' Veronica said puzzled.

'Yeah, it's like belly up. If someone were dead in the water their belly or in this case, tits, would be up. It means that something isn't working, gone wrong—'

'I get it! I get it! Oh, that is hilarious!' Veronica laughed fit to burst.

'But I thought you'd think it was vulgar?'

'It is, but so funny too!'

Sarah watched Veronica rocking with laughter, her face red, tears streaming down and worried that Veronica had been pushed over the edge by the whole crazy situation. 'Good, well, anyway, we need to sort out a few Stitch ground rules.'

Veronica ignored her.

'Veronica, can you please listen?'

Veronica laughed a while longer and then noticing Sarah's stern expression took a few deep breaths. 'Okay. Go on I'm all ears. All ears.' She took another breath and cocked her head on one side. 'Imagine if a person was made up entirely of ears, now that would be most odd.' She grinned stupidly at Sarah.

*Yup, deffo on the brink*. 'Right. Listen carefully. We must not at any time divulge to people that we are Stitches or any information from our own time. That is a big no no. If that happens we are liable to be warned to stop by being inflicted with fits of laughter, flatulence, nausea, or any number of embarrassing things.'

'Oh, dear. Have you suffered any of these afflictions?'

'Yes, I was given the giggles in 1940, and flatulence in 1913. It was very difficult to cover up I can tell you.'

'Ah. And I revealed quite a bit to that Geraldine creature, didn't I? So why didn't I have any of those things inflicted upon me?'

'Probably because she thinks you are a crackpot and didn't believe a word. But no more of it, okay?'

'Well, really! Me a crackpot and she looking like a phantom or one of the living dead?'

'She thinks you're a crackpot because of the things you were saying, Veronica. I mean, what would you think in her shoes?'

'I wouldn't be seen dead in her ugly boots.' Veronica shuddered. 'Or yours either. Why are you dressed like that? Does everyone in the 1970s dress like that?'

Sarah explained that when a Stitch goes on a mission they find themselves dressed in the fashion of the day, and in the seventies only punk rockers dressed in that way. 'To be honest, I don't know much about 1979 because, as I told you, I was only just born. I guess the most shocking thing for you to hear about this year is that Britain elected its first woman Prime Minister.' Sarah figured it wouldn't hurt to spill those beans as Veronica would get a memory wipe when she got back to 1939. Sarah checked herself. *If* she got bloody back.

'My goodness! Did she do a good job?'

'Some folk loved her; others hated her, like my family. She closed down the mines and decimated the steel industry and coming from Sheffield, that was a huge blow. But enough of that, I need to find out who I have to save and then get gone.'

'But I just don't understand how it all works,' said Veronica dejectedly. 'You look like you, well apart from the ridiculous hair and make-up, but Geraldine obviously thinks you are someone else, someone who lives in that house. Yet she called you by your name.'

Sarah's heart sank. This would not be easy to explain. She'd only just about got her own head around it. It had taken John a few goes to get it across to her as it was. She stretched her legs out and thought about how to start. 'Right, Veronica, this is a bit hard to swallow so pay attention.'

'I *always* pay attention. And don't talk to me as if I was a child in class.'

'Sorry, force of habit. Okay, what normally happens is that a Stitch goes back in time and they kind of "become" a person alive at the time. They have the same name too. So when I go back in time it always has to be a Sarah. No idea what would happen in your case. Veronica isn't that common, is it? Anyway, the Sarah I become is close to the person that the Stitch is sent to save. They could be a relative or a friend. But in order not to alarm anyone, the Stitch looks exactly like that person to their friends and relatives, yet the Stitch stays entirely themselves. I am thankful I always have all my own bits. They don't inhabit that person's body. And when they look in a mirror they of course see themselves.'

Veronica thought for a while and then said, 'But what happens to that person's body if they aren't inhabited? Is it just an empty vessel floating around in the ether or something?'

'Ha! That's more or less what I asked John a while ago. He didn't know absolutely because the Spindly Ones play their cards very close to their chests ... if they have chests. Anyway, as I understand it, a Stitch sort of works in tandem with the person from the past. They don't possess the body, but have a kind of spiritual and cerebral link.'

'Sounds a bit odd to me.'

'A bit?' Sarah chuckled. 'I'd say a lot!'

'Don't the people in the past remember what happened after the Stitch has gone again? And you still haven't said what happens to their body.'

'Okay, I'm getting to that. Because your connection is one of brain and spirit not physical, there is a melding of minds but not a physical meeting of bodies. The spiritual link makes them feel like they are dreaming, and they might remember some of what is happening, like you might remember a vivid dream for example. But after I have completed my mission, the actual memory of the dream fades quite quickly, more or less, depending on the person. And as I said, when I am in the past I feel and see my own body, but the Sarah in her dream state still has hers at the same time. This is, like I said, because you aren't them, physically, but you're like a spiritual presence outside *but* alongside them in tandem. She isn't an empty boat floating in the ether or whatever you said.'

'I said vessel. And I really am finding this hard to grasp.' Veronica shook her head.

'That's because it is. It is outside all human experience and if I hadn't experienced it first-hand, I wouldn't have believed it either.'

'Hmm. And how do you know who to save?'

'Again, it is tricky and often you just have to go with your gut instinct. Sometimes there are physical signs like when you get punished for divulging information about the future. In 1940, during the Blitz in Sheffield, I got itchy feet and in 1874, when I was sent to help a family of homesteaders in Kansas, I got the worst attack of the hiccups. Mind you, it was a wonder that I didn't just pass out as I had to help deliver a baby on a dirt floor with no medical assistance.'

Veronica's eyes widened but she said nothing.

'Sometimes Stitches get nothing at all to go on apart from their intuition.'

Veronica remained quiet for a while and Sarah could almost hear the cogs turning in her brain trying to order the information into coherent understanding. The breeze blew against her spikes and she wondered if her hair would ever be the same again.      Her mum had bought a newspaper once all about the year she was born and Sarah had thought that the punks looked dangerously exciting. Now that she was one, she just felt faintly ridiculous, but perhaps that was because she was thirty-four. Punk rock was the domain of young folk she guessed. Young folk? Gosh she was beginning to sound like the puzzled woman sitting next to her.

'Who exactly are these "powers that be" or "Spindly Ones", then?'

*Great, more questions.* Sarah groaned. Now she realised how John must have felt when she was grilling him. 'I really have no idea. John said they are infinitely powerful and keep time running smoothly.' Sarah picked up a little stone beside her foot and skimmed it along the pond sending a few ducks squawking. 'Not doing such a great job now, are they?'

'But you must know more than that,' Veronica barked.

'I don't actually. And John's dad told him to never

question or seek more answers about them, as bad things would happen.' Sarah was looking forward to the next bit. When John had told her she thought he was joking at first. 'You know when people say "pressed for time", meaning you are too busy or running late?'

Veronica nodded.

'It originated from a Time Needle who was far too curious for his own good. One word is wrong, it isn't pressed *for* time, it's pressed *in* time. This guy was actually "pressed *in* time". He was flattened like a butterfly in a lepidopterist collection.'

Veronica's eyes grew round. 'Crikey! God forbid that should happen!'

'So, don't ask any more questions.' Sarah smirked.

'Oh, that's a shame because I do have a very important one.'

Sarah sighed. 'You are very much like I was in the question department, Veronica. Such curiosity even under the threat of being flattened must be a teacher's trait. Okay, make this the last one. I want to find out who I have to save, save 'em and bugger off home.'

'Why do holes open up in time?'

'Ah, yes. I like the answer to this; it fits right in with my love of history.' Sarah turned to face Veronica on the bench and felt privileged to impart such knowledge. 'The most generally accepted theory is that all the dimensions of time are linked by a living, breathing thread. From the beginning of time until the present, the deeds, emotions, memories and spirits of the players on this vast stage of history all become part of this thread. John explained that it is like a strong, tightly woven cord of human essence, keeping time interlinked, balanced and enabling progress to the future. Isn't that beautiful?'

'Hmm. You said generally accepted, why don't you know for definite?'

Sarah felt disgruntled by her less than enthusiastic response. Had this grumpy Stitch no soul? 'Not impressed with that, then? And as I have already said, the Spindly Ones are very secretive. It doesn't do to know too much. We can only piece together the bits of information they give us.'

Veronica gave a heavy sigh. 'But you still haven't said why holes appear.'

'Give me chance. Okay, the holes appear because the link between past and present in certain areas becomes weak. As you probably realise, it's very important to know where we all come from and to learn from our mistakes. Also, we all know on Remembrance Day that we should be grateful to those who have made sacrifices for the wellbeing of others and stuff. Well, too often people forget. They just pay lip service to the past. Then holes open up in time's thread and can only be strengthened by the bravery, determination and love of people like me, and perhaps one day like you, Veronica.'

'Me ... do you think I will be a Stitch in the end?' Veronica asked.

Sarah noticed that the old trout's eyes were moistening. Good it was about time she realised how bloody important and beautiful all this was. 'Maybe. I don't know. You have to prove you are up for it. Stitches must go in and demonstrate that they are prepared to undergo traumatic situations in order to save the lives of others. The past isn't dead and gone, Veronica, it's crucial for our passage to the future and even our very existence.'

'Thank you for explaining it all, Sarah.' Veronica wiped her nose and turned her excited eyes on Sarah. 'And right now, by God, I actually feel like I want to be a Stitch!'

'Well, good for you! And right now I suggest we walk back to the squat and try and see who the hell needs saving, okay?'

Veronica jumped up from the bench and did a mock salute. 'I will do all I can to help you. Veronica Ratchet at your service!'

Sarah smiled and nodded. But as they walked back through the park, Veronica gushing on about the marvels of time travel and her ideas for finding out who they had to save, Sarah wondered if that would be such a good idea. Ratchet had already created merry hell in Sarah's classroom and freaked Gerry out with her ramblings. What was needed here was a promise from Veronica that she would keep her mouth well and truly zipped. But something in Sarah's gut told her that knowing Veronica, the zip would bust under the pressure. And she was all out of ideas on what to do next. John would know.

Her husband's handsome face surfaced, a look of longing in the verdant green of his eyes. How she wished she was in his arms, safe and warm in their bed, away from this waking nightmare. *Oh, John, I wish you were here.*

# Chapter Ten

Much as he would have loved to be, John of course wasn't there. At that very moment he was sitting in a comfy chair in his dad's sitting room under strict instructions to calm down. Harry had been a little surprised to see him screech up to his front door in a cloud of dust and gravel fifteen minutes earlier and since then had listened patiently while John had vented his spleen about the incompetence of the powers that be.

Afterwards, as well as insisting that John calmed down, Harry also insisted that he made his son something to eat and was busily rustling up leftover stew and dumplings while John did a little silent stewing of his own. John regarded the amber liquid in the heavy cut-glass tumbler in his right hand, swirled it and downed it in one. As if by magic, his dad's head appeared round the door. 'That's the last you're having until you've eaten, lad. You'll be no use nor ornament sozzled.'

John raised his eyebrows. 'How the hell did you know I'd even poured a whisky?'

'Dads know everything, as I hope you will discover.' Harry smirked, his blue eyes dancing. 'Now dinner will be about ten minutes. Just sit quiet and gather your senses.'

John's senses were so jumbled it would take an army of gatherers to sort them. All he could think of was Sarah's worried face as she tried to make Veronica comfy in the wardrobe. God, he'd make sure she was *permanently* bloody comfy if he ever set eyes on her again. She had caused nothing but mayhem since she'd first reared her stupid mop of a head. But some sense came back to him. It wasn't all Ratchet's fault, was it? She seemed to be as much caught up in this awful Cross Stitch malarkey as Sarah was.

The empty glass in his hand begged to be re-filled but he knew his dad was right, so instead of leaping to the drinks cabinet, he absently tapped the edge of the glass while his thoughts galloped over the jumps. The rapid 'pink, pink, pink' his fingernail made against the glass competed with the thud of his heartbeat as he wracked his brain about how to help his lovely Sarah. After a few more minutes he thought he had the beginnings of a plan.

'Now, do you feel better after that?' Harry asked, pushing his plate away and pouring his son a glass of wine.

Despite his worries John had enjoyed it and even had a second helping. Like Sarah, he tended to eat rather than starve when he was upset. 'It was another Harry Needler triumph.' John took a long swallow of wine and looked intently at his dad. 'What do you say to sending an email or two on my behalf?'

Harry ran his hands through his grey salt and pepper hair and blew heavily down his nostrils. 'You don't beat about the bush, do you? I don't know, John. They said they wouldn't talk to you because you had been rude. They aren't stupid. They'd know that you are using me to get answers.'

'Not stupid? Well, they haven't been particularly clever lately have they?' John flashed his eyes and put his glass to his lips.

'But what do I say?'

'Well, first it might be helpful if we knew where in time she was. I would like to know why it's happening too if you can wheedle something out of them.'

'The thing is,' Harry took a sip of wine as if he wanted more thinking time. 'They told you to just sit tight and wait, that Sarah would do her best and be back.'

'That's not good enough for me. I want to try and do something to help if I can ... especially if ...'

Harry leaned forward his face eager for more. 'Especially if ... what?'

This was just what John had hoped for. The more he let his dad into his confidence the more he would be likely to offer help. 'If she is in the same, er ... situation as that other Stitch Mum once told you about.'

'You mean you think she *is*—'

'Don't say it, Dad. I have no idea, but if you say the word it will become all too real and then if it isn't true ...' John looked away and ran his hand across the stubble on his chin.

'I get you.' Harry heaved a sigh and pushed his chair back. 'I'll see what I can do, but stay away from the whisky bottle.'

Not even the slightest tremble disturbed his hands as they busied themselves making coffee. How they remained calm like that while his heart did the tumble dryer act in his chest, John didn't know. Waiting for anything that was important had never been his strong point.

Harry was back quicker than John expected though and it wasn't good news. The powers had of course realised that Harry was acting on John's behalf and were not best pleased. The only bit of new information he'd gleaned was that Sarah and Veronica were on a mission in Bristol in 1979.

'They won't tell me anything personal about Sarah, even though I told them what your mum said about the other Stitch.'

'What, and that was it? Not who they had to save, how long they would be there or anything?' John watched his dad's face for any sign of the ENF, but his dad shook his head and his face remained open and honest.

'I knew Sarah was due to go on a time trip to 1979 but not for a few weeks. Why would it have been brought forward? And what has Veronica Ratchet to do with it all?

Right, I'm going in. Somebody's got to look after her.' John slammed his coffee cup on the table and stood up.

Harry grabbed his arm. 'You will do no such thing! Remember what happened last time when you went back in time without express permission?'

John pulled his arm away and glowered at his father. 'It's not the kind of thing you forget in a hurry.'

'No, it bloody well isn't. And this time it could be more than a mangled hand that you receive in punishment!'

'I know, but what about Sarah!'

'Sarah will be okay, I feel it somehow. And if it hadn't been for her pleading with the powers you would still have that claw instead of a hand. *Then* where would you have been, eh?' Harry guided John into the sitting room and forced him into the chair. 'Of course you want to protect her, but she is an independent woman – strong and confident. Trust her. If you don't and go charging back to 1979 like a mad bull, she might be lost to you forever.'

Again under strict orders to calm down, John relaxed back into the comfy chair and closed his leadened eyes. The clatter of dishes and a fake cheerful whistle came from the kitchen as Harry put on a command performance of 'everything will be all right, lad'. John felt a little smile tug at the corners of his mouth. Nobody could ask for a better dad. And he had to admit to himself that Harry was right.

If he went back to 1979, all guns blazing, there would be no second chances after last time. The smile disappeared when he remembered all the hoops that the powers had put Sarah through to ensure that she was the right woman for him. She had come up trumps in the end and the age old rule that forbade Needles and Stitches to be together apart from a few exceptional circumstances had been overcome. She'd been allowed to retain all memory of her stitching and they had been allowed to marry.

It had not been easy though and John had been severely punished when he'd gone back to 1928 to save Sarah from rape, and possibly serious injury. The powers were furious, said he should have known better, but given the circumstances he had no choice. But he did have a choice this time.

John opened his eyes and gazed across the room into the amber flames of the open fire. This time he had to be strong. As far as he knew Sarah wasn't in danger and, as his dad had said, there would be serious consequences if he disobeyed the rules. He guessed it could be a memory wipe for her and possibly him too, not to say a physical punishment. The physical punishment he could bear, but the idea that he might not even remember having met Sarah at all ...

A lump of emotion pushed its way into his gullet and sat there, heavy as a cannonball. The amber flames reminded him of whisky but before he could think about getting one, the cut-glass tumbler appeared in his hand courtesy of Harry.

'You look like you need that,' Harry said, and the warm reassuring weight of his dad's hand on his shoulder doubled the size of the cannonball. John took a big gulp and dislodged it, the fiery liquid burning a path to his belly.

'Cheers, Dad. I did.'

'So are you resigned to do the sensible thing, sit tight and wait for Sarah to come home?' Harry lowered himself into his favourite armchair by the fire.

'I guess so.' John finished his drink and clenched his jaw. 'But if she comes to any harm, I swear to God I won't rest until someone pays for it.'

Harry levelled his compassionate gaze at his son and nodded. 'And I swear to God that if she does, I'll bloody help you.'

# Chapter Eleven

Outside the squat again, Sarah raised her hand to knock on the peeling painted door and glanced at Veronica. 'So remember, keep to our story and then stay quiet, okay?'

'Of course. I'm not stupid, but I'd rather not say what I have to … Isn't there something else we—'

'No, there isn't. Be quiet now,' Sarah hissed and knocked.

Gerry's head appeared round the door. 'You forgot your key again?'

'Yep, I need to be more organised. So can we come in?' Sarah tipped her head to Veronica.

Gerry rolled her eyes and stepped to the side.

'I guess so, but Ollie and Laz are back. They weren't too keen on having another house guest, to be honest. Especially one with such a, let's say, colourful imagination.'

Two serious looking punks, presumably Ollie and Laz, were draped lazily over an old green Chesterfield sofa that looked like it had been salvaged from the Blitz. Stuffing bulged from seams and the tall and very slim men resembled stick insects on some exotic plant leaf. Both had the regulation spikes, though shorter than Sarah and Gerry's, chains, black eye make-up and piercings, but Sarah noted that the younger one had very attractive blue eyes, pleasant features and a half smile on his lips. The other one looked like a bulldog chewing a wasp.

Sarah nodded at them and perched on a smaller settee in a similar condition, she indicated that Veronica should do the same hoping that she wouldn't get a flea bite or worse.

'This is your mate, then?' The wasp eater inclined his head towards Veronica, his hair spikes wobbling slightly.

'Yes, this is Veronica, she's going through a tough time

at the moment and I would really appreciate it if she could stay with us for a bit and—'

'Ain't she got a tongue in her 'ed?' Bulldog snapped.

'I have indeed, young man. Would you mind telling me your name so I can address you civilly?' Veronica smiled and folded her hands demurely in her lap.

'Jeez, you weren't joking, Gerry. This bird sounds like the bleedin' queen!' Bulldog chuckled and then looked at Veronica intently. 'My name is Laz and I would like to know more about you and why we should let you join our little clan.'

'Right, Laz … is that short for Lazarus? You know the man who Jesus raised from the dead?'

'Eh? No, I hated the name my parents gave me – Larry. It makes me sound like a bloody lamb or something. So I changed it to Laz. Cool, yeah?'

Veronica frowned. 'Cool? I wasn't aware that names had a temperature.'

Laz looked at the others and then snorted with laughter. 'That's a good 'un, Ronnie. You ought to be on the stage! Deadpan and everything.'

Veronica looked questioningly at Sarah and Sarah signalled with her eyebrows for her to get on with it.

'Okay,' Veronica began haltingly and rolled her eyes up to the left as if she was reciting lines from a play. 'I think I should be allowed to stay because I have been into some weighty drugs … no, I mean heavy drugs that have given me a bad trip. I was on a trip when I said those odd things about the war and stuffing.' Laz frowned at her. 'No, sorry, I meant stuff. I have nowhere to go because my aged man, er … no, old man, beat me up,' Veronica finished, smiling triumphantly at the fact that she'd remembered most of the story word for word.

Ollie leant forward and spoke to Sarah, his smile gone, blue eyes chipping to steel. 'Where did you find her? Down the docks again where you found your other … let's say more intimate friend?'

Gerry thrust a cold bottle of beer into her hand which gave her thinking time and as she sipped it, Sarah had the strong feeling that the 1979 Sarah and Ollie had been lovers. There was still more than a flicker of passion burning for him too, but something had gone horribly wrong between them. Given his question, she surmised that 1979 Sarah had cheated oh him.

'Yes, actually. That's where I find all my waifs and strays.' Sarah sighed and attempted a smile.

'Hmm, and how is that mangy dog, Steve, then? Not seen him sniffing round you for a few days.' Ollie flashed a nasty smile but Sarah could see an ocean of hurt behind his deep sensitive blue eyes.

Laz sneered. 'Yeah, I heard you arguing in the early hours the other morning. I bet he's dumped you, ain't he?'

Gerry frowned at him and shook her head quickly as if to warn him to shut up.

'Ah, he has then. Well, you had it coming, love. What goes around and all that.' Laz grinned and patted Ollie's shoulder chummily.

Ollie nodded and slumped back into the sofa. Unsure of a response Sarah took another sip of beer and hiccupped loudly.

'Careful, Sarah, we don't want you to choke, do we?' Ollie said quietly, his death stare suggesting that's exactly what he wanted.

'So can I stay here with you all a while?' Veronica's reedy tone broke the uncomfortable silence.

'Don't see why not. You make me laugh and that's always a good thing.' Laz chuckled.

About to say thank you, Sarah just hiccupped violently again. 'You'd better go and have a drink of water, love,' Gerry said, taking the beer. 'Hold your head upside down and drink from the other side of the glass. Works wonders for me.'

Sarah stood and caught Ollie's eye again. He was watching her intently, the hate replaced by love. Realisation hit her between the eyes like a sledgehammer. *Bloody hell! The hiccups – it's him I have to save!*

She beckoned to Veronica and the two of them made their way to the kitchen. Veronica found the cleanest glass on the drainer and ran water into it. Sarah tipped her head upside down and took a sip. 'Thanks, *hic!* I think I, *hic,* know, *hic,* who I have to, *hic!* save.' Sarah straightened up and faced Veronica.

'Are the hiccups a sign, like you said?' Veronica patted Sarah's back which irritated rather than relieved the hiccups.

Sarah, red-faced, nodded vigorously and swallowed another hiccup along with more water. Gerry came in and joined Veronica in patting Sarah's back. 'Will you both, *hic,* bloody sto-*hic*-p that plea-*hic*-se?'

Veronica knitted her eyebrows and planted her hand on her hips. 'Now, really, Sarah. Geraldine and I are only try-*hic*-ing to help. *Hic!*'

'Blimey, Ronnie, looks like you got 'em too,' Gerry said, smirking. 'Can't be the beer because you didn't have one.'

Sarah and Veronica looked at each other agog and did a synchronised *HIC!* Gerry shook her head and went back to the other room. Veronica took Sarah's water and gulped it down.

'Hold your breath, that works some-*hic*-times,' Sarah said.

Both women held their breath. Sarah wanted to burst out laughing at the red-faced bulging eyed face in front of her, all topped off with a crazy haystack. Veronica looked like a deranged clown.

Veronica released her breath slowly and said, 'Do you think I have to help you save someone?'

'I have no idea. Anything's possible in this unorthodox situation.' Sarah sighed, noting the absence of hiccups. 'But we agreed that you would stay put here, with your mouth shut, out of harm's way, so let's stick to the plan. It's probably safest.'

'But who needs saving?' Veronica said, puzzled.

'I reckon it's Ollie and so I'm going back in there to keep tabs on him.'

Veronica looked crestfallen. 'Yes, but what shall I do?'

'Sit at the kitchen table and read that magazine, make a cup of tea, *anything* except spew out more nonsense about 1939.' Sarah pointed a finger. 'If anyone talks to you, just say you don't feel well and keep quiet, okay?'

Veronica gave her a doleful stare and then made a big show of scraping her chair back and plonking herself down.

As she stepped back through the living room door, Sarah caught the tail end of a conversation about Ollie meeting a dealer. *Just marvellous ... not.* She'd suspected drugs would feature in the set up, but it looked like Ollie was off to score some right now. Still, perhaps that was her mission, maybe she was meant to save him from an overdose or something. Trouble was, she had the feeling that he wouldn't take too kindly to her tagging along if the 1979 Sarah had just dumped him for someone else.

'I'll be off then,' Ollie muttered avoiding Sarah's eyes and pocketing a wodge of notes from Laz. 'Cheers, Laz, I'll bring you yours later.'

*Right, this calls for drastic action.* Sarah's heart raced up the scale and her tummy did a somersault. 'Um, Ollie. Can I have a private word, please?'

Ollie narrowed his eyes. 'What about?'

'Well, if I told you now it wouldn't be private would it?' Sarah shot him a hopeful smile.

Ollie looked at Laz and Gerry and shrugged. 'Okay, but

you will have to walk with me, I'm late already.'

Sarah told him she'd have to get her bag and ran back into the kitchen. Veronica was exactly as she'd left her, looking horrified at the problem page in a magazine.

'I can't believe how utterly shameless these girls are. Nothing but whores if you ask me—'

'Just shut your face and listen. I'm off out with Ollie, this might be my chance to save him so do as I said before, remember?'

'Well, how rude? And of course I remember, you only told me a few moments ago—'

Sarah held up her hand in a 'palm-face' gesture and ran from the room.

Veronica finished the magazine and drummed her fingers on the table. This time travelling lark was turning out to be pretty boring. Sarah, it seemed, was to have all the exciting work while she was left at home like a modern day Cinderella. But then, she'd never been one to go to the ball, had she? Her mother had seen to that. All those years fetching and carrying and then she'd become her nurse when mother had contracted TB. Before Veronica had known it, her youth was behind her and so were her chances.

Catching sight of her reflection in the hall mirror, Veronica had to concede that her chances had never been marvellous, not with her looks. When she was little her mother had once said that she looked like a horse. How could a mother be so cruel to their own child? As an adult, Veronica realised that all the insults and brow beating had been to undermine her confidence, a way of keeping her tied to the house and to servitude. But then along came Edward and with him the always longed for, but never expected, prospect of romance.

Poor Edward was all alone in 1939 though, wasn't he? *And you are too concerned about saving your own skin to go back there. Shame on you, Veronica.* But then what did she expect? Self-preservation had been paramount during the dark years of Hettie Ratchet's reign. That's why she'd turned down the stitching lark in the beginning, always looking out for number one and—

Veronica's thoughts were interrupted by the rise and fall of angry voices from the other room and she crept nearer to listen.

'But you said I could play the guitar like an angel the other day ... you said I had prospects!' Geraldine yelled.

'But that was before Jakey Harris said he'd join the band last night ... Jakey Harris, Gerry! He once backed the Stranglers before they got famous!' Laz growled back.

Geraldine's voice returned, quieter, but Veronica could detect the desperation in it. 'And so, what, you thought you'd drop me from the band just like that?'

'Just for now, love. We'll still be together as boyfriend and girlfriend—'

'Boyfriend and girlfriend? Where are we, in the fucking schoolyard?'

'Don't be like that. You know how I feel about you, babe—'

Veronica heard something crash across the room and Geraldine yell, 'Don't you dare "babe" me! And don't come anywhere near me! I hate you and your crappy little band!'

'You broke me favourite chair!'

'I'll break more than a chair in a minute. GET OUT!'

Veronica heard footsteps approaching. *Yikes!* She dashed back to the kitchen table put her head down on the magazine and pretended to be asleep. A door slammed, and then a wail of despair cut the silence. A few minutes later Geraldine plonked herself down opposite Veronica, and snuffled and sobbed quietly to herself. Taking a quick peep from under her lashes, Veronica spied a whisky bottle on the table and a very long, strange smelling cigarette in the other woman's fingers.

'So dumped again, eh?' Gerry sighed. She touched Veronica's arm lightly. 'I know you're asleep, my old mop-head, but it helps to talk to somebody.' Gerry took a swig from the bottle and sucked on her cigarette.

Veronica snorted inwardly. *Mop-head? Well, really! And that damned cigarette smells ... smells ... hmm, quite nice actually.*

'Serves me right, I guess, for dumping my boy on my parents. But what would you have done if you had a kid at sixteen, eh, Ronnie? Social workers all over it, parents treating you as if you were The Whore of Babylon?' Gerry swallowed more whisky, drew a lungful of smoke, held it and in release said, 'Cut and run that's what, just like me.'

*A child at sixteen?* My God, if Veronica had been her mother she would have given her a good hiding! Veronica found herself trying to breathe more deeply to catch a whiff of that cigarette. She'd never smoked in her life, but she could definitely see why people did. It was sooo relaxing.

'And then at last after years of living on the streets, into drugs ... and worse, being picked up and dumped by the world and his wife, I finally get a house and a man who seemed to care. But you know what was best of all? I thought I might get somewhere with this guitar lark.' She put her lips close to Veronica's ear. '*Actually* be someone, you know? Huh! Fat chance.'

Some time later Veronica took a cheeky peek at her watch and found an hour had passed, but Geraldine was still talking ... well, slurring mostly. A good part of the whisky had gone and she'd rolled up another two of those cigarettes. Veronica found that she had to keep resisting the urge to giggle. Not at anything Geraldine was saying, as all that was pretty grim, but just giggling for no apparent reason. The idea that dancing in bare feet on the cold lino might be a fun thing to do also had begun to flit across her mind intermittently.

She had never had these kind of frivolous thoughts before and began to worry that she was going a bit odd. The worry was edged with a warm fuzzy glow though, so not really worry at all. And now the position of her head on the wooden table was beginning to make her neck ache. Could she turn her head and still pretend to be asleep? Just as she was about to try it Geraldine tapped her arm again.

'There was one really happy day in my life though, Ronnie, that was a day to remember. In my head ... the memory of it is wrapped in the finest blue silk and placed in a jewel-studded box. I was twelve, it was summer and we went on a school trip to the docks down the road here. It was before boys, teenage angst, pressure from parents or anything and I just felt free, happy and as if my life was stretching out to infinity before me, you know?'

Veronica didn't know, but she liked the idea of life stretching out. At thirty-nine she felt that life's elastic was due to snap soon-ish. Her dad had died at forty-two, her mother five years ago at fifty-four ... dear God she was beginning to feel a bit maudlin now. What she needed was another sniff of that ciggie, Geraldine to shut up, Sarah to save Ollie and then she could go home and start making the best of the time she had left with Edward. Geraldine seemed in no hurry to shut up though.

'That school trip was bloody fantastic!' Gerry giggled and took another swig of whisky. 'We had a boat trip then we walked up to the bridge and Kelly Hall pretended to push me off!' She chuckled again and began to laugh hysterically. 'We got told off by Miss Grant and Naomi Thorpe was pulling faces behind her back the whole time! Such a happy day.' Gerry's voice took on a wistful air. 'If only I could turn back time and start afresh from that day ... things would have been so different for me.'

Veronica rolled her eyes. Time is something you didn't fool around with as she had learned to her cost. And if she didn't turn her head soon, her neck would seize up.

'You know what, Ronnie, me old bird, I think I might pay a visit to the bridge now. Relive that day and then ... and then ... float away across the clouds ...'

Even in her woozy state the tone of Geraldine's voice ran a cold finger of warning down Veronica's spine. What did she mean by that?

Geraldine pushed back her chair, turned in a circle and sang *Somewhere Over the Rainbow* quietly to herself. Then she left the kitchen.

Veronica sat upright and rubbed her neck. How odd that this modern creature knew the song from that new *Wizard of Oz* film back in her time. People said how marvellous it was. Perhaps she and Edward would go and see it. But what on earth was the young woman doing now? She could hear Geraldine banging about upstairs and then ... nothing. A few minutes later she had to pretend to be asleep again as Geraldine came in and put something on the table next to her face. Then she heard her go into the hall and the front door slam.

On the table was a pad of paper. Veronica read:

> *Right guys. I'm checking out ... Today was just a bridge too far and when you find out what's happened to me, you will understand my cryptic little note.*
>
> *Sorry to do this to you, Sarah, you were a real mate. Have a happy life. PLEASE don't make such a mess of it the way I have.*

*Love G xx*

The cold finger of warning became an ice block. Veronica jumped up, her hand fluttering to her mouth. That note looked pretty final to her. But what the hell was she to do? She'd promised Sarah she'd stay put, but if Geraldine was off to do something terrible ...

Before she could talk herself out of it, Veronica grabbed a coat from the back of a chair, ran out and followed the hurrying figure of Geraldine down the street.

# Chapter Twelve

The sunshine that Sarah had enjoyed earlier in the park with Veronica had done a disappearing act. Down by the waterfront the wind whipped off the river and across her bare arms like knives. Now early evening with dark clouds rolling in, the run-down wharfs and alleyways of the decaying industrial harbour area looked foreboding. It was certainly not the ideal place Sarah wanted to be hanging around.

Briskly rubbing her arms, she watched Ollie stride over to a huddle of men at the end of an alleyway. He slapped a few on the back and then a moment later threw his arms up in a gesture of exasperation. Voices were raised but she couldn't catch what was said and then Ollie came back over to her, his face like curdled milk. 'Just brilliant! Because you made me late, the dealer's gone. So no score for me or Laz tonight.'

Really? Could it be that easy? Had she averted a drugs overdose just by making Ollie late? If so, that was her ticket back to John! And anyway why shouldn't it be easy? God knew she deserved to be cut a bit of slack.

Ollie was still glowering at her. 'I suppose you are happy about that, aren't you? Probably made me late on purpose. You're like bloody Snow White since you dumped the heroin.'

*Yay!* She was so pleased that the 1979 Sarah had quit drugs. It also gave her a response in an otherwise unknown territory. 'I *am* pleased as it happens. It's a mug's game after all ... you could end up dead and colder than this bitter wind.'

Ollie rolled his eyes, shrugged his leather jacket off and wrapped it around her shoulders. It smelled of lemon and aniseed and felt strangely comforting. She wondered if his arms wrapped around her would feel comforting too. *Eh? Hang about … no!* The 1979 Sarah must have made her think that. Honestly, she was a newly married woman!

Ollie stepped closer and as she looked into his cool blue eyes she began to wonder some more about his arms and his mouth so close to hers too. This misplaced 'affection' malarkey had happened to her when she'd gone to 1874 Kansas, she remembered, but the feeling of attraction for the guy there hadn't been as strong as this. Sarah figured that it was because the 1979 Sarah and Ollie had been in a sexual relationship, and very recently. She swallowed and folded her arms protectively across her chest.

Ollie stepped even closer until she could feel the heat of his breath on her cheek. 'Why would you care about what happens to me anyway, Sarah? Thought all you cared about now was Steve.' He traced a crimson painted nail across her jawline.

Sarah gulped, stepped back and intuition made her blurt, 'I'm over Steve. I made a mistake. It's you she … I mean I loved, but I just couldn't cope with your drug taking any more.'

Ollie raised his eyebrows and a daft soppy grin shone the light of innocent youth through the darkness of his carefully erected rude-boy punk image. 'Love? You never talked about love!' He picked Sarah up and whirled her round. 'If you had I would have tried harder to quit!'

Sarah looked into his face wreathed in smiles and nodded. 'Well, I do, so will you try harder now?'

His face grew solemn. He raised her hand to his mouth and tenderly kissed the back of it. 'If this means you're giving me another chance. I'd do anything for you, Sarah.'

Sarah felt the depth of emotion of the 1979 Sarah, but she needed to keep her distance. 'No. It has to be for you, Ollie, okay?' To avoid the inevitable kiss, Sarah took his hand and turned for the road. 'Come on, let's go home.' And as they walked, Sarah prayed with all her might that she soon would be.

A few minutes later they crossed a footbridge and a little way further off Sarah noticed a huge bridge suspended between two steep cliffs. Underneath a wide muddy river meandered, dotted with a few small boats. Sarah immediately recognised it as Brunel's Clifton Suspension Bridge as she'd taught the kids about him many times during their lessons on the Industrial Revolution. It would be great to go and have a closer look, but she could go and visit it any time when she got back to the present. And that was all she could think about at the moment, forget bloody bridges.

She quickened her pace dragging Ollie along with her. He'd try to slow down a few times to kiss her but she'd told him that they had to take things slowly and they would have more time for all that later. Waiting at a crossing they were surprised to find a biker waving them over at the lights.

The man flicked the visor back from his helmet and studied them with concerned grey eyes. 'I think I just saw one of your lot as I crossed on the bridge. Looked like they wanted to jump but a few folk were gathered round.'

'One of our lot?' Sarah said.

'Yeah, a punk. Think it was a woman ... had pink hair.' The lights changed and the man sped off.

Sarah and Ollie looked at each other opened-mouthed and at the same time said, 'Gerry!' Sarah's thoughts went into free fall. Was Gerry the one she was supposed to save after all and not Ollie? But she'd felt *sure* that it had been Ollie, all the signs had been there and the gut feeling she'd had too. And if Gerry was about to jump from the damned bridge there was no way she'd get there in time, not on foot anyway. Oh hell, what should she do? All she wanted was to go back to John, thought she would be doing so very shortly, and now this!

'Come on, we have to get up there!' Ollie grabbed her arm and started towards the bridge.

Sarah shook her head and stopped. 'We won't get there in time, in fact *how* do you get up there?'

'Eh? What do you mean how do we get up there? We've been up there hundreds of times, but you're right, we need some kind of transport. Shit I don't know which buses go …' Ollie's voice trailed off and he turned in a circle putting his hands to his head.

It seemed obvious to Sarah. 'Taxi?'

'Oh, yeah! I have the money that Laz gave me for the gear! Great we can flag one down, shouldn't be too long on this bit of road.'

Great wasn't really the word Sarah would have used for the situation. It really was the living end. One minute looking forward to being in John's arms, the next tearing up to a bloody bridge to save yet another life. Bloody stupid Gerry, if she wanted to sodding jump, then let her. Immediately Sarah felt her moral compass swing into life. That was a terrible thought and so unlike her. But then she had been stretched to breaking point lately.

Sarah put her hands behind her head and looked up at the darkening sky. This was all above and beyond, but she'd said that before, hadn't she? She blew heavily down her nose and resigned herself to more trials and tribulations. She deserved a medal. Did the Spindly Ones give out medals? If they did, they would be all twinkly and suspended from staunch, yet wispy threads of humanity. Jeez, now she was going nuts.

Ollie, a little way up the pavement, waved madly at an approaching taxi and it slowed to a halt in front of her. It looked like she was going to get that closer look at the famous bridge after all, unfortunately. *Okay, once more unto the sodding breach ...*

The 'sodding breach' was so much worse than she expected. And given that she knew that Gerry was probably about to jump off the Clifton Suspension Bridge, that was saying something. The scene before her as she stepped out of the taxi and ran onto the bridge was like something out of a film. Dusk had settled, hastened by the ever gathering rainclouds, and little lights had come on all along the bridge. From the radio of a parked car, the strains of *I Will Survive* escaped through the open window. Sarah remembered her mum telling her that the song was a smash hit in that year. She joked that she sang it when she was in labour with Sarah. How ironic that it was on the radio now, given the circumstances.

A sizeable crowd had gathered at the end of the bridge and about a third of the way along, a figure – a figure with pink spiky hair – clung to the railing on the edge, looking over the river far below. Standing next to the figure – and the 'so much worse than she expected' –was the form of a tall, and now that she thought about it, spindly figure, running its hands repeatedly through giant haystack hair. Veronica Ratchet.

'Oh my God, no.' Sarah's breath caught in her throat and she leaned against Ollie for support. Of all the people anyone could have picked to try and talk down a suicide jumper, Ratchet would be the last. Why the hell hadn't she listened and stayed put? Damn her, when did she *ever* listen? A few more moments of Ratchet's babbling and Gerry would jump. Hell, anyone *not* suicidal would jump!

Sarah started forward again; she had to shut Ratchet up pronto, but she felt Ollie's restraining hand on her arm. 'Hey, stay here. A guy in the crowd told me the police will be here soon. They have professionals who know what they're doing.'

'It might be too late by the time Veronica's finished. You stay here and wait for me.'

A sense of the surreal descended as Sarah threaded through the crowd and began to walk towards Veronica and Gerry. Thunder growled in the distance and apart from a light wind chattering around the bridge struts, the only other sound was Sarah's footsteps on the tarmac.

A few seconds later, Veronica turned, saw Sarah and relief washed across her anguished face.

'Sarah, thank goodness,' she gasped.

Sarah closed the short gap between them and looked up at Gerry. Gerry slowly raised her gaze from the water and to Sarah. 'Hello, Sarah, you're clever.' Her voice was flat, monotone. 'Deciphered my note and got here in record time ... pity it's been for nothing.'

'Note?'

'Yes, Sarah,' Veronica piped up. 'The one she left on the kitchen table for you all. I followed her here and—'

'Yes. When I told you *expressly* not to. What have you been saying to her?' Sarah hissed.

'She's been saying nothing to be honest, it's me who has been bending *her* ear.' Gerry smiled sadly and then peered between her legs down at the swirling water as if mesmerised.

'You said nothing?' Sarah looked at Veronica in astonishment.

Veronica nodded her head and shrugged. 'I was worried I'd say the wrong thing like I always do.'

Relief flooded through Sarah. Perhaps she might still have a chance.

'So if you didn't get my note, how'd you find me?' Gerry asked and stretched her one arm up to the sky.

Sarah quickly told her and then took a tentative step towards Gerry.

'Er, don't come any closer. You think I'm too drunk and stoned to know what you're doing here?' Gerry shot Sarah a glance of pure venom.

Even in the disappearing light Sarah could see that Gerry's pupils were large and black, and coupled with the whiff of booze on the breeze she didn't need a rocket scientist to tell her what a sorry condition she was in. *Drunk and stoned, just marvellous.* From the films she'd seen where jumpers were talked down she remembered the main thing was to keep calm and not to alarm the suicidal person in any way. She told herself to *try to be as normal as possible ... yeah, right.* Glancing to her left she saw that the crowd had grown but no evidence of police yet. *Even more marvellous.*

Sarah swallowed and forced a tremor out of her voice. 'I am here because I'm your friend, love. Life can't be so bad that you want to end it, can it?'

Gerry looked at her sidelong, shook her head and gave a humourless laugh. 'No. I'm just up here for the bloody view, you daft cow.'

'But what happened after I left with Ollie? You were fine before that.'

Gerry began humming *Somewhere Over the Rainbow* and then stopped. She looked at Veronica, her blue eyes dark with pain. 'You tell her, Ronnie. I'm all talked out.'

Veronica quickly told Sarah that she had pretended to be asleep and heard everything, which she now shared. She had confessed to Gerry on the way to the bridge that she hadn't really been asleep and that they should go back and talk about it, but Gerry wouldn't see reason.

'But death *is* reason, Ronnie. It's my sad, grubby, worthless little life that has *no* reason.' Gerry looked down again and shivered.

Sarah guessed that the most important bit of the sorry tale was Gerry having to leave her son with her parents and feeling totally rejected. The rejection today from Laz was just the last straw. But how to tackle it? Sarah felt completely out of her depth. *Okay, here goes.*

'There's no wonder you're distraught given all that's happened to you, love. But there are ways round it. Have you tried to contact your parents lately to see if you can see your boy?'

'No point. What good would I be to him anyway?' Gerry's eyes filled up and spilled over. 'He was born on my birthday, you know. That was last week but I didn't tell you lot. Birthdays are sad for me 'cos of him ... I was twenty-one and he was five.'

Bingo. Seemed her intuition was right about the boy. 'You *would* be good for him, Gerry, you're his mum,' Sarah said, feeling her own eyes moisten.

'Mum!' Gerry's face coloured up, her eyes flashing in anger. 'What kind of mum dumps her son and runs off when things get tough? What kind of mum shacks up with men for drugs, what kind—' She broke off, silent tears coursing down her face. Sarah was worried that the more upset she got the more likely she'd lose her grip on the railings, or perhaps just jump to end the pain. Shit what should she say next! She looked at Veronica who was anxiously biting her nails and shifting from one foot to the other. No help there then.

'Come on, Gerry. Let me help you back over the railings and we can at least talk about it ... please, before it's too late.'

Gerry stopped crying and took one hand from the railing. 'It's already too late.'

Sarah's heart lurched as she watched Gerry turn and look at the water once more. And then Veronica stepped closer to the edge.

'Right, that's enough of that, young lady. Just take my hand and climb back over, this minute!'

Sarah's mouth dropped open. Had she gone bleeding

bonkers! Gerry wasn't one of her kids in the schoolyard. 'Veronica, what—'

'But what's the point?' Gerry said in a small voice.

'The point is that forty odd years ago people in the last war died to make your life better and now you want to chuck it away! Well, that's disrespectful. In fact, *bloody* disrespectful, to use a vulgarity.' She looked at Sarah and winked. 'Those people were fighters, and if you do this today, that boy of yours will always have to live with the fact that you didn't fight for him. For God's sake, don't you have *any* feelings for him at all?'

Gerry slapped her other hand back on the railing. 'Of course I have feelings for him,' she shouted. 'I love him! I can still see his face, smell that lovely baby smell he had ...' Tears welled and rolled again.

'Then get your miserable arse back over here and fight then, damn you!' Veronica's beady eyes were bright with emotion, her mouth set in a determined line and, for once, Sarah thought she actually looked quite beautiful.

Gerry looked at them both trancelike. Thunder grumbled in the near distance and the first fat raindrops splashed down mingling with her tears. For Sarah, time seemed to stop and all she could hear was the thudding of her heartbeat in her ears and the faint wail of a police siren coming up the valley. Then, incredibly, Gerry gave a half-smile and held her hand out to Veronica. Sarah's stomach did a few somersaults but she stepped forward too and together they both practically dragged Gerry over the railings and back to safety.

'My God, what a fright you gave us!' Sarah wrapped her arms around Gerry's shaking frame and hugged her tight.

Veronica sank to her knees next to them and turned her face to the rain. 'Thank God,' she whispered.

Sarah knelt too and gave her the biggest bear hug in the world. 'You did it, Veronica! You stuck your bloody schoolteacher's head on and you sodding did it!'

'Watch your language, madam!' Veronica laughed and hugged Sarah back. 'Looks like we both did a bit of good stitching today, eh?' She nodded at a smiling Ollie running towards them.

Sarah grinned, realisation dawning. 'That's right. Two people needed saving today more or less at the same time and one Stitch couldn't do both. You should be so proud you pulled it off, Veronica.'

Veronica beamed and hugged her again.

Sarah closed her eyes and breathed a sigh of relief. 'Thank goodness it's all over, me old Ratchet.'

When Sarah opened her eyes again she was standing in her kitchen in front of a stunned but delighted John.

# Chapter Thirteen

John nearly dropped his coffee mug when he turned from the toaster and saw Sarah standing by the kitchen door. The hot liquid slopped on his hand but he barely noticed it. All five senses were tuned to his beautiful wife, safe and back home again.

He set the mug on the table and crossed the distance between them in three large strides. She shot a shaky smile at him, but he could tell by her moist eyes and trembling hands that she'd been through it. 'My poor darling,' he whispered, feeling his throat thicken. Drawing her gently towards him he looked into her beautiful blue eyes and kissed her gently on the lips. 'Are you okay?'

He felt her arms go round him and tighten as if she'd never let him go. She rested her head against his chest and released a deep sigh. 'I have been better, but now at last I'm back in your arms, thank God.'

After a hot bath and breakfast, Sarah told John the entire story of the impromptu trip to 1979. Most of why it happened was still a huge mystery to the pair of them. John, this time, was as much in the dark as Sarah. He normally knew roughly when a Stitch was due back from a trip and if they had been successful because the powers would email.

However, because he was in the doghouse with them at the moment, they had remained silent, apart from the odd message regarding the other Stitches that he was needling for. One, Karen Hillary, had temporarily got stuck in the middle of the Crimean War. Thankfully she'd managed to complete the mission and come back without John having to go and sort it. That's *all* he would have needed, dodging bloody cannonballs while being beside himself with worry about Sarah.

He'd had a sleepless night after he'd come back from his dad's and was on his fifth coffee when Sarah appeared, but as soon as he'd held her close, all the tension drained out of him and he at last began to feel a bit more like John Needler, instead of a raging bull on amphetamines.

'So,' Sarah said, sipping her tea. 'I reckon that I was sent back to 1979 with Veronica because both Ollie and Gerry needed saving at the same time, so two of us were needed. Also, because of this unexplained Cross Stitch, I think the whole thing seems largely out of the Spindly Ones control. 1879, 1939 and 1979 all got jumbled up in one big time-travelling disaster.'

John could see the logic in that, if there *was* logic in such a mix-up, but he had the strong feeling in his gut there was more to it. Nevertheless, he decided that his gut had to keep schtum on that front. Time would tell. He smirked at the ironic thought and Sarah immediately pounced on it.

'What's the smirk for? Do you know something about all this that I don't?'

'Nope. But I will send an email later to see if I can get any more out of them.'

Sarah stood and moved round the table to sit on his lap. She smelled fresh from the bath and the heat from her soft curvaceous body coming through the thin silky dressing gown ignited a flare of excitement in his.

'You were so brave standing up to the Spindly's like that, hon,' she murmured in his ear as she slipped her hand under his shirt and traced her fingers across his chest.

'I was so bloody angry I didn't even think about the consequences.' John moved a damp tress of honey-blonde hair away from her neck and placed a kiss in the well of her throat. Brushing his lips along her neck he inhaled the warm familiar smell of her and ran his hand along her thigh. Last night he'd lain awake tossing and turning, worried sick about where Sarah was and if she was in danger. He'd yearned for her touch and to feel her body against his again, just like this. It was inconceivable to him that he'd never hold her again; he knew he couldn't have gone on if anything had happened to her.

'Hey, John,' Sarah said, putting a finger under his chin and lifting his face to hers. 'What's wrong? You look like somebody died?'

'I was just thinking what I would have done if you had been stuck there ... never come home ... I—'

'That's enough of that talk.' Sarah stood and held her hand out to him. 'I *am* back and we are together again, and come hell or high water, we will *always* be together.' She walked to the door. 'Now, thankfully I'm not teaching today, so come on, I have a job for you to do.'

'Eh? Can't we just relax a bit before you have me fetching and carrying and—' John stopped as his wife dropped her dressing gown to the floor, a cheeky smile on her face. He jumped up and hurried up the stairs after her, enjoying the view of her pert behind swaying as she climbed. He grinned. 'Now *this* is the kind of a job I like.'

A few hours later after making love and a restful sleep, Sarah, desperate to get back to normal, had gone grocery shopping. John had been given strict instructions to try and find out more from the powers by email. Surprisingly, it seemed he was forgiven and he'd found out quite a bit about Veronica, Gerry and Ollie, and he was sure Sarah would be pleased to hear it. However, any personal information had been withheld, so John hadn't pushed it. There was no use getting on the wrong side of them again.

Up to his ankles in sludge, John carefully levered up another bedraggled looking bunch of carrots. The last week had turned his field into a quagmire and harvesting in those conditions was not his favourite job. Still, there had been more than a nip in the air that morning, a sign that winter was walking towards them in frosty boots. In a few weeks the swede, parsnip and leek would be ready, and the heated greenhouses were full of exotic vegetables and herbs for the local restaurants.

John straightened, wiped the sweat from his brow with a muddy paw and looked out across the rolling hills edged with stone walls and dotted with sheep. Glowering rainclouds gathered in a corner of the sky like school bullies conspiring to muscle in and nick the dinner money of the watery October sun. All around was still and silent, save a rook's bark and his own heavy breathing. Inhaling deeply, the pungent aroma of the damp earth connected him to the land and John felt a swell of happiness in his belly. He loved his work, life was good and hopefully due to get better if his dad's hunch was—

'Hey, John, I'm back!'

John turned to see Sarah waving from the doorway of their cottage, her hair lifting on the breeze, dressed in blue jeans and a red shirt. His stomach flipped and his heart grew heavy with love at the sight of her. He raised a hand and grinned stupidly. Without doubt she was the most beautiful woman in the world.

'Well, stop gawking and come and tell me what you found out, then!' She turned and went indoors. John stuck his fork in the ground and chuckled. Yep. The most beautiful woman in the world ... but with the sharpest tongue.

'Chocolate and walnut cake, you are a star!' John smiled as he saw the cake Sarah had placed on the table. 'And my favourite coffee too, you are spoiling me,' he said, slipping his arms around his wife's waist as she busied herself with the cafetière.

Sarah tapped his hands. 'Get those mucky paws washed and sit down. I am all ears to know what you have to say.' She turned and gave him a wistful smile. 'Veronica thought that was a really funny phrase. She said "imagine what a person would look like made entirely of ears". I miss the old trout, unbelievable I know. Hope she made it back okay.'

'Mmm. That cerk is de best yer,' John said, his mouth full.

'I think you'll find it's cake not cerk.' Sarah licked the chocolate off a walnut and tossed it into her mouth.

John washed the cake down with a mouthful of delicious coffee. 'Okay, miss perfect, at least I haven't got chocolate on my nose.'

Sarah dabbed at her nose. 'Where?'

'Nowhere. Fooled yer!'

John received a withering look. 'Right tell me what you found out before I pour coffee on your head.'

John pushed his plate away and leaned back in his chair. 'Okay, you were right about the double save bit. Ollie and Gerry. But the main reason you were pulled back with Veronica was because if you hadn't, she'd have never become a fantastic Stitch.'

'Eh … she became a fantastic Stitch? Old scaredy pants and "I look after number one" Ratchet?'

'Yup. She went on loads of stitching missions, was allowed to keep her memory, married Edward and lived happily ever after. Seems like she deserved it after the merry dance her mother led her, poor cow.'

John briefly told Sarah about the way Veronica's mother had treated her.

'Blimey, no wonder she was a bit spiky. Talking of spiky, why wasn't Veronica dressed as a punk?'

'Can you imagine how freaked out she'd be if she'd looked in a mirror. She nearly had a meltdown as it was!' John laughed. 'Anyway, the main thing is you gave her confidence to try and save Gerry and save countless others later. Seems a little speech you did about why holes open and the thread of humanity and stuff really struck home. She greatly admired you, Sarah, wanted to emulate you.'

Sarah blushed and her eyes moistened. 'Can't see why, I was hardly the nicest person. All I could think of was getting home to you.'

John put his hand over hers. 'That's not surprising, love. You were under so much pressure just whisked off like that.'

'And have they explained how that happened? Why everything went crazy?'

'No. They aren't sure, still. My dad reckons that they don't have total control over time and space, they are like guardians of time really, but they can direct. Same as Needles and Stitches, they can't coerce people to do stuff. "Time waits for Norman" is a good example of that. We have to want to do it.'

A snort escaped Sarah's nose. 'Yeah, right. I couldn't wait to be dragged from my wedding to 1939 and then dumped again in 1979.'

John spread his hands and nodded. It didn't sound logical to him either. Sarah regarded him across the table her mouth pursed into a rosebud. She looked as if she were gearing up for more difficult questions, so he jumped in first.

'Talking of 1979, do you want to know what happened to Ollie and Gerry?'

Sarah brightened. 'Of course. Hope it was good.'

'Yep, it was fab. Gerry was reunited with her son, trained as a teacher and married a really lovely guy, an artist who influenced her son. The son grew up to be a world famous graffiti artist making influential social comment through his work.'

'You mean Jinksy?'

'Yep, the very same! And Ollie married Sarah, they had three kids. One of the kids is making a real difference in the developing world. He's instigated an innovative charity that raises money for education and social welfare, mainly in India and South America, I think. So lives are being enriched and I guess saved daily because of his efforts.'

'That is *so* brilliant and if I hadn't have made his dad late for a drug deal he might never have been born.' Sarah beamed.

John lifted her hand to his lips. 'That's right, my little swamp duck. So missing the wedding, contending with a rampaging Ratchet in your classroom, being catapulted back to 1979 and finding yourself with two foot spikes for hair, sent on a mission to a suspension bridge to talk down a suicide attempt ... all that was plain sailing. *So* brilliant, yes?'

Sarah thumped him on the arm. 'Don't push it, pal.'

John was relieved to find that his and Sarah's life returned to normal over the next few weeks, well as normal as their life ever could get. The last few days, however, Sarah had begun to look drawn and she complained of stomach cramps. He virtually had to drag out of her that morning that she had been feeling dizzy and sickly of late too. She hadn't told him as she didn't want him fussing. She thought it was perhaps just stress and being busy at school. Well, fussing or no, he decided that it was time he tackled this head on.

John found her in the garden hanging out the washing. He watched her closely for a few seconds and as she stretched to peg a shirt on the line he was afforded a good side view of her torso ... yep she certainly looked as if she could—

'Wanna give me a hand, handsome?' she called.

'A bit optimistic, aren't you? Nearly November and black clouds rolling in over t' hills?'

Sarah gestured across the countryside. 'The cows are still standing up, they're optimistic too. Cows know about drying washing.'

John walked over and handed her the pegs.

'What's up with you, pensive features?'

This would be a good a time as any to broach the subject,

120

John reckoned. 'Erm ... just thinking ... you know this not feeling well thing, sickness, heartburn, cramp and stuff?'

Sarah glanced at him and held her hand out for another peg. 'Ye-s?'

'It's just that I think ... well, not think exactly, but I feel it could be possible that ...' His voice tailed off. What if he was wrong, what if she was really ill ... cancer or something?

'Ye-s ... spit it out.' Sarah bent and selected a pair of jeans from the wash basket.

John stretched and put both hands behind his head. *Just go for it, at least it will all be out in the bloody open at last.* 'Sarah, could you be pregnant?'

The jeans whacked him round the face as a sudden gust of wind turned the rotary clothesline into a weapon. She put her hand on the line to find a gap for her knickers. 'I think I might have told you before now if I was, my love.' She gave him a sad little smile. 'I did think that at first, too, but my periods have been as regular as clockwork, more's the pity.'

John felt two lead weights thump into his stomach. One courtesy of the fact that the hopes he'd held since his dad started all the hints about the other Stitch on their wedding day had been dashed, and two, because he was now really concerned about some sinister illness. Then a thought occurred.

'Oh, right. But I hadn't noticed them getting in the way of sex though?'

'That's because they have been quite light and only a few days or so in duration. But that happens with me from time to time.' Sarah put her arms around him and laid her head on his shoulder. 'If there was the slightest possibility, don't you think I would have told you – shouted it from the rooftops?'

'Yes, and that's why I haven't said anything before now. I wanted you to be the one to spring it on me all bright-eyed and bushy-tailed,' he muttered, kissing the top of her head. He felt her grow rigid in his arms.

'Well, I'm sorry to disappoint, then,' she snapped and pulled away.

*Great, John. Step all over her feelings with your big size tens.* That's the last thing he wanted to do. 'Oh, sorry, love. That came out all wrong,' John said to his wife's retreating back. 'But I want you to get a check-up. Whatever is making you ill needs sorting.'

'I told you, it's probably overwork and stress.' Sarah flounced through the patio doors and into the kitchen. 'Comes with the territory of teaching.'

John caught up with her at the kitchen sink, gently took her in his arms and searched her face. Unshed tears stood in her eyes and he felt an ache begin in his heart. 'You might be right, but I want to be sure. And I am *so* sorry. I'm such a big oaf for upsetting you like that. I know you want a child as much as me ... probably more.'

Sarah nodded allowing the tears to spill over and run down her cheeks. 'I know. I'm sorry too. The symptoms are classic, but then the periods ... I couldn't let myself believe for one minute that I ...' she finished on a heartfelt sigh.

John held her tight, stroked her hair, muttered platitudes, but the sadness surrounding her was almost palpable. It seeped into his pores and pumped up his own ball of misery until it grew large and heavy in his gut. But what about the tales of the other Stitch who's experience was so similar? What about the hedging of the powers when he'd asked them directly about Sarah's condition. John figured it was time to tell her, even if it got her hopes up, he couldn't keep it to himself any longer. He released her and pulled out a chair. 'Sarah let's sit down and have a cuppa. I have a strange tale to tell.'

'But why didn't you tell me all that right away?' Sarah flung her arms up in exasperation. 'I *knew* you had the bloody ENF on, even though you said you didn't.'

'Because as I said outside earlier, I thought you would be the first to know and would want to be the one to tell me, not the other way around ... especially not courtesy of the Spindly Ones. You would have loved that.'

'Okay.' Sarah sighed. 'I can see that, but are you saying that all this Cross Stitch thing has happened because I could be pregnant, then?' Sarah folded her arms and leaned back in her chair, her expression unreadable.

John shrugged. 'It's really unclear because as you know the powers wouldn't tell me personal details ... but I thought it could be part of the reason. Still ... now you have told me your periods are regular, we must go to the doctor's, okay?'

Sarah grimaced and shook her head. 'You think I have a serious illness now, don't you? Great.'

'Probably not, love. But I'm not a doctor. We do need to get to the bottom of it.' John reached for her hand. She gave it and he felt a tremble in her fingers.

'Yes, okay,' she said with a sigh. 'And to tell you the truth, I've been worried sick too. I'll try and get an appointment for this afternoon.'

Dr Stewart regarded them over the rim of his spectacles, his kind brown eyes intense. He'd given Sarah a thorough examination and now held the urine sample that Sarah had just presented him with. 'Right you two, sit tight. Just going to test this, shouldn't take a minute.'

'What are you looking for, Doctor?' Sarah said, gripping John's hand so tight he thought she'd cut off all circulation.

'This and that. I can't find anything physically wrong with you, so I'm looking for sugar ... and so forth.' He turned and went to the other end of the room.

'This and that ... and bloody so forth?' Sarah whispered to John. 'Hardly a man of science, is he?'

A few minutes later the doctor straddled a wheeled stool and shot himself across the floor towards them, barely concealed excitement on his face. 'So do you want the good news or the good news?' He paused to watch their tentative smiles spread across their faces. 'Okay you don't appear to have diabetes or kidney problems, everything looks normal.'

John and Sarah looked at each other, and back at the doctor. He just sat on the stool and grinned at them inanely. Was that it? Wasn't he going to say more?

John cleared his throat. 'So what's causing the problems, doc?'

'From what you've told me I very much doubt that it's going to be seen as a problem, in fact quite the contrary.'

'For goodness sake, tell us,' Sarah said, a tremor in her voice.

'You, my dear, are pregnant.' Dr Stewart chuckled and held out his hand to them both. 'Congratulations, you are going to be parents.'

As if in a dream, John watched him shake hands with Sarah and then felt his own hand being pumped. 'But ... I—' he began.

'What about my periods?' Sarah almost yelled.

'It is uncommon, but not unheard of for a woman to have periods throughout the pregnancy. When you told me this earlier, along with the symptoms, I was already on that track, and then upon examining your abdomen, well ...' Dr Stewart's grin grew wider '... the urine test confirmed my diagnosis.'

John looked at Sarah and he saw his shock and joy reflected tenfold. She practically launched herself at him, laughing and crying at the same time. 'Oh, John, John ... I can't believe it!'

'Me either, but God, what fantastic news!' John's voice caught in his throat, his heart pounding adrenaline though his veins. He was going to be a dad, a *dad*!

From somewhere up on the ceiling he heard Sarah ask, 'So how many weeks ... how can we tell if my periods are—'

'We can't. That's why I'm sending you for a dating scan as soon as it can be arranged.'

The past week had been the longest in their lives whilst waiting for the scan. Although they had been mostly floating on a cloud of euphoria, they were dying to tell friends and family, but daren't jinx it until they had news that all was well. Sarah had convinced John to wait and he had to admit to himself that she'd been right. He knew exactly how Harry would have reacted. He would have been round there every few minutes, asking questions, getting onto the doctor to see if they could speed things up, asking if they had chosen any baby names, telling them stories about 'he knew a woman who' until they would have been driven mad by it all.

But at last, now in the darkened scanning room, soon all would be revealed. John drew his chair closer to the bed and caught hold of Sarah's hand. Their eyes locked as the nurse started the machine and slid the microphone over the jelly on Sarah's tummy. All they could hear were a series of crackles and then John held his breath as on the screen above him the shape of a tiny foetus appeared. Then a second later, a faint but rapid, *dub-a-dub-a-dub-a-dub* and growing stronger by the second filled the room. A gasp escaped their lips simultaneously and then tears of joy streamed down Sarah's face.

'A heartbeat, John ... oh my God.'

John found himself swallowing and dashing at his eyes too ... there was a beautiful child, *their* child.

'Now, as you know, you will have your next scan at twenty weeks, so a little way to go.' The nurse smiled and moved the microphone lower on Sarah's abdomen. 'I'll have to take some measurements, but I would estimate you are around thirteen weeks, Sarah.'

'Thirteen weeks!' Sarah exclaimed. 'Wow, that's a shock, further than we thought, then.' She looked shiny eyed at John.

'Yes … and if I am not mistaken …' The nurse moved the microphone again. 'You're in for another shock. There's two of 'em in there.'

John thought that someone had fiddled with his eardrums and switched them to fantasy mode. 'W-hat did you say … two?'

'Yes, Mr Needler, you are going to be the father of twins.'

# Chapter Fourteen

The 'little get together' had grown into a monster. Enjoying a rare warm and sunny early November day, relatives and friends spilled into the garden, the field, the kitchen, the patio. In fact every little corner of the Needler's cottage and surrounding land was heaving with those intent on celebrating their happy news.

Once the shock of twins had sunk in, the two of them were crazy with happiness and decided to invite a few close friends and family over. Because they were so overjoyed, however, a few became thirty or so, but the atmosphere and feel-good vibes surrounding them today was so fantastic, it made up for the less than low-key affair they had planned.

Sarah, comfy on the sofa, sipped lemonade and grinned at her mum over the rim of the glass. Gwen grinned back, flushed from the champagne and excitement of the occasion and prepared to trip another light fantastic across the patio with Harry.

Harry had been like the cat who'd got the cream and a dog with two tails all rolled into one since he'd heard the news. There had been lots of 'I told you so's', and 'I knew a woman who's,' but mostly he'd just talked non-stop about how thrilled and tickled pink he was for them both.

Both Gwen and Harry had shed a few tears with their respective offspring in private, because their great joy couldn't be shared with Sarah's dad or John's mum, but for the most part, the last few days had been some of the happiest Sarah could remember. And now the party was like the wedding reception they had never had. Brill.

Ella, her mouth full of party food, waved from the kitchen door and Sarah budged up to make way for her sister. She flopped down, her auburn ringlets bouncing like springs, and nudged Sarah's arm. 'Great do, our kid.'

Sarah smiled and slipped her arm through Ella's. 'It is, isn't it? I am so happy I can't tell you.' Sarah searched her sister's face. 'And you seem much happier too these days, things better with Jason?'

Sarah hoped so as Ella and Jason had come very close to splitting up a few months ago. He'd been unemployed for nearly a year and the poor guy had been almost destroyed by it.

'Yes, thank goodness. They couldn't have been much worse, as you know. Since he got this new job he's a new man. Talking of which – *they* seem to be getting very friendly lately, have you noticed?' She inclined her head towards Gwen and Harry and then searched Sarah's face, her forget-me-not blue eyes twinkling with mischief.

'What … you mean Mum … and John's dad? Don't be bloody daft, you've had one too many, I think.'

'You look at them and tell me I'm wrong, then.' Ella nodded her head at them again.

Sarah glanced over and, blimey, she had to admit they *did* look quite cosy together. The fast track playing earlier had finished and now they were dancing a little closer to *The Long and Winding Road*. They weren't full-on in each other's arms having a smoocherama or anything, but Harry had his hand in the small of Gwen's back and she had her right hand on his shoulder, her left hand clasped in his right as they swayed to the melody. Harry leaned forward and whispered something in Gwen's ear and she tossed her tawny curls and giggled coquettishly. Bloody hell – her mum looked about twenty years younger and so did Harry.

Sarah felt her sister's elbow in her arm again. 'Well. Am I right, or am I right?'

'Er … I guess you might have something, but it's never

right is it?' Sarah said. 'I mean at their age, and she being my mum and him being John's dad ... I mean, it's weird.'

'Stop being such an old misery! They are only in their mid-sixties and Harry is still quite a handsome man in a Harrison Ford kind of way.' Ella grinned. 'And what does it matter about her being your mum and him being John's dad? It would be better for the twins to have both grandparents married.'

'Married? Are you nuts?' Sarah gasped.

'Okay, perhaps I'm getting ahead of myself, but it would be nice if Mum met someone to share her life with, little sis.' Ella leaned over and kissed Sarah's cheek. 'And given the fact that Dad's gone, I couldn't think of anyone better than Harry, to be honest.'

Later that evening in the quiet of their bedroom as Sarah and John lay in each other's arms, she told John what Ella had said and at first he laughed out loud.

'Dad and Gwen, are you pulling my chain?'

'That's what I thought when Ella suggested it ... but they did look cosy together.'

He was silent for a moment or two and then cleared his throat. 'Hmm, well I think your sister might be barking up the wrong matchmaking tree,' John said, propping himself up on his elbow and pinning a strand of hair from Sarah's cheek behind her ear. 'Still, at least you see your sister. I wish Lucy lived a bit nearer. You've not even met her yet.'

'You miss her, don't you?' She stroked his face. 'Didn't Harry say she would be popping over soon?'

'Yeah, but she's said that for nearly two years although France is hardly the other side of the world. But I'm always so busy with the market garden and Lucy in helping her new husband get the riding stable business up and running that we never have time to visit each other. Time just gets away from you, doesn't it?'

129

The irony of that last remark wasn't lost on Sarah but she just said, 'It does.' Sarah knew John talked to Lucy on the phone every so often but it wasn't the same. Lucy had even missed the wedding because she was ill with shingles and had to cancel at the last minute. Poor John. Sarah would find it impossible if Ella was away.

'Yep. I just miss her.' He sighed. 'And if what your sister says about our parents turns out to be true, I can't see as it would do any harm, can you?'

Sarah remembered the way her mum's eyes had sparkled and her girlish laugh. 'Um, no, I guess not.'

The next day dawned, and brought chilly and bright weather with it, much more in keeping with November. It also brought Harry Needler tapping at the kitchen door not long after eight o'clock. Sarah was already up, wide-awake and making coffee, but John sleepy-eyed and yawning opened the door in his dressing gown.

'Dad, what are you doing here so early on a Sunday?'

Harry ran his hand through his curly grey hair and looked at his watch. 'Oh, thought it was later.' He slipped past John and nodded at Sarah who stood just behind him in the hall. 'Look, I thought I'd better pop over as soon as because I remembered something that might be useful about that other Stitch.' He paused to take in his son and daughter-in-laws' bemused expressions. 'You know, the woman who—'

'Yes, we know, Harry. Come on in and have a coffee,' Sarah said, leading the way.

Harry sipped his coffee at the kitchen table, his lively blue eyes staring somewhere over Sarah's shoulder. John waved a hand in front of his dad's face. 'You with us?'

'Eh? Oh yeah, I was miles away wondering if Gwen got

back okay ... I ordered her a taxi from here last night but it was quite late and she was a bit squiffy.'

'I think we would have heard if she wasn't, Harry,' Sarah interrupted, wondering if he was just around here to find out more about her mum. Her protective feathers were definitely ruffled at the thought of Harry trying to elicit personal information about her mum from them.

'Yeah, of course,' Harry muttered, taking another slice of toast from the rack. 'Grand woman, your mum.'

John and Sarah shared a meaningful glance.

'Okay to the point. This other Stitch, as you know, just like you, Sarah, left her body behind on the first trip. But when I was lying awake in the wee-small hours I remembered something.'

Harry took a bite of toast and a sip of coffee. In her head, Sarah screamed, *get on with it!*

As if he had heard her, he said, 'Apparently that was because she was only in the very early stages of pregnancy and the trip could have damaged the baby. I suppose that was the same with you.' Harry pointed a crust at Sarah.

'That makes sense, but why was that so important for you to come tearing round here early on a Sunday morning, Dad?' John yawned again and Sarah remembered he'd had quite a few over the eight the night before.

'I haven't finished yet.' Harry frowned at John. 'Then later on the poor lass was sent on another trip – just one as far as memory serves, but she had no choice in it. And this time she went as normal.'

This wasn't news to Sarah and she was getting fed up of Harry's melodrama. 'In case you haven't noticed, I have already *been* on another trip, Harry, and I had no choice in it either.'

'Yeah, but this lass was just a three-tripper, like most Stitches, not a committed life-longer like you ... she'd already done three, Sarah. She'd had a memory wipe and everything, so finding herself back in time just like that was a huge shock. The powers sorted it quick smart though, and she had a normal life after, but if that happened to her—'

'Dad, I don't really see how her story is helpful to our—'

Sarah noticed the warning look her husband shot his dad. 'No need to protect me, John. I understand what Harry's saying.'

Sarah's heart was thumping up the scale. If pregnancy had sent her time travel trips haywire, plus the Cross Stitch thing chucked into the mix, perhaps her experience was set to get much worse than the other woman's.

'You need to get on to the powers pronto, John.' Sarah wasn't surprised to hear a tremor in her voice. 'Get a guarantee that they'll leave me and our babies the hell alone.'

An hour later John came back into the kitchen with no trace of the ENF. Sarah knew that was a worry in itself. He studied her face, his beautiful eyes full of concern, and he rubbed the stubble on his chin which looked even darker now against his wan face.

'Well?' Harry said.

Sarah was thankful he'd said something as she was struggling for words.

John lifted both arms in a heavy shrug and released a long sigh. 'They remembered the Stitch that Dad was on about and confirmed what he said. As usual they only gave me bits, even though I kept my temper and tried to wheedle more out of them. But the gist is, they can't confirm nor deny that you will be sent on another trip.'

A flare of anger brought Sarah to her feet. 'What! But they *must* know what happens in the bloody future!'

'Try not to get upset, love, sit down and I'll make you a cup of tea,' Harry soothed.

'Tea? Tea! I need more than bleedin' tea!' She looked at John. 'What else did they say, for God's sake?'

'Basically what we talked about before. They don't have total control and can only direct, so—'

'Direct? What are they, time cops? Do they stand in space wearing white gloves and blowing a damned whistle?' Sarah knew she was getting beside herself with anger but she couldn't help it.

'Calm down, Sarah. I won't tell you any more until you sit down and take a few deep breaths,' John said in his no nonsense 'that's it and that's all' voice.

'And want it or not, I'm making you that tea.' Harry smiled.

Sarah sat and gripped the edge of the table until her finger ends went white. That was preferable to screaming at the top of her lungs. 'Just tell me, John.'

'Okay, but there's not much more … they said that they would endeavour to—'

'Endeavour?' Sarah said, feeling a giggle of hysteria caper up from some dark place labelled 'I'm out of control now'. 'Really? Who uses words like that any more?'

John narrowed his eyes and continued in his no nonsense voice, 'They would endeavour to keep you off missions until at least a year after the twins are born, but they can't promise and they can't reveal what happens because that would be personal information about—'

'The future? Yes, now where have we heard that before?' Sarah spat out, the hysteria replaced by a stab of anguish.

John drew up a chair and slipped his arm around her. 'Look, I know you're upset, I'm upset, but—'

'Well, you seem to be pretty calm about it!'

'You want a biscuit with that tea?' Harry called, his head in a cupboard.

'NO!' They yelled in unison.

That brought the ghost of a smile to Sarah's lips and she felt a little better.

John smiled too, his emerald eyes twinkling reassurance. 'I'm not calm inside, my love, but I have to be strong for you. If we both lost it, the whole thing would get blown out of proportion.' John kissed her cheek.

'I don't think it needs much blowing,' Sarah muttered.

'But nothing has happened yet. Might never happen.' John kissed her shoulder.

Sarah turned and looked him square in the eye. 'It might not, John, but it's more than clear that the powers don't know why the hell all this is happening. Yes, I'm pregnant, but so was the other woman and they sorted her out quickly. Why can't they do the same for me?'

'I don't know, hon.' John took her face in both his hands and kissed her lips. 'But the most important thing they said was that whatever happens, the babies won't be harmed.'

'They had bloody better not be,' Sarah growled. 'Or I will rip the power's spindly little bodies limb from limb!'

The great thing about maternity clothes was that you always knew they would fit. Sarah picked a piccalilli coloured top from the rail and screwed up her nose. Perhaps not. There was bright and breezy and bright and queasy. This was deffo the latter. Since the news about the twins, the last week had sailed by on the *S.S. Ecstatic*, the initials standing for Sarah Stupidly.

John walked around with a permanent smile on his face and Sarah pulled her top up, stuck her belly out and gawped at herself side-on in the mirror umpteen times as day. Her perpetual question of 'has it grown, do you think?' was becoming redundant. She had only now to look at John and he would say, 'same as it was a few hours ago'. He never seemed to get bored with it though, and he was just as soppy as she was about looking in the shops or online for anything to do with their forthcoming arrivals.

It was at John's suggestion that she get a 'few bits' for herself on one of her days off that she was here in the maternity section of Dorothy Perkins, rifling through the sales rails. Sarah loved a bargain and amused John with her, 'the original price was X and I got it for Y'. He always said there was no need for her to get stuff in the sales, but she liked to hunt about – made her feel like she was getting one over on the fat cats. Spying a rather fetching pair of green maternity trousers at the other end of the section she decided to throw caution to the wind and have a look at the non-sales items. *I will only be doing this once after all*. She smiled to herself.

Three or four steps towards the rail her legs turned into concrete blocks and butterflies in her tummy sent a flutter of wooziness into her head. Sarah stopped and swallowed hard, this felt only too familiar and it wasn't morning sickness. Sweat beaded her brow and fears about what might be about to happen crowded her brain like the heavy mob, but with a herculean effort she took a few steps further and … the rail got further away.

A bone shaking roll of nausea sent her senses reeling and *please, please, nooo*, screamed inside her head. What she was experiencing was so similar to the time she'd gone back to 1913 it was untrue. But now she had thrown in nausea too. Sarah tried to calm her galloping heart with the reasoned thought that nowadays, thankfully, the process of time travel was relatively painless and stress free … it had been just in the early days that she'd had a variety of experiences. She figured it could be the fact that she was expecting which was making the difference. She shook her head and took a deep breath. Perhaps all this was just a symptom of pregnancy and she was letting her imagination get the better of her.

Steadying herself with the nearest rail she closed her eyes and tried to calm herself, but unfortunately no matter how much she tried to deny it, the movement of the shop floor under foot forced the terrible truth and Sarah's eyes open. She looked down at the disintegrating floor swirling and breaking up beneath her and oh my God, yep, there was no doubt about it now – she was deffo being sent on a mission. Sarah began to sink, and with her, any hopes of she and their babies being left the hell alone.

# *Chapter Fifteen*

Just as in the 1913 trip, Sarah descended in some weird time vortex. She looked up. The sale rail and the trousers she'd wanted to buy grew smaller and then faded, along with the light, shoppers and annoyingly cheerful music designed to make folk spend, spend, spend. Soon all that was left of her world was a tiny pinprick of light and then nothing. Darkness was all ... darkness and ... Sarah sniffed ... fried chicken?

Aware of solid ground under her feet, heat and a weight in her right hand, the darkness gradually brightened until Sarah could see a scene slowly appearing as if someone had switched on the demister to clear a car windscreen. At last she could see in glorious Technicolor, a 1950s American diner full to bursting with 1950s diners, all busily eating, gesticulating and making their way to and from red leather seats in booths. A few harassed looking waitresses in green dress uniforms, white scalloped edged aprons complete with white pin on hats, tended their flocks like demented Bo Peeps, and a grumpy looking mountain of a man in a ketchup-stained apron wiped down the counter.

Into her ears, hitherto blocked of sound, the familiar *Rock Around the Clock* blasted from the jukebox in the corner, and then upon seeing Sarah staring open-mouthed, the grumpy looking man yelled at her in similar volume, 'What in the world are you doing standing there with the frying pan in your hand? Can't you see we're waiting on orders here, Sarah?' He knitted his bushy black eyebrows together and then ran his hands through a shock of grey hair.

Sarah looked at the frying pan in which half a dozen partially cooked fat sausages reclined and then brought her eyes back to the man. 'Um … orders?' Sarah noted her accent was identical to the man's deep southern states one.

'Jeez, girl, what's a matter with you? Git yourself back in that kitchen and ask Larry to help you.' The man shook his jowls and dabbed at his forehead with the cloth. 'You ain't been the same since you came back from yo' aunt's in New York … with high-falutin' ideas about changing the world.' He jabbed a stubby finger. 'I tell you, daughter of my best buddy or not, if you carry on like this, yo' out, git it?' The man's brown eyes shone with quiet anger.

Sarah nodded and fled, her nose and ears leading her in the direction of the kitchen via the smell of fried chicken and the clatter of pans.

On autopilot Sarah watched her hands push open the half-saloon doors until they swung inwards allowing access to a small but frantically busy kitchen. Two black women sporting *Kitchen Assistant* badges bustled to and fro washing up a huge pile of dishes and preparing vegetables, and a tall skinny red-haired man with his back to her – presumably Larry – flipped burgers on a hot griddle.

Numbness of feeling and screaming desperate despair jostled each other for prominence in Sarah's mind. For the moment, thankfully, numbness guided her actions and she walked forward to put the heavy pan on the hob. Looking down she saw she was wearing a long white, stain spattered apron, brown tight trousers and sneakers. Sarah wiped her greasy hands down the apron, glanced across at Larry and found him regarding her with keen hazel eyes.

'So did you find the pepper for the sausages?' His accent was the same as grumpy man's and her own.

'Um … no … I …' Sarah trailed off and looked at the sausages starting to sizzle gently around the edges. What was it about her and kitchens? She'd ended up in them in three of her trips now.

'You need to shape up. When I said get some pepper I

expected you to leave the damned sausages on the stove, not wander off *with* the fry pan like some loony tune.'

'Yeah, my mind is full of stuff at the moment, I guess.' Sarah hoped that sounded plausible given the stuff that grumpy man was saying about her. The heavy blanket of numbness was still managing to smother the fevered yelps of despair, and she told herself to imagine that she was improvising in a play or something. Sarah clocked the look of disdain on Larry's youthful but pockmarked face ... hmm that could be quite a challenge.

'Did Big Josh see you?' Larry flipped a burger onto a bun and handed it to one of the women.

Sarah presumed that was grumpy man. 'Yeah, he said I had high-falutin' ideas and I'd better get on with the job or I'm out.' She reached for a spatula and turned the sausages.

'Can't say as I blame him.' Larry waggled his head sagely. 'You know we're short-staffed in here with Joe away. And he don't like the talk of this equal rights for negroes you come back with. Nobody does in these parts. Not me so much as I had a negro friend when I wuz a kid 'til my pa put a stop to it.' He nodded briefly at one of the assistants and chucked a piece of steak on the griddle. 'But others are talkin' 'bout you. This is Alabama not New York.' Larry sidled up to her and lowered his voice. 'You don't wanna go git you a burnin' cross on your lawn, or worse like old Willie Boomsnart.'

Sarah raised her eyebrows. Boomsnart? Really? Any other time she would have laughed or made a joke about such a comical name, but now her blood ran cold despite the heat in the room. Alabama – check, 1950s – check, burning crosses outside your house – check ... she must be slap bang in the middle of one of the worst periods of American history. A neon sign flashed in her head – *Segregation alive and well and living in this town, yes siree.* Instinctively both her hands flew to her belly as if to protect her unborn children. My God, she had to get out of this hellhole.

'Hey, don't look so scairt. I'm just warnin' you, is all. And don't mind Big Josh, his bark's worse than his bite. There's no way he'd fire you after how yo' pa rescued him in the war an' all.'

'Um ... I was just thinkin' about poor Willie.'

'No need to get a breeze up. That won't happen to you. They only lynched him on account of his belly achin' on his commie radio show.' Larry pointed a knife at her. 'So, just keep yo' mouth closed and be grateful that a slip of a girl like you gits to be a short-order cook. Must be the only one for miles around.'

'She shapin' up, Larry?' Big Josh's boom so close behind nearly made Sarah drop the sausage pan.

'Yup. She done finished those sausages now and she's gonna start on the bacon next, ain't you?' Larry flashed a meaningful look.

Sarah nodded. 'Yup, sure am.' With shaking hands she put the sausages on a plate that one of the kitchen assistants was patiently holding and took the bacon Larry shoved at her.

'Pleased to hear it,' Big Josh muttered, standing just over Sarah's right shoulder. God, she couldn't cook with him there, hell she couldn't even keep her hands steady. All she wanted to do was escape, because no matter who she was here to save, she couldn't risk any danger to her babies and Klu Klux Klan country was certainly a dangerous place to be.

As she placed the rashers in a pan she turned to quickly retrieve her spatula on the counter and smashed to the floor a plate of pancakes complete with blueberries and cream. She felt Big Josh's exhalation of breath on her neck and his big fist slammed down onto the counter beside her. 'Damn it all, Sarah, that's it! There's nothing for it, Claudette will have to take over, git in there.' He pointed to a door marked 'staff'. 'Git a uniform on and serve some customers. We can't have you in here if you can't cook!' he bellowed.

Sarah hurried through the door and found a few uniforms hanging in a locker. Her heart was doing a sledgehammer impression and her immediate plan, such as it was, was to do a runner. If she put a uniform on and went out into the bustle of the diner, she figured that her chances were quite good to slink unnoticed out of the place. *Yeah, then what, Sarah?*

She had no clue, but perhaps she could try and find a quiet place to think and plan a way to get home somehow. Perhaps John was right at this moment negotiating safe passage back with the Spindly Ones. God, she hoped he was. In her situation, they wouldn't refuse to get her back, would they? She'd already endured a Cross Stitch, hadn't she given them enough faithful service? Surely they wouldn't have deliberately placed her and the babies in this awful situation? No, of course they wouldn't. *Right, deep breaths, in … out.*

A few minutes later Sarah stood in front of the mirror and an extra from *Happy Days* looked back at her. A white scalloped pinned hat sat atop heavily lacquered hair. This bouffant style at the front was drawn into a ponytail of bouncy swinging blonde curls at the back. Bright red lipstick and darkly drawn arched eyebrows made her look like a drawing of a child's idea of glamour. This picture was completed with the green uniform-dress, white scalloped edged apron and bobby socks. The shoes at least were sensible, black flats – good for doing a runner.

Walking back into the diner was like walking into a crowded railway station. Big Josh must be raking it in. Though a few grumpy faces indicated the shortage of staff and Sarah's mess-ups were causing long delays in service. The door handle to the outside was almost in reach as she threaded her way through the counter queue and dashing waitresses. Tucking her chin to her chest she hurried the last few feet … and then felt a rough hand on her wrist.

'Where's my goddamn burger? You think I've got all day?'

Sarah looked into the shark-eyes of another man-mountain, but younger and much angrier than Big Josh. 'Please let go my wrist.' She made her face deadpan, but inside, a thousand butterflies wearing spike heels had just alighted. This guy wasn't playing with her.

After a painful squeeze he released her. 'If you don't git my burger *now*, I'll do more than squeeze yo' wrist. We don't like yo' pinko kind round here,' he growled.

Sarah shuddered and made for the door again, only to find a wall of aproned belly blocking her way. 'Where you goin' now, Sarah?' Big Josh hissed in her ear. 'If you don't get JB's burger he'll be late for his shift on the bus and then he will make your life hell.'

Sarah realised by the fevered look in Big Josh's eyes that he was scared of this bus driver. Perhaps he dressed up of an evening in a white sheet and pointy hat.

Damn it! She'd have to go to the kitchen now and get this piece of slime's food before she could make her escape. On the way she passed another waitress. 'Please, er,' Sarah read her name badge, 'Jolene. Would you get JB's burger, I need to go to the restroom and he's awful mad at being kept waiting.'

Jolene narrowed her cat-green eyes and smacked her gum at Sarah. 'Nope. Since you stopped waitressing and became an uppity short order cook with grand ideas, you ain't had no time fo' us. Git it yo'self.'

Shit, shit, shit! Sarah cursed silently as she pushed past Jolene and hurried to the kitchen. All she wanted to do was escape and now she had to get food for a racist bus driver ... Sarah halted in her tracks and a light bulb snapped on in the history section of her brain. JB? Wasn't the name of the bus driver who asked Rosa Parks to stand up to make room for white passengers James Blake ... JB? Oh my God!

With the burger plate clasped tightly in her hand, Sarah hurried back from the kitchen a multitude of thoughts tumbling around her head. What if she'd made him late and then Rosa Parks wouldn't get on his bus, wouldn't be asked to move, wouldn't refuse and ergo wouldn't spearhead the Montgomery Bus Boycott which triggered the Civil Rights Movement championed by that giant of history, Martin Luther King? Jeez she could have single-handedly set integration back years, just because she was 'selfishly' thinking of her babies and trying to escape instead of trying to figure out who she had to save.

*Hang on, Sarah, this makes no sense.* Making him late hardly equated to life saving … unless if he'd have gone early, he might have stepped under a ladder and had a hammer drop on his head or something. So actually, perhaps making him late meant that he was saved from the hammer and Rosa does get on his bus? Perhaps that's it? She was buggered if she knew and as she approached JB's table she heard Big Josh, who had just set a mug of coffee down by his newspaper, say, 'And this one is on the house on account of yo' been kept waitin' … the burger too. Can't have you late for work, JB.'

'I ain't workin' today, Big Josh. Got me some time off. But I'm on late afternoon tomorrow.' JB took a swallow of coffee and eyed Sarah with disgust. ''Bout time, set it down here and git me some ketchup.'

Sarah did as she was asked wondering what the hell was going on if he wasn't even working today. Perhaps the momentous day was tomorrow after all then. Did that mean she had to stay here overnight? That thought made her want to heave. Placing the ketchup down she started to walk away.

Big Josh held up a finger. 'I think you have summin' to say to JB, here, Sarah.'

Really? She could think of a few choice words he needed

to hear, but it was clear what she was being asked. 'Sorry to keep you waitin', JB.'

JB looked down his nose at her, his dark eyes alive with malice. 'JB, sir.'

Goodness he was asking for a slap now. Swallowing her pride and anger, Sarah said, 'JB, sir.'

A few hours later Sarah was still taking orders and racing about like a headless chicken. JB had gone, but she figured that finding a quiet place to plan her escape to the future wasn't an option now, not with so much at stake. Perhaps John would suddenly appear having found a willing 'passing the time' Stitch and whisk her off home. But with her luck lately – conception of the twins excepted – that was not a likely scenario.

She was ready to drop but eventually the lunch rush was over and the handful of customers now coming in just wanted mostly pie and coffee. Big Josh was still tossing her mean looks whenever she caught his eye, but now as she wiped down a table by the window, he came over and took the cloth from her hand.

'Looks like yo' Jesse's here.' He nodded outside to the street where a young man was looking at them from the window of a battered pickup. 'A few minutes early, but I guess you can git.'

Sarah nodded but wondered who the hell Jesse was. Please don't let him be her husband. 'Thanks, Big Josh.'

'And if you promise that you'll stop acting like a crazy person I might jest let you back in the kitchen tomorrow, okay?' A ghost of a smile played at the corners of his mouth.

'Yes, thank you ... I will.'

The passenger door creaked open as Sarah approached the pickup and the young man gave her a toothy grin and a friendly wave. His face was round and pink and a yellow baseball cap seemed to meld with his unruly hair the colour of corn.

Sarah slid into the sun warmed seat beside him and looked up into his light blue eyes. She immediately warmed to him and felt instinctively there was no romance between the 1955 Sarah and him, but there was definitely love.

'Had a good day, sis?' Jesse grinned and pulled away from the kerb.

*Ah, phew, thank goodness for that.* Her frazzled emotions wouldn't stretch to another act. 'Yup it was real good, thanks.' No use in going over the whole rigmarole of what had happened. The least she said about anything at all, the better.

'Really?' He looked at her in disbelief. 'So you have forgotten all this talk about savin' up your pay, goin' to college and gittin' an education?'

Sarah's spirits rose a little. Good for old Sarah. 'No, I ain't forgot, just no point in being miserable 'til I do, is there?'

Jesse nodded, apparently happy with that and concentrated on his driving.

At a stop sign a little while later, Sarah took stock of 1950s Montgomery. They must be on the outskirts of the city she guessed as the buildings were smaller and not as tall as the ones she could see in the distance. On a nearby building a sign for a swimming pool proclaimed *Whites Only,* and on a station building across the street a sign on the pavement announced *Waiting Room Whites*à *Colored.*

Of course, as a history teacher, Sarah knew that segregation was enforced in all walks of life: schools, leisure, buses, drinking fountains, even in death as whites and blacks had separate cemeteries at the time, but to actually see it for real made her sad and furious in equal measure. Fear of communism due to the Cold War was ever present in newspapers and on TV, in books and in culture in all its forms and sadly in schools too. And at the exact same time in history huge leaps were planning to be made for mankind, in science, technology and medicine. On every jukebox and radio rock and roll thrilled the 'new teenager' and lifted the spirits, and classic films like *Oklahoma!*, *The Seven Year Itch* and *Lady and the Tramp* were playing to packed audiences at the cinema. Yet segregation was allowed to continue.

'Gee, Sarah, your face might set like that if the wind changes, girl.' Jesse chuckled as the lights went green and he moved the bone rattler off down the street again, just as Elvis's *That's Alright Mama*, came on the jukebox in a nearby bar.

How ironic. *This* was not all right. The pain that the inside of Sarah's cheek between her teeth was causing couldn't suppress her fury any longer. 'Don't you get angry at all this disgusting discrimination, Jesse?' She flung her hand at more signs as they passed. 'I mean, how can one group of people be so mean to another just because of the colour of their skin, it sure beats the hell out of me!'

Jesse shook his head. 'Don't start all this again, it won't do no good, and probably will do bad. Pa loves his sister but he ain't pleased you come back from a visit to her with all this talk of change in yo' head. You know we is just as sorry about segregation as you, but like Pa says, it will change over time, and there's nothing we can do fo' now.'

A harrumph escaped her lips, but from now on Sarah decided to button them. Luckily Jesse had been sympathetic but what would she have done if he hadn't have been? Best keep quiet and hope that tomorrow would bring her a clue and please God … home again.

Home for now turned out to be a pumpkin farm. A small but cosy homestead nestled against a backdrop of pumpkin fields and tall trees. Once inside, Sarah feigned a headache and quickly ran up the rickety stairs. She had no wish to have a conversation with 'our pa', whose dungaree clad frame she'd glimpsed chopping up something in the kitchen. Larry called after her that 'our ma' would send up a tray later if she felt up to it.

Having found her room after three attempts, she closed the door and leaned her back against it. Wall to wall pink gingham, frilly curtains and fluffy teddy bears almost gave her a real headache, and she flopped down on the edge of the bed to stare through the window at the uninspiring winter landscape and the occasional truck passing on the distant road. Warm for her idea of winter though, and Sarah had gleaned from Jesse that it was the first of December tomorrow. If memory served, that was the day that Rosa made her stand, or sit, to be more precise.

Sarah released a heavy sigh and then from the corner of her eye she spied an envelope marked *Sarah* on the dresser and her stomach turned a somersault. It couldn't be. She leapt from the bed and snatched it up. It was ... it was John's handwriting. Ripping it open she read:

> *My poor darling, you must be at your wits end! The powers are very apologetic and have no clue as to why this has happened to you as never before have they encountered such an erratic and unusual departure. They normally have some indication but not this time. Yes, they couldn't confirm or deny you would travel again, but they were banking on at least having some control over it. They are flummoxed.*
>
> *Anyway, they have promised to get you back tomorrow and are working round the clock to sort it. Don't ask me how, as usual they don't tell me everything, but suffice to say they are going to get another Stitch to 'pass the time' with you. So don't worry about letting anyone down. The thing is, Sarah, you have to be outside the diner at 5 p.m. tomorrow. That's the only slot they can do.*

*I miss you so much even though you have only been away for a few hours. And I'm so angry and frustrated that I can't be with you, hold you, kiss you and tell you I love you, but you know how much I do, don't you? They let me come back for a few minutes to put this letter in the bedroom but not a moment more. I was going to stay and damn the consequences, but Dad thankfully talked me out of it as he did last time. God knows what would have happened if he hadn't … probably would have made it all worse. I am such a hot head where you are concerned, but that's because I love you so much.*

At this point the writing became blurred and Sarah dashed at her eyes and held the letter to her thumping heart. God she *so* needed John right now, the pain of separation was almost physical. She looked back to the letter.

*So try to sleep, you and our babes need to rest. And obviously try to avoid conversation with Sarah's family. Tomorrow I suppose you will have to go back to work, but be outside at 5 p.m. Whatever you are doing, just leave, and don't let Big Josh or any of them stop you. It will soon be over, sweetheart, believe me. Be strong and take care.*

Sarah held the letter for a few moments more and then tucked it down her top. That would take some explaining if any of the family clapped eyes on it. She felt so much better now, closer to John too. Even if she only had a letter next to her chest for comfort he felt nearer somehow. It was a real and physical link to her life back home. And what was he panicking about? Of *course* she'd be outside at 5 p.m. tomorrow. That was her chance to get home as quickly as possible. Where else was she going to bloody be?

# Chapter Sixteen

Back on short-order duties all day, Sarah was beginning to wonder if she would ever be able to bring herself to eat bacon, burgers or sausages ever again. A mountain of them had passed through her pan, griddle and skillet since 7 a.m. and now it was getting on for four in the afternoon. Even the lull after lunch hadn't been so much of a lull but a pause for breath, and now orders for burgers had started up again. It was a wonder that there were any cows or pigs left in the whole of Alabama – the demand from Big Josh's Diner was enough to sustain supply from Georgia too.

Still, one more hour and hopefully she'd be back home in the cottage with John. And God help the Spindly Ones if they sent her anywhere else before the babies were born. In fact, the way she felt now, she never wanted to do another mission as long as she lived.

At four-thirty she was about to take an afternoon break as her plan was to skip away and hide by the dumpsters in the back lane until five. Sarah figured that there was no other way that it would work. She couldn't just down tools and walk out at 5 p.m. with Big Josh and Larry hot on her tail. They were already suspicious of her clam impression because the 1950s Sarah was a regular chatterbox by all accounts.

Sarah had kept her lip buttoned at breakfast too before Jesse had given her a lift to work. She'd just nodded and smiled at our ma and pa, grunted when required to utter a word. There was no way she wanted to put her foot in it again and be thrown in jail or something for 'pinko' talk.

On the way down the corridor, Big Josh appeared at her side as if by magic and said, 'Before you have yo' break,

Sarah, JB wants you to serve him. Asked for you personally.' Big Josh looked a bit sheepish but Sarah could tell there would be no wriggle space for her here. Nevertheless she tried anyway.

'Aw, Big Josh, can't Jolene or Muriel do it? I'm dead on my feet and I don't have my uniform on —'

'Nope. He wants *you* so he can make a point. Git a uniform on. It won't take long and thar'll be a little summin' extra in yo' pay packet come the end of next week. You worked hard today and no uppity talk neither.' Big Josh folded his arms across the vast expanse of belly and fixed her with a kindly, but no-nonsense stare.

A few moments later she waited patiently by the side of JB's table as he flicked through his newspaper deliberately ignoring her presence. She cleared her throat. 'What can I get you, sir?'

A few more flicks, a rub of the chin and then, 'You can get me a good honest southern girl's values and a smile now and then.' JB's leer slimed around her body like a physical caress. She wanted to shower. 'You're a purty girl, Sarah, when you smile. Use it more often.' He put his hand on her arm and squeezed it gently.

A recoiling step back knocked her hip into another table and a smallish unkempt guy whom she'd noticed earlier sitting at it slurred, 'Washh where you're puttin' your ass, lady.'

Sarah looked at his grey eyes swimming in a sea of alcohol, his slumped shoulders carrying the weight of the world, his tar black fingernails and jacket stained with who knew what – the personification of dejection. 'Sorry, sir.'

'You watch yo' mouth, boy.' JB slapped his rolled up newspaper on the man's arm. 'She don't have to put up with no slurs from the likes of a damned hobo.'

*That's rich coming from a sexist racist pig such as yo'self, JB.* Sarah wanted to say but of course didn't.

The clock above the counter chimed 4.15 and wishing to cut short any retaliation from the little hobo guy, get JB's order and get the hell out, she said, 'Your usual burger, Mr JB, sir?' and flashed him a smile that would have brightened the pits of hell.

'Now that's the smile I was talkin' about, purty lady.' JB grinned. 'Yup, and a side order of fries, please.'

*He said please? Wonders will never cease.* Sarah ran off in the direction of the kitchen. On her return JB tried to get her to 'set a spell', but she excused herself saying she had other tables to wait. She preferred him nasty and spiteful to amorous, but now she had no choice but to take more orders and the clock was ticking.

Upon passing the Little Hobo's table a while later, Sarah heard the tail end of a nasty exchange between him and JB.

'There ain't no excuse for being a bum, no matter what hard luck story yo' peddlin',' JB snarled and made ready to leave. 'And next time you come a stinkin' my eatin' place up, I'll git a few of my friends to make sure you have a bath … in the Alabama River.'

'Think yo' such a big man, dontcha?' Little Hobo drained his cup and wiped his mouth with the back of his hand.

JB thrust his face inches from the other man's face and growled, 'That's 'cos I is a big man, little pecker.' JB prodded him hard on his right shoulder. 'And don't you forget it.' Then he raised a hand in Big Josh and Sarah's direction. 'See ya'll later, off to work now.'

An icy finger drew a length of Sarah's spine. *Off to work.* She hoped that the Spindly Ones had secured a Stitch to keep him safe until Rosa Parks got on his bus in the city. Sarah wiped down the table next to Little Hobo's and shook the finger off. It was 4.50 now and if they hadn't got someone to take her place it was tough. There was no way she was staying here a moment longer.

Little Hobo pushed his cup to the edge of the table and stood up. A mask of anger and embarrassment hung on his face and the icy finger found a new target of her abdomen when he mumbled to himself, 'You'd better watch yo' back, Mr JB. I'll show you who's the bigger man.' Then he strode purposefully through the door and slammed it behind him.

An urge to drop everything and run after him was akin to a team of wild horses trampling across Sarah's consciousness. Again, the thought that a 'passing the timer' would be found calmed her a little, but as she watched from the window she saw Little Hobo pick up his pace and then duck down an alley. Oh God. He looked on a mission ... and not a good one.

The clock ticked down the final minutes of the hour. The wet cloth clasped to her chest began to seep through her uniform. Sarah threw it down on the table and raked her hands through her ponytail. *Shit ... SHIT!* What if they haven't managed to find anyone?

'What's up, Sarah? Poor dear, you look real agitated,' Jolene said in her ear. She sounded about as concerned as the breeze.

'I ... I have to go.' Sarah's brain was fighting with her heart and the heart was winning. She couldn't leave it to chance, could she? Couldn't just walk outside and wait to be taken home while Little Hobo might at this moment be ...

'Yeah.' Jolene waggled her head and planted her hands on her waist. 'Well, I for one will be glad to see the back of yo' negro loving ass.'

That choice comment made her mind up. There wasn't much time and it was now or never. Sarah turned to face Jolene and shoved the flat of her hand hard in her midriff. 'Out of my way, you nasty piece of work. After today yo' nice white little world is gonna be rocked forever and I don't mean by Bill Hayley and his sodding comets!'

Jolene said something like, 'Oomph' and was sent sprawling into the next table and onto the lap of a very surprised customer. A clatter of crockery followed soon after and as Sarah steamed out of the door, she heard bellowing from the lungs of Big Josh, 'SARAH, GODDAMIT! YOU'RE FIRED!'

Being fired seemed the least of her worries as she sped across the street and down the alley that Little Hobo had taken. Though it was a fine and fairly warm winter's day, the alley was gloomy, flanked by dumpsters and dustbins – no trash cans, funny how her language tuned in and out to American English – and the damp, moss-patterned walls running at either side seem to close in on her.

*What was that?* She stopped and cocked her head to one side. Apart from the rustle of a sleek black rat in a newspaper near her feet there was nothing. Sarah stiffened, stamped her foot and the creature scuttled away. Lucky she wasn't the screaming type or the whole of Montgomery would be alerted to her presence. Moving as quickly as she could without making a clatter in her flat plastic shoes, she stopped at the corner and peered around it at yet another alleyway twinned with the one she'd just traversed.

The thought of her unborn twins made her stop and take stock. This was crazy. It must be only just after 5 p.m. ... she could run back and—

'You just try it, you little bastard, and I'll knock you to the pearly gates!'

*Oh my God, that's JB's voice.* Sarah slunk along the alley and hid behind a particularly large dumpster full of what smelled like rotting cabbage. Holding her nose she peered round it and her breath caught in her throat.

In the backyard of what looked to be a greengrocers, judging from the wooden crates strewn around, Little Hobo crouched commando style and moved crablike from side to side about three feet in front of the hulking figure of JB. In his right hand Little Hobo held a flick knife, while his left taunted JB with a gimmee gesture. JB was crouched a little too, had his shirtsleeves rolled up and arms stretched out in front, hands quivering as if he were about to grab Little Hobo and pull his neck.

Sarah released her breath slowly and tried to stop her sledgehammer heart from breaking through her chest. What the hell could she do to help JB? She didn't particularly want to help the nasty vicious scumbag, but if Little Hobo somehow managed to kill him, then everything would go tits up with the bus boycott and the rest would be history – a nervous tic tugged at the corner of her mouth – *but not as we know it, Jim*. Gawd, surreal thoughts were a trademark of hers when she was in a tight spot.

His back to her, Little Hobo did the crab dance again, and JB, his arms still stretched, open and closed his fingers, almost ready to pounce. It struck her that they looked a little like a lobster and crab performing a mating ritual. Hmm, but then crabs and lobsters don't mate you dumbkopf! *Oh come on, Sarah, concentrate, you need to stop this!*

What she needed was some kind of a weapon to clonk Little Hobo over the head with ... and then an idea came to her courtesy of another black rat clambering into a trash can a few steps back into the alley.

Blimey the trash can lid was weightier than she expected. Sarah set it back on the ground to get a better grip on the greasy rim. She had one chance at this and if she dropped it on her foot that would be it. One, two, three steps ... and then she was out in the yard, the lid hefted above her head.

Upon seeing her a flicker of triumph passed through JB's eyes but he skilfully kept his face deadpan. He smiled coldly at Little Hobo. 'Come on then, you little shit, I ain't got all day.'

Little Hobo lunged at JB and simultaneously Sarah lunged at Little Hobo, bringing the lid down on his head with a resounding *thunk!* Little Hobo sank to his knees and then toppled over onto his side like a puppet cut from its strings.

'You sweet thing!' JB yelled, grabbing her and swinging her round. 'And what you doin' creepin' round the alleyways? 'Taint no place for a lady?'

'Set me down, JB, I need to check I ain't killed him!'

JB set her down and hooked the toe of his boot under Little Hobo's back. Little Hobo rolled over and lay still. 'You ain't killed him, and that's a shame. He's jest out cold.'

Sarah eyed the trash can lid still rocking slightly from side to side on the ground and felt like swinging it a second time, this one would be aimed square in the face of the smug- faced bastard before her. And right now as he leered at her, eyes bright with adrenalin, she felt like killing him.

'You'd better git to work, JB. I'll call for a doctor.' Sarah was surprised how calm she sounded.

'First I need a sweet kiss from your purty lips, honey-pie, to send me on my way.' JB took a step forward.

'One more step and I'll scream rape.' Even though her voice was low, Sarah could tell by his shifty eyes that the threat had unsettled him.

He held his hands up. 'Jeez hot and cold, eh?' He gave a wheezy chuckle. 'Okay, I'll be back tomorrow, darlin', and I don't take no for an answer.' JB put his jacket on and sauntered off down the alley.

Sarah leaned against the wall to steady her shaking legs and let out a long sigh of relief. Thank God he was going off to drive that bloody bus. It seemed like she had completed the crazy mission against all odds and a little tickle of victory capered up from her depths. She turned her face up to the sky and took a minute to gather her wits and then looked back to the prone form a few feet away. *Okay, now for the doctor*. A groan from Little Hobo stopped her in her tracks.

'Hey you, please help me,' he said with a croak in his voice.

Cradling Little Hobo's head in her lap she gingerly touched an egg-sized lump growing at the top of it.

'Ouch!'

Sarah cringed. 'Oops, sorry. I'll run to a phone and get a doctor.' She made as if to get up.

'I don't need no doctor, just some water. Did you see what happened?'

Sarah looked into his kind grey eyes now almost clear of alcohol and realised that beneath the scruffy beard that this guy wasn't as old as she had originally thought. Early thirties, tops. She shrugged in answer to the question; she could hardly say what really happened, could she? 'Um … I'll get you some water.'

Little Hobo smiled and Sarah realised something else. This guy would be real handsome if he was spruced up. She felt the 1950s Sarah's heart skip a beat. Now wouldn't it be good if they had a happy ever after?

'Thanks, um … you been so kind to me and I was rude to you in the diner. I'm sorry for that. What's yo' name?'

'Sarah, what's yo's?'

'Gary … Gary Owen, like the song.' He shot her another heart-stopping smile.

Sarah smiled back and then stopped. His face began to pixilate and morph into someone else's. Panic prickled through her, accompanied by a floating sensation. What on earth was happening now? It was as though she was being suspended from above looking down onto a prone body, but before she could make out exactly who she was looking at, the hard alley floor gave beneath her knees and she toppled sideways into a soft bouncing … bed? Her vision cleared and with it, the recognition of the face. On the pillow next to her sleeping peacefully was her darling, John. *John! Thank God she was home!*

The floating sensation made way for a lead weight in every limb and though she struggled to keep them open, her eyes began to close. With a huge effort she reached out, switched the bedside light off, touched John's face and then immediately fell into an exhausted and deep sleep.

# Chapter Seventeen

The sliver dawn light trickling through the curtains and onto the pillow next to him was playing tricks with his vision. It must be the 'twilight' moment between a dream and wakefulness because he could see Sarah's sleeping face a few inches from his own. John shut his eyes again and yawned. He had hoped and prayed she'd come back safe to him over the last few days, it was only natural that his brain was projecting his wife sleeping soundly next to him in his first waking moments. But she wasn't back, was she? No, she'd chosen to ignore everything he'd said, stay in 1955 and go off on a hare-brained life saving mission.

A movement in the bed next to him popped his eyes open and startled him fully awake. Turning onto his side he looked again and even in the scant light he could see that it *was* Sarah, one arm thrown over the side of her face, one of her legs tucked over a pillow –the typical Sarah sleeping pose – and from her slightly parted lips, her soft breathing now bordering on a snuffly snore.

A torrent of love and gratitude flooded his heart and he reached out to take her in his arms but then he stopped. She must be exhausted, she might not take kindly to being woken so early, she could have only just got back for all he knew. Five o'clock in the afternoon in 1955 had turned out to be 11 p.m. here and John had stayed awake waiting, a pent up ball of anxiety until a text from the powers at 1 a.m. had sent him to the whisky bottle and oblivion.

*John. Sorry to say that Sarah missed the deadline. She has decided to take the mission herself and we will endeavour to reward such dedication with a swift and safe return.*

Watching her lovely face as she slept, John realised that it wasn't just fear of disturbing her sleep that prevented him from taking her in his arms. A little boat of annoyance had set sail on the torrent of love and was growing ever nearer on the horizon. Damn her. How could she put her life in jeopardy like that, not to say the twins? Hadn't she realised he'd be beside himself with worry? Had she learned nothing from the 1928 trip last year? Suddenly wanting to put distance between them he scooted to the side of the bed, slipped his dressing gown on and left the room.

An email on the laptop told him the whole story, and boy wasn't Sarah the flavour of the month with her Spindly Ones? How brave, dedicated, selfless she'd been, etc. Worked with her gut instinct ... John felt the little boat of annoyance turn into an ocean liner. God, how selfless? He'd say selfish was nearer the mark! Sarah had actively put herself and their unborn babies in harm's way. His hand shot out and slammed the laptop lid down. He needed coffee and air.

The reds and golds of autumn predominant on the rolling hills all around was now giving way to the more barren greys and browns of winter. John stood on the decking, pulled his dressing gown closely about his neck and heaved a heavy sigh. He noted that the sigh hung in the cold November air – a physical embodiment of his frustration. A huge gulp of coffee burnt a path down his gullet and fanned out through his chest. The heat failed to warm him, however, as the chill of ocean liner persisted.

How could Sarah have been so cruel? Two days of hell had left him hollow inside and now he learns that she chose to stay ... chose to keep him in turmoil. But then lo' and behold, she appears peacefully sleeping like an innocent angel.

The patio door sliding back halted his thoughts and he turned to see Sarah watching him, full of sleep, hair stuck up, bare foot, bundled in his favourite sky-blue dressing gown that brought out the colour of her eyes.

At the sight of her his ocean liner shrank to boat size again and she stepped out and ran to him, flinging her arms tight around his neck.

'John, oh thank God I'm back. I missed you *so* much, my darling!'

Every atom of his being said, hold her, kiss her, tell her that you love her … but quiet anger stiffened his arms and silenced his words.

She looked up at him, a frown furrowing her brow. 'John, what's wrong?' She rubbed his arms. 'Hey, sweetheart, you're freezing, why are you out here on such a cold morning?'

Holding her firmly at the top of each arm he moved her away from him. 'Not as cold as you, sweetheart.' He was gratified to see the sarcasm in his voice put a stop to a half-smile fluttering at the corner of her mouth.

'Eh? John, what's wrong?' She took a step toward him again, but he sidestepped and marched to the house. 'John, hey come back.'

'Ha! That's rich, Sarah!' he flung over his shoulder as he wrenched the door open and flounced into the sitting room. 'For *you* to come back, that's what I have been bloody praying for the last forty-eight hours and what did you do to make it happen, eh? Fuck all, is what!'

Sarah ran in and managed to stand between him and the door to the kitchen. She held up her hands. 'Okay, stop right there and sit down and tell me why you're so angry with me.'

John sat down on the sofa more from the shake in his legs than because she'd asked him to and yelled, 'You ask me what's wrong! You actually have the cheek to ask that? You chose to forego safe passage home to me and instead went off down an alleyway to sort out some knife-wielding drunk, risking your life *and* our babies' lives!'

Sarah's face blanched and she flopped down on the arm of a chair. 'God … when you put it like that, I can see why you're so angry. But I didn't have time to think properly. My gut feeling knew what Gary intended to do and I was scared there wouldn't be enough time for a passing the timer to get there.' She raked her fingers through her tousled hair. 'Don't you see, John, the whole Civil Rights Movement, Rosa Parks—'

'Oh, please! What do you want to be? A Super Stitch?' John registered the anguish and pain on her face but couldn't help himself. 'Because I think you really do have a superhero complex – pity you didn't have a billowing cloak and a mask!'

She pursed her lips and shook her head in defiance. 'They might not have found a passing the timer—'

'They would, Sarah. *Somebody* would have done it! And you were protecting the wrong man anyway! JB was short for James Brace. Not James bleedin' Blake!'

Sarah's mouth gaped open. 'But ... but who was Brace then?'

'Just a goddamned bus driver.' John threw his hands up. 'The guy you whacked, Gary, was the one to save. He was a former lawyer, couldn't cope after his wife had left him and became a bum. The whack on his head seemed to have brought him to his senses. That of course was helped along the way by Sarah. He changed his life, wrote a book about social injustice and became a brilliant Civil Rights lawyer.'

Sarah threw her hands up too. 'So I did good then. Saved the guy who I was supposed to save! What's the problem?'

*God how damned big-headed was she?* John folded his arms and tried to keep a lid on his temper. 'You are missing the point. You had no clue he was the one – just launched in. Sarah Super Stitch, cape flying, all based on gut instinct and saved him by accident. What would have happened if Gary had spun round and stabbed you in the belly?'

Sarah lowered her head and picked at her nails, her hair curtaining her face. 'I ... I don't know.'

John noticed a tear appear on the end of her chin but felt no remorse. 'No? Well, I bet you can hazard a very good guess.'

She tossed her head up and glared at him through shimmering eyes. 'Would I have been actually hurt? I mean, I know I am me when I travel, but people see the other Sarah, so perhaps it is her body that would have been wounded—'

*She was taking the piss now.* 'Are you mad? You know there is both a physical and cerebral link – you both would have been hurt, and didn't you give a thought to the poor 1950s Sarah?'

'Yes, no, I don't know!' Sarah stood and began to pace the carpet. 'I told you that I didn't really have time to think. And besides, everything is muddled – my gut instinct was messed up because everything has gone haywire lately with my travelling, as you well know! But it was all good in the end.' Sarah lowered her voice and sat down again. 'You said that Sarah helped Gary back on his feet ... she must have been okay, then?'

Her hunched and thoroughly miserable posture poked a sliver of conscience and pity into his heart. 'Yeah she was grand.' He sighed. 'She never went back to the diner, worked at a car wash instead. Then she bumped into Gary a while later in town and confessed that she'd clonked him on the head to save him from prison. He'd already started to climb out of his pit and had moved towns to avoid JB and his hench mob. He'd only come back to collect his things, so it was lucky they met. They got talking and he discovered that she was more than just a pretty face, so they started courting. He helped her through college, and after she went to work for him. They made a formidable team and married in 1958.'

A bright little smile curled her mouth as Sarah blinked back tears. 'So that's great, no? As I said, the whole think was mixed up because of the pregnancy and stuff—'

'Yes, Sarah, but that's only part of it. No matter how you dress it up, in the end *you* chose to do it.' John jabbed a finger at her across the room. 'I explained to you a while ago that no Stitch can be totally coerced into a job. Even though you promised them you would be a life-longer. What you do *during* a mission to a large extent depends on free will, *you* have to allow it.'

'But I was so worried about what might happen and—'

John was heartily sick to the stomach now of her denial and her wilful disregard for herself, their babies, and yes, if he was honest, for him too. 'Well, I'm up to here with it!' He chopped the side of his hand at the air above his head. 'Sick of it. You ignored all the warnings that last time in 1928 and so I had to come to bloody rescue you, nearly getting permanently disabled as a result. But I did it because you needed me and I would die for you – still would! So how many more times will I be required to?' He thumped his hand down on the coffee table.

Sarah flinched and silent tears began to course down her face.

John swallowed a lump and felt his own eyes moisten, but his anger was too great to relent. His voice was almost a whisper. 'This time, Sarah, this time you have gone too far. Our babies ...' John felt his throat close over and he couldn't bear to look at his wife's tortured face any longer. He turned, stormed through the door and slammed it shut against her anguished wail.

# Chapter Eighteen

The roar of an engine and screeching of tyres some time later were the only things loud enough to break through the volume of Sarah's sobs. Then the shock that John had gone without trying to resolve the situation, or even comfort her in some way, brought her to her knees on the sitting room floor. There she rocked to and fro hugging herself tightly, the sobs now stuck in her chest and her whole body shuddering with despair. He had always been the one to calm things, said that an argument left as a molehill grew into a mountain. Well, this one was already a mountain – the summit invisible above the clouds.

Sarah rubbed her eyes and prepared to get off her knees but then a little sparkly object under the settee caught her eye. Flicking it out with her fingers she found it to be a silver horseshoe from their wedding cake. How had it got there? Was it a sign that her luck was going to change ... or had it just fallen off someone's plate at the impromptu reception they held here? Sarah feared it was probably the latter. Her luck seemed well and truly on vacation at the moment. *Right, if in doubt, make tea.*

Tea normally helped her think but today her brain and thought process resembled a bowl of cold spaghetti. One train of thought curled around another and then got lost under the heavy weight of the whole. The whole being that she had royally buggered up this time. At least that much was clear. John was right. Everything he said was true. How could she have risked her babies? Obviously she hadn't consciously chosen to put them at risk, and it was true that everything had happened so quickly it made her head spin, but in her haste to do the right thing, she of course had done just that – risked the babies.

Another sip of tea and still she'd found no real defence for her actions save the genuine belief that she was saving the Civil Rights movement. That should have been enough in normal circumstances, but there was more than just her at stake nowadays. The superhero complex ... perhaps he was right about that too. For so long in her life she'd been the under- confident mouse, worried about upsetting anyone, dragging her life behind her ex Neil's, like it was a errant bit of loo roll tucked down her pants. Then John had appeared with a new life, a new love, and everything had changed beyond all recognition. John's belief in her had given her confidence and, it wasn't too dramatic to say, a reason for living.

But oh my lord, he must have been furious to bring 1928 up again. That was the last time she'd stuck her neck out for glory and alongside John's awful punishment, it had been touch and go if the powers were going to give her a memory wipe and allow her relationship to continue with John. They had though, on condition that she would take missions for the rest of her life.

Through the window the sun and wind played chase with clouds over the hills, turning the landscape alternately light and dark green. The clouds and wind looked like they were winning a few moments later as they brought dark reinforcements from the north and the sun eventually gave up and played elsewhere.

A long sigh of resignation escaped Sarah's mouth. Perhaps she should play elsewhere for a bit – go back to her mum's for a few days, let John calm down. A twist of sadness in her gut propelled yet another lump into her throat. Perhaps she should go back permanently. If she stuck around John and this crazy pattern of time travel continued for her, who's to say that she wouldn't find herself in dire straights again? Even though next time they definitely wouldn't be of her own making, no matter what was at stake, he would be tempted to come to the rescue, in fact the babies would mean that he definitely would and this time there would be no forgiveness. The Spindly Ones had made that pretty clear last time.

Sarah stood, wandered back into the sitting room and picked up a large framed wedding photo of her and John from the sideboard. Because the actual day had been a shambles they had dressed in their finery and had a few shots taken on the Monday. John was carrying her over the threshold, his head on one side, dark curls messy in the wind looking down with eyes full of love for her and hers were a mirror to his. The love she'd felt for him on that day was as big as the sky was now, as big as the universe, but what good was that if she would ultimately destroy him?

In her heart of hearts she new damned well that John loved her too much – would never let her leave, especially now she was carrying his babies, so it might be just as well to ask for a memory wipe for both of them. That way neither would be hurt, she would still have the babies and perhaps a fake memory of who the father had been could be planted. She and they would be happy, John would be happy because he wouldn't remember anything, and that would be that. Even though her heart felt as if it was being lacerated with metal barbs, she ran upstairs and packed a bag before she could change her mind.

Gwen's face was a picture. On second thought, no, it was more like a version of Ratchet's Munchian visage when Sarah had spilled her beans over coffee later that day in her mum's chintz palace – her and Ella's name for Gwen's conservatory. And Sarah had to admit, as only a few of her beans had been spilled because of the inability to share the time-travelling experience, it was quite a reasonable response.

Gwen sat opposite Sarah in a white rattan backed chair,

wringing her handkerchief —now soggy in places – and shaking her head in disbelief. 'I still don't understand you. What do you mean it's not working? You have everything you have ever dreamed of and now the twins! How can it *not* be working?'

Sarah sighed and hugged a cushion to her chest – an explosion of flowers emblazoned on its cover. 'As I said … I just don't feel like I am right for him. He deserves better.'

'Well, right at this minute, I agree with you.' Gwen flapped the hanky. 'How can you just up and leave him like that?'

Sarah shook her head. 'Let me remind you, he left me.'

'But only because you argued about something, which you still refuse to explain to me, I might add. He's not taken any of his clothes or belongings, has he?' Gwen narrowed her eyes and inclined her head to Sarah's holdall by the chair. 'Unlike you, missy.'

'No, but it's for the best.' Sarah knew it all sounded pretty lame and just wanted to go up to her old room and be quiet for a while. Somewhere in the house the phone began to ring but Gwen shook her head when Sarah rose to answer it.

'How can it be for the bloody best? I bet the twins wouldn't think so!' Gwen stood and pointed a finger at the slight swell of Sarah's tummy.

*Okay that's it and that's all.* If she stayed there being talked at like a five-year-old she'd say something she'd regret. 'Mum, I know you are upset and have a right to be. But for now I need to go upstairs and just get my head sorted for a few hours.' Sarah stood and moved to the door.

'No. You *will* sit down and tell me the real story, my girl.'

Sarah ignored her and stepped forward.

'So what's it like time-travelling then?'

The ground shifted under her feet and Sarah clutched at the edge of the sofa. *What the …* Turning slowly to face her mum she managed to squeak, 'Pardon?'

Gwen's face set in a scowl and she pointed to the chair. 'You heard me. Sit down and spill it.'

On legs that felt like they belonged to somebody else, Sarah shuffled back to the pink and yellow floral sofa and sank down feeling her bottom become enveloped in its over-puffed cushions. This *cannot* be happening. She lifted her eyes and found her mum's sapphire-blue ones fixed onto hers like two probing searchlights. Where to start? There was no use trying to blag her way out of it. Her mum was too clever for that. So, if in doubt, ask a question and Sarah had a few hundred forming an orderly queue on her tongue.

'How ...' Sarah cleared her throat of treacle and tried again. 'How do you know about that?'

'Oh, I'm pleased you didn't try to wriggle out of it, that's something I suppose.' Gwen picked up the teapot, refilled her cup and raised her eyebrows at Sarah. Sarah nodded, not because she wanted more tea, but just to give her hands something to do. Currently they were gripping the edge of the seat so hard she was afraid the cushion would pop, shooting little balls of kapok across the room to land in her mother's lap.

'No point is there. Just tell me, Mum.'

Gwen settled back in her own seat and sipped her tea, a faraway look in her eye. The phone rang again. Both women ignored it. Then Gwen said, 'Okay, I had dinner at Harry's the other night and the next morning when I got in the car I realised that I'd left my watch on the sink in the bathroom. I ran back in, but Harry was on the phone so—'

'Whoa, whoa, hold on a little minute there, Mum,' Sarah gasped, holding her hands palm up at Gwen. She could hardly believe her ears. 'You had dinner and then you were *still* there in the morning?'

Gwen clucked her tongue and folded her arms. 'Oh, please, we are both well over eighteen and responsible adults. And I think your news is a little more earth shattering to be honest, don't you?'

'Er ...' Sarah began and then clammed up. She did have a point.

Gwen nodded in satisfaction. 'So, as I said, Harry was on the phone in the kitchen and I went to go upstairs to get the watch, but being a nosy old cow I stopped to listen because he was washing-up and had the thing on speakerphone. He was talking to John. Evidently John was worried about you being stuck in 1955 ... well, you can imagine what went through my head.'

Sarah couldn't. 'I ... Blimey, Mum, what happened then?'

Gwen sighed and dabbed at her nose with the soggy hanky. 'I listened to the whole conversation thinking that the pair of them were unhinged, or had taken some mind-bending drugs that John had grown in the hothouse or something.' She took another fortifying gulp of tea. 'Boy was Harry surprised when he'd finished the call and saw me standing in the doorway. He tried to concoct some daft story about them rehearsing for a play, but though I've not known my Harry for that long, I know when he's spinning a yarn.'

The words, *my Harry* and the way her mum had said them left Sarah in no doubt that the relationship was serious. But for now she shelved that realisation – there was a more pressing matter at hand. 'Did Harry tell you ... about me, about John, then?'

'Yes, he had no choice. And the truth seemed even more bloody crackers than the fib if you want to know. Mind you, he said you had reacted in a similar way last year when John dropped the whole time bombshell on you.' Gwen sat forward in her seat and whispered, 'But when Harry disappeared right in front of me to prove he was telling the truth I nearly wet me pants.'

Open-mouthed, Sarah took a moment to process that last bit. The powers would do their nuts! Harry should have known better and would likely suffer a punishment. 'I can't get my head around all this, Mum. Harry could be in real trouble because—'

Gwen flapped a hand in dismissal. 'Oh, I know all about the powers or Spindly Ones as you call 'em. They *were* a bit narky, but I promised to keep quiet about it all. To be honest, I didn't have much choice as they threatened a memory wipe if I didn't.'

*A bit narky ... I bet they bloody were.* 'Hmm, well I had no idea Harry could be so reckless. He's always been so cool and rational.'

Gwen twinkled and flushed. 'Yes, well he says I bring out the devil in him.'

'Okay, too much information, Mum.'

'And talking of information, missy, have you thought how you would explain to John why you have decided to break his world apart and take his babies? Let's have the real story, now that you know that I know ... that was a song, wasn't it?' Gwen attempted a watery smile.

Sarah sighed and spilled the whole thing including her idea about memory wipes.

A thunderous look appeared on Gwen's face and she slammed her cup down on the tray. 'Well, my God! When did you turn into the most selfish woman on the planet, not to say the stupidest?'

Sarah really did feel like a five-year-old now. An angry five-year-old to boot. 'What do you mean, selfish and stupid? I'm doing it to protect John, or haven't you been listening?'

'That's the stupid bit, well one of them. If you think taking a father from his children and depriving him of all that goes with it is the right thing to do, then you must be potty. Of course, as you say he wouldn't know about this, so what's the harm? Well, duh!' Gwen waggled her head from side to side. 'I would remember everything. Ella would, Harry would, the whole set of family and friends

170

would, colleagues at work would, or were you going to ask for a memory wipe for half of bloody Sheffield?'

A tide of crimson burned its way across Sarah's face and neck. In her befuddled and sorry for herself state she'd not considered any of that. Perhaps she really *was* stupid after all. Tears of humiliation and sadness welled and she still felt like a five-year-old. A lost and troubled one.

'I ... I have absolutely no idea,' she managed and stared at the flower patterned rug under her feet.

'Oh, my poor love,' Gwen muttered and hurried across to sit beside her. 'You're hormones are raging, you've had morning sickness, you're worried about the birth I expect, and that's enough for any new mum to contend with.' Gwen enveloped Sarah in her arms. 'But you, my poor baby, on top of all that have had to cope with being dropped back in time, here, there and every bloody where to save folk's lives. No wonder you can't think straight!'

Being held like that, her head on her mum's chest, feeling her steady heartbeat beneath her cheek, its comforting thump in her ears, Sarah began to feel that things weren't so bad, or could be sorted at least. Her mum had that affect. Always had ... when she was five, and now. 'Thanks for being so understanding, Mum.'

'You don't have to thank me for that, my girl. That's what being a mum is all about, something which you are soon to discover.' Gwen took her daughter's face in both her hands and looked into her eyes. 'And we'll have no more talk about leaving John. Now that I know about your adventures it will be a lot easier for you to cope ... we'll work through this somehow.'

Sarah all of a sudden realised it didn't matter that her mum knew about the time-travelling, in fact she was quite pleased. 'Oh, Mum. I do hope so.'

Gwen gave a little nod. 'Right, you'd better get back home and unpack before John comes back. Chop, chop.'

Sarah planted a sloppy kiss on her mum's cheek, grabbed her suitcase and ran to the door – just as it burst open.

'Sarah! Oh, thank goodness,' Harry gasped, his hair dishevelled, his face flushed. 'Our John's been going crazy wondering where you are.'

John appeared over his dad's left shoulder looking in similar anxious state. 'Sarah, thank God! I was convinced you'd been whisked back in time again!' He pulled her to his chest and wrapped his arms around her so tightly that Sarah thought he'd cut off her air supply. Then John glanced down – held her away from him. 'What's the little suitcase for?'

The wounded look in his lovely green eyes was too much for Sarah to bear. What on earth was she going to say to him? Moments ago her situation had looked much brighter with her mum on her side and in the know. Now it looked infinitely much worse.

'Er ...' she began and then found she couldn't get the words past the lump in her throat.

'Not to worry, John,' Gwen said, stepping forward and guiding them both towards the sofa. 'Our Sarah just got a bit upset about everything and thought a couple of nights away might calm it all down. We talked it through, and in the end she thought that the best idea was in fact to go back and see if she could work things out with you. She was just going home when you came in, weren't you, love?'

Sarah nodded. Thank the lord for her mum.

'But we rang and rang. Why didn't you answer, love?' Harry said, plopping down on a chair.

'Busy putting the world to rights and drinking tea.' Gwen chuckled. 'Talking of which, who wants a cup?' Everyone nodded and Gwen went off to make it.

John pulled Sarah to him and rested her head on his shoulder. 'Please don't think being apart will ever solve things, hon. I know you have every right to want distance between us. I was a right pain in the arse and I'm sorry.'

'So am I. You had every right to be angry after my superhero antics. I just need to learn to follow my head more ... especially where the children are concerned.' She snuggled down further, comforted by his familiar smell and light kisses along her hairline.

'Dad put me right.' John tipped a wink at Harry. 'I was working off my mood digging the bottom field and he popped over for a visit. Said he had a feeling that I needed someone to talk to – must be telepathic.'

'Aye, well someone has to set you straight from time to time. Just like my Gwen did for you I'll warrant, eh?' He smiled at Sarah.

A knowing look passed between Sarah and John. *My Gwen, eh?* Before Sarah could stop herself she sat forward and said, 'So, you and my mum are an item then, as the phrase has it these days?'

Harry flushed redder than he had earlier and coughed. 'Um, aye ... aye we are. You two okay with that?'

A giggle threatened to caper up from her tummy as she looked at this man in his mid-sixties nervous as a child, but she kept it down. Despite her earlier misgivings Sarah realised that she was okay with it. If her mum had to find another man, she couldn't have picked a better or more perfect one for her than Harry. Fighting with another giggle she said in her best teacher's voice, 'That would depend what your intentions are, Mr Needler. Are they honourable?'

Harry cocked his head on one side and shot her a wicked smile. 'Most of the time, love, aye.'

Gwen came in with another pot of tea and home-made Victoria sponge cake. Sarah put her feet up and nestled back against John. Harry had told him that Gwen was in the know about their time-travelling roles and though John had been as shocked as Sarah, he was okay with it. He had said that he shouldn't have been surprised that Gwen would cope with it all given that she was Sarah's mother … *Gutsy and nosy in equal measure*. Sarah kissed her husband on the cheek. Things seemed to be looking up at last. A beep from John's jeans pocket interrupted her thoughts and he stood to check his text message.

'Your laptop around, Gwen? The Spindlies have some information for me that will be better read on a larger screen apparently.'

'What now? Hope it's not more bad news,' Sarah muttered as John went off to the study.

Two pieces of cake and a cup of tea later John reappeared. His expression did nothing to raise Sarah's hopes of good news.

'Sit down, lad, have a cuppa,' Gwen soothed, pushing a cup towards him.

John nodded and sat next to Sarah. 'You've got sugar on your lip.' He smiled raising his fingers to brush it off.

'Never mind prevaricating, John. What's the story?' Sarah felt a little dark shadow of anxiety sweep in.

John took a sip of tea and sighed. 'Well, they have apparently found out what the problem with your erratic travelling is, Sarah. They eventually had to consult a higher power,' he paused, and everyone looked at each other agog. 'And they have concluded that it is because of twins.' He turned to Sarah and took her hand. 'We are lucky enough, my darling, to be expecting one of each – a boy and a girl!'

The shadow of anxiety was banished by a warm glow of sunlight. 'But that's fantastic! Why the long face?' Sarah said.

'Because one is destined to be a Stitch and one a Needle. This means they are pulling in opposite directions, even at this early stage and that's what's causing your crazy trips.'

Sarah scratched her head. She kind of liked the idea, expected it really, that her kids would carry on the tradition at the same time as being worried for them, it wasn't a straightforward life after all. But why this pulling apart?

'I don't get it. We work in harmony to achieve our goals, well, when we can.' She said rolling her eyes. 'So why is there a problem with the littlies?'

'As far as I can glean it's the hormones, intuition, susceptibilities, feelings and attributes that a Stitch and Needle have that makes them good at their job. The thing is, they are equal but opposite skills. Needles find and direct, Stitches save and complete. The twins are developing all this mentally as well as developing physically ... and so, unfortunately, they have sent the whole thing off the scale.'

'But hasn't this happened before in all their time dealing stuff? And what higher power did they consult?' Gwen asked.

'No to the first question and no idea to the second,' John said, picking up a bit of cake. 'As we know it happened to a woman who Mum and Dad knew years ago, and that was because there were in essence two people travelling through time and space. It was nowhere as bad as Sarah's experience though and now we know why.'

'Have they said that there will be more trips?' Harry asked quietly.

John munched his cake. 'This is your best cake yet, Gwen.' He attempted cheerily.

'Answer your dad, John.' Sarah folded her arms and prepared for the worst. The expression he was wearing was his best ENF yet.

John swallowed his cake as if it were made of lead. 'No. In fact they said there would probably be one more ... they aren't too sure.'

Sarah jumped up so fast it made her head spin and the coffee table shake. 'Damn them! If *they* aren't sure, what chance do we mere mortals have?'

# Chapter Nineteen

With November in its last week and the first snow dusting the peaks around the cottage, Sarah figured it was perhaps safe to breathe a tentative sigh of relief. Since the day John had discovered the reason for her impromptu trips, she had stayed thankfully in the present. The powers had further divulged that, although they couldn't be absolutely certain because the future wasn't always clear even to them – yes, really, and the old thing about not telling them too much about their personal future as they had said more than they should already – there didn't seem to be any trips in the offing. Moreover that if by some huge misfortune there *was* to be another mission, it was likely to be in the few weeks following her return from 1955. And that was ... Sarah ran her finger down the calendar on the kitchen wall ... exactly seventeen days ago.

The very best news of all, however, had come in the email John had received just last night. The powers had said that after much deliberation, once the babies had been born they had decided to release Sarah from the promise she made to them after the 1928 debacle. That promise bound her to take missions for the rest of her life. Now there would be no more, unless she wanted them. Apparently she had gone above and beyond, what with all the unpredictability, not to say danger, lately, and it was thought that she had earned her freedom. Just perfect. Now she had the choice of if and when. Of course, technically, she had always had the choice, as John was fond of telling her, but to pick and choose more, or not to take any at all was everything she could have hoped for.

From the corner of her eye she noticed her reflection in the hall mirror just outside the kitchen door. The black and white stripy jumper she wore over black leggings did accentuate the round, and sideways on, the bump looked definitely bumpish. But at four months, it would do wouldn't it, being twins and all. Twins. And one of each too! Sarah hugged herself and sighed with contentment. Even now she had to metaphorically pinch herself. Little had she known last year back in 1874 Kansas, when she was looking at her 'son' Artie and wondering if she would ever be lucky enough to have a child, that in a short while she would have two! It still hurt so much when she thought of Artie, but heartache came with the job she realised.

Now, to use her day off shopping for more things for the little guys, or to just put her feet up, read a good book and then make a hearty stew for when John came home? That was the question. As she finished the washing-up, a flurry of snow lace-patterning the window made up her mind. Feet up time ... and perhaps a choccie or two with a nice cup of tea.

A knock at the door chucked a house brick into her flat-calm peaceful mood. She groaned. *Please don't let this be a visitor ... let it be a cold caller, at least I can tell them to bugger off.*

In her mind a surreal picture of a cold caller was presented as she made her way to the front door. A block of ice with a clipboard and name badge stuck to it and a man's frosty head perched on top. She grinned. Well – it was cold and snowing. The grin froze on her face as she opened the door on a vast empty plain as far as the eye could see. Gone was the driveway and the road a little way off, gone were the rolling snow covered hills of Yorkshire.

Sarah, heart thumping like a sledgehammer, tried to shut the door, but found she couldn't move. A gust of wind took her breath away, and in the distance, but moving closer as if on huge rollers, was a series of town dwellings cowering under the huge black whip of a tornado towering into the greeny-yellow sky. Then the wind dragged Sarah from her home and forced her to the dirt floor. She closed her eyes and curled into a ball. *Oh no! Please, not again!*

John stuck his head out of the greenhouse, surveyed the darkening sky and shivered. That wind had got up, and with the snow behind it, the day felt positively Icelandic. He glanced at his watch – nearly four o'clock. Time for a nice cuppa and perhaps a bit of late-afternoon delight with his darling wife. To hell with the accounts he'd got pencilled in for later, they would be there in the morning.

Crunching up the driveway he tossed his wellies into the porch and then another shiver ran through him and this time it had nothing to do with the weather. Why was the door wide open on such a bitter day? And why was Sarah's slipper upside down just inside the entrance? He took a small step inside and picked up the slipper. 'Sarah? Sarah!' John raced to the kitchen, the living room, upstairs, everywhere, all the while calling her name but nothing. Sarah wasn't there. What the hell had happened to her?

In the kitchen John gripped the back of a chair and tried to quell the panic in his belly and calm his ragged breathing. The coffee pot felt lukewarm under his hands and a winter recipe book was open on the table. *Perhaps she'd just popped out to the shops for something, no need to get beside yourself.* He shook his head and balled his hands into fists. So why was the door wide open, her slipper just abandoned like that and where was the other? A *beep, beep* from the phone in his jeans startled him. A quick scan of the text message left his heart racing and his legs weak. Collapsing into a chair he let out a roar of anger. Damn it all to hell! With shaking fingers he punched the keys on his phone.

'Dad? Guess what's happened now. They've only sent Sarah on another bloody trip!'

'Oh, no lad ... where?'

John raked his hands though his hair and thumped his fist on the table. 'That's the best bit. They said they hadn't foreseen it, and it is not clear where Sarah has gone – just that the year is 1966!'

'Eh? How can they not know? I don't unders—'

'You're not the only one! I think they should be called the powers that "have been". Totally bleedin' incompetent! Apparently it's because of the twins making things impossible – typical of them to pass the buck! Anyway, they are trying to find out where she is and will let me know.'

'Blimey! They have lost the plot big time!' Harry said excitedly, and then did a fake cough and came back with, 'But don't worry, they will find her. Don't you panic, lad.'

'Yeah, right. I'll try to remember that, Dad. Now, let's put our thinking caps on … any memorable things happening in 1966? Knowing the bloody powers lately they might mean 1066 for all we know. They might have sent her to the middle of the Battle of Hastings!'

Harry sighed and then said, 'Oh, wait, there is one obvious one!'

'There is?'

'Think about it.'

'I can only think of the World Cup?'

'Yup. England beat Germany 4-2!'

John thought his dad had been at the beer early. 'The World Cup? Why would anyone need saving there, apart from the German side, of course?'

'No idea, but it's the only thing that sprang to mind. You could scan the Internet for important events and—'

'No time, Dad. I'm going back to Wembley 1966, right now.'

'You can't, John! You know you'll be punished. Besides there might be lots of other places she could have gone. My world history of 1966 isn't great.' The anxiety in Harry's voice came across loud and clear.

'Don't care. I can't just sit here and wait to hear that Sarah is hurt, trapped or worse.'

'But it might not be an important event, even. You know that. And thinking about it more clearly now – why on earth *would* Sarah be there?'

'I don't know, Dad, but what choice do I have? I am not hanging about risking the twins and Sarah. I nearly went mad when she went off to 1955. The powers can't help it seems. They don't even know what's going on any more and it might be too late if I stick to their stupid rules. Speak to you when I get back. No doubt the powers "that were" will be in touch with you before then!'

The strains of choral music drifted and halted abruptly. Then a banshee wail crashed through her stupor, assaulted Sarah's ears and roused her rudely from unconsciousness. Sirens? Was she back in 1940 for some reason? But that music had been real ... perhaps she had died and gone to heaven.

She opened her eyes, lifted her head and looked up at the weird olive sky and the grand building in front of her. The town she had seen earlier had gone, somehow it had moved ... but the tornado hadn't. In the far distance she could see its towering column wide, black and angry tearing up the ground and buildings like matchwood.

That sight twisted her gut and sent the 'fight or flight' adrenaline pumping through her veins. Being no worthy opponent of such a force of nature, in a split second she chose flight. But where? A sign just in front of her told her that the grand building was *Washburn University* – that would have to do.

She pulled herself to her knees as a knot of people ran towards the entrance of the building, some carrying musical instruments. They glanced briefly at her as they passed and one woman yelled, 'Don't you hear the storm siren, woman? Seek shelter, get to the basement!'

Another voice yelled, 'It's on the ground and coming fast!'

Once on her feet, the ground trembled under her, or was it just her knees? Fat raindrops came out of nowhere and spattered painfully on her arms as she set off after the others, her heart thudding, her mind racing. Why did this have to happen now? Hadn't she suffered enough ... and the twins. God, if John had thought 1955 was dangerous he must be doing his nut by now!

The mystery of the choral music, and indeed where she was, became clear as she hurried along next to a tall man and woman who she thought resembled the farmers from that painting. What was the painting called? American something ... Gothic, she thought. Whatever it was called, the farmer man carrying the pitchfork was a dead ringer for the guy prattling on next to her. Perhaps they had jumped out of it; anything was possible in this nightmare.

'Good job we heard that siren over the sound of the choral recital, me bein' a bit hard of hearin' an' all.'

'Yes, dear,' the woman said absently. Sarah could tell she wasn't really paying attention, just concentrating on hurtling down the steps to get to safety.

'Time Topeka gotta better warnin' system. There gotta be summin' better, ain't there? Men goin' into space, an' all? There's even talk of a man *walkin'* on the moon in a few years, so there's gotta be summin', ain't there?'

'Probably, dear.'

*So, Kansas again ... must be some kind of spiritual link with this bloody place. Perhaps I should change my name to Dorothy.* Sarah shook her head and continued down the flight of stairs. Just then she got a twinge in her belly – almost like a stitch and a wooziness washed over her like a lazy wave on the shore. Panic sprang into her heart and she had to stop for a moment to catch her breath. She noticed the black and white striped jumper and black leggings had been replaced by dark green slacks, a floral long-sleeved smock and a pair of red kitten heels. Pity they weren't covered in glitter and then she could click her heels together and ask to be delivered straight back home. Everyone rushed past, either not noticing that she was in trouble, or too worried about their own safety.

Soon alone on the steps, she sat down, leaned her head on her knees and tried to think calm thoughts. Was there any wonder she felt like this? She was pregnant after all and in the middle of the scariest trip of her life. Placing her hand on her little bump she took a few deep breaths and began to feel much better, but before she could continue her journey, a clatter of feet behind her, and a yell of anguish jerked her head up. A man with a mop of white-blond hair tumbled past her and lay prone on the landing just in front of her.

'Oh my goodness! Are you okay?' she said into his ear as she knelt by his side. Nothing. Damn it, what should she do next? There had been a fist aid course a few years back for the staff but she hadn't paid as much attention as she should have because it was her era of depression after Neil and Karen. They had so much to answer for. If she couldn't help this poor guy who had a look of ... now, who was it? The face of the person just danced out of reach at the back of her memory, and the guy did have his eyes closed, so hard to place.

*Never mind who he reminds you of, Sarah, do something.* Right. Listen for breathing. Sarah put her ear to the guys nose and yes, deffo breathing. His chest rose and fell gently too. Good. So ... what now? The next step came flooding back to her. I know – put him in the recovery position. That was it! Hmm the man was tall, heavy – not fat, but muscular, in his mid-thirties she guessed. So if she didn't get the technique right he would be hard to shift, and that tornado sounded even closer now.

Gulping down a ball of panic, Sarah shoved her hair

behind her ears and put his arm across his chest. Then it was the bendy leg thing, wasn't it? Sarah bent his knee and then attempted to roll him onto his side. A groan stopped her mid-roll and the guy pushed himself up onto his elbows and regarded her groggily. As soon as she looked into his bright blue eyes she had it. He looked like an older version of Artie, 'her son' from 1874 Kansas!

'Are ... are you okay?' she said a little breathlessly, touching his shoulder briefly and noting that her American accent was back.

'Yes thanks, ma'am. My leg feels a little painful though,' he muttered. As he struggled to his knees, his mouth twisted to the side and he sucked air through his teeth when his foot made contact with the floor.

Sarah noticed that his ankle was puffing slightly when he rolled his sock down to examine it.

'Here lean on me.' She pulled his arm around her shoulder and leaned into him. 'Let's get you down these stairs and into the basement.' The air of confidence hanging on those words were all for show, however. This guy was heavy and God knew how far this damned basement was.

'You are so kind, ma'am. It was my own stupid fault that I fell – shouldn't have been runnin' so fast.'

'Hardly surprisin' in the circumstances. That's it; you're makin' good progress ... er?' She glanced up at him.

'Arthur, folks call me Artie. And your name is?'

The shock of hearing that name nearly struck her dumb, but she heard herself choke out. 'Sarah.' It was impossible. It *couldn't* be Artie, he would be in his nineties now.

'That's a nice name. My great-grandmother was called Sarah.' He flashed a grin that took her breath – it was the spit of Artie's.

'Just a few more steps now. There's the basement.'

They entered the large basement where people were settling on the floor, some were chatting some were silent and hugging each other, all wore signs of fear and anxiety on their pale faces.

One particularly pale young man nodded at Artie, beads of nervous sweat stood on his brow. But then he blinked a few times and said, 'Evening, Professor Johnson. You might not get my homework if this goes badly.'

Artie put his hand on his shoulder. 'Evening, Dexter. We'll be safe here, so no excuses on that essay.'

Though neither Dexter nor Artie, nor anyone else could be absolutely sure about their fate, Sarah could tell by the genuine smile on the young man's face that Artie had given him hope with those few words. She could also tell that Artie must be a damned fine teacher with the respect he commanded in this terrified student.

So was he 'her Artie's' grandson? His great-grandmother had been Sarah, so it was certainly possible. She couldn't be sure that Johnson had been her Artie's last name but it did ring a bell. And she had certainly saved him just now, so it had to be more than coincidence didn't it, so could she go home? Before she had time to order her thoughts, the noise of what she could only describe as an approaching train met her ears and this time there was no mistaking the movement of ground under her. Even the wall seemed to shiver under her touch as she put her hand against it.

Right, no messing, she'd ask him outright and then try and get back. 'Artie, was your grandfather the famous senator?'

He looked a bit startled, then grinned. 'He was indeed, Sarah. The finest. And the finest grandfather, too. I miss him every day. Glad that you remember his name.'

'Oh, I will never forget it, Artie.' Sarah's voice trembled and she lightly touched her hand to Artie's cheek. He frowned, puzzled, but before he could say any more, Sarah walked away and hissed to the ceiling, 'Okay you spindly sons of bitches. Get me and my babies out of here and to safety right now!'

A floating sensation enveloped her, and the ceiling she'd hissed at turned into wisps of fog as she passed through. Sarah closed her eyes, smiled and relaxed into the transition. Thank goodness, the Spindlies had listened; she'd soon be at home safe with John. A thump, a rattle and an ear-splitting crash said different however. Immediately she felt a jolt in her shins as solid ground once more met her feet. Sarah opened her eyes but couldn't see very much, as thick brown dust hung heavy in the air and irritated her lungs. She coughed and leaned against a smooth hard surface which felt like a wall, and as the dust began to settle, a ruin of a cellar was partially revealed.

What on earth had happened? Had the tornado struck before she could escape? But where were the rest of the people in the shelter? And this place was smaller than she remembered. The wail of a siren started up a little way off and once the dust had completely settled and sunlight filtered through a huge hole in the ceiling, Sarah could see she was no longer in 1960s Kansas, she could also see she wasn't alone. A hunched figure in the corner got shakily to its feet, a figure whose haystack mop was rusty with brick dust, a figure that was unmistakably ... Veronica flippin' Ratchet!

# *Chapter Twenty*

'Sarah Needler! Oh, you have no idea how glad I am to see you!' Veronica shot her a horsey whiter than white smile enhanced by an orange brick dust 'fake tan' and her dark eyes shone with emotion. Sarah was just about to say that the sentiment was definitely not reciprocated, punctuated by a half a dozen expletives as Veronica stepped forward, but then another explosion outside and nearby took the poor woman's legs from under her and she ended up flat on her face.

Luckily Sarah was still leaning against the supporting wall which still lived up to its name or she'd have followed suit. Deafened and shaken by the blast, she scrambled over the rubble as quick as her trembling limbs would carry her to where Veronica lay prone and unmoving. The thump of her galloping heartbeat pushed the silence from her ears as she put her hand on Veronica's shoulder, and curses that had been lined up on her tongue just moments ago gave way to prayers. *Oh please God, let her be all right*!

Was she just out cold ... or worse? Putting her ear to Veronica's back she listened for a breath as she held her own. Yes! Yes, thank goodness, she was breathing. A perfunctory glance at her limbs confirmed they were all there and didn't appear to be broken or bleeding, and then for the second time in a few hours, Sarah prepared to put someone in the recovery position.

Just as she rolled Veronica onto her side, her eyes opened and she began to cough and take big gulps of dusty air which then made her cough some more. 'Sarah, it really is you ... I thought I was ...' she coughed again, '... hallucinating.'

'No, it is me,' Sarah said, placing Veronica's arm over her shoulder and slipping an arm around her waist. 'But as fond of you as I have become, I wish you were hallucinating because to be honest, I really don't want to be here in this damned war again. What are we, 1940?'

'1941 ... May.' Veronica grunted spitting a globule of spit and dust onto the rubble.

'Marvellous.' Sarah sighed and tightened her grip around Veronica's waist. 'Here let me take the weight, do you think you can stand ... walk?'

'Just about.' Veronica puffed air from her cheeks, heaved herself upright and dusted down her very un-Veronica-like blue trousers. 'I'm okay now, just a bit shaken.'

Sarah took Veronica's hand and the two women took a few clumsy steps towards a mountain of rubble above which a blue sky played chase with clouds. Thankfully all now seemed quiet on the western front. 'Where are we?'

Veronica peered down at Sarah in disbelief. 'In a bombed out cellar.'

'Yeah, I *did* realise that. No, I mean where in England?'

'Oh, right. Southampton, not far from the centre.'

'Fantastic. My day is just getting better and better. Washburn in the middle of a tornado and now instead of going home I'm catapulted to one of the most heavily bombed cities in Britain during the Second World War!'

Veronica's face beamed with pride. 'Well, that's because of the important docks we have here and, of course, the Spitfire factory. You should have been here last year, it was an absolute nightmare. Bombing us morning noon and night they were.'

Sarah's mouth dropped open. Had the woman gone mad? 'I should have been here last year? Oh, yes, that would have been fabulous, what a shame I missed the chance of getting flattened nearly every day!'

'No need to get on your high horse. I'm just glad you agreed to help me today.'

'Help you? I didn't agree to help you.'

Veronica wiped the back of her hand across her mouth and looked decidedly shifty. 'Oh dear ... I see. I thought it was a bit odd that you didn't know where you were and so forth.'

Sarah folded her arms and gave Veronica a hard stare. 'Okay, out with it. Just what exactly is happening?'

A huge sigh escaped Veronica's lips and she sat down on a boulder. 'Well, I'm looking for my Edward, you see.' She pulled a hanky out of her jacket pocket. 'We were in town shopping when the sirens started; they've not come for a while and certainly not in daylight for ages. You remember that your John told us that my Edward would be invalided out of the Home Guard and have that shard of glass through his foot?' Sarah nodded. 'Well, that was last year. Hell of a mess his foot was in and he's still in a bit of pain with his limp and all ...' Veronica's voice tailed off and she gazed into space.

Sarah was beginning to get impatient and it was all she could do to stop herself from yelling at Veronica to get on with it. She also had an awful feeling in her gut that she wouldn't be back home in the few moments she'd originally thought she would be when she'd left Washburn. 'So what happened next?'

'Oh, well, being the hero he insisted on leaving the public shelter and going to see if anyone needed help. I begged him to stay but he wouldn't listen. They had sounded the "all clear" but then about twenty minutes after he'd gone the sirens went off again.' Her voice wavered and she dabbed at her eyes with the hanky.

'I'm really sorry about that, Veronica, but can you explain about me agreeing to help?'

'Yes, sorry. I was sitting there thinking about how I'd changed over this past year or so since I'd become a Stitch. I'm much more confident in my stitching abilities and less of a cowardly custard.' Veronica smoothed out the material on her trousers. 'I even wear slacks now, very unladylike my mother would have said. My proudest moment came just a few months ago. I saved a really important person by preventing him from getting on the *Titanic* just before it sailed. Would you believe how smelly some people were back in 1912? I bet they hardly ever washed.'

'Yes, I know, Veronica. I have been back to that time period before, and will you please get to the bloody point!' Sarah sat down on a pile of rubble opposite and shoved her fingers through her dusty hair in frustration.

'Hmm, not sure I like your tone, Sarah.' Veronica saw the look of fury in Sarah's eyes and hurriedly continued. 'Anyway, I was also thinking about how much I admired you and what you've achieved as a Stitch so far. I was wondering what you'd do in my situation, sit in the shelter worrying, or get up and find Edward.' She smiled at Sarah. 'So I got up and left the shelter.'

Though Sarah still hadn't got to hear why she'd ended up here, she did feel glad to know that she'd inspired the old trout. John had told her she'd admired her and gone on to do a great job, but to hear it from Veronica herself warmed Sarah's heart. She felt a genuine respect and admiration for old Ratchet-face. Such a far cry from the early days. 'And then ...?'

'Then the oddest thing happened. Well, two things happened. Firstly, as I was poking about the rubble and asking anyone if they'd seen Edward, I got an image in my head of you floating up to a ceiling with a smile on your face, and I just said out loud, "Oh, Sarah, I could do with you here to help me". Secondly I heard an explosion as I was walking down a street and must have fallen into this cellar.' She shrugged. 'You know the rest.'

'But that makes no sense! I know that my stitching life has become ridiculously crazy because of the twins, but you "seeing" me and needing my help just as I was returning home is just so ... so random.'

'Twins? What twins?' Veronica frowned.

Sarah had forgotten that Veronica didn't know about her pregnancy so decided to show rather than tell. She undid the buttons of a blue gabardine Mac she found herself to be wearing and smoothed her hands over her bump under a floral dress.

'Oh my goodness, you're pregnant!' Veronica clapped her hands and leapt up, her face beaming with happiness.

'Yep, and it's twins – a boy and a girl!' Sarah laughed as she received a spiky all elbows hug from Veronica.

Veronica drew back, her face a picture of bamboozlement. 'Eh? How can you possibly know that before they are born?'

'We can do those things in my time. Pretty amazing, huh?'

'My giddy aunt!' A hand fluttered to Veronica's mouth. 'It's more than amazing, it's a bloomin' miracle.'

This happy moment between them was lovely but Sarah really had to get to the point of why she was here. 'Right, so you think Edward is around here somewhere?'

'Yes. This is the direction he was headed. A member of the Home Guard told me he'd seen a man with a limp pass down this street.'

'And what? I'm supposed to save him? Because that's the only conclusion I can come to.'

Veronica shook her mop-head and a little puff of brick dust haloed briefly in the air giving her the appearance of a very puzzled lion. 'I have absolutely no idea. It seems odd that you would be allowed to do a personal saving just to help an old friend ... even though ...' Veronica's face crumpled and she blew hard into the hanky. 'Even though it is to be my wedding day tomorrow.' Then she gave a strangled sob, sat down again and buried her face in her hands.

Blimey! No wonder the old trout was upset. Sarah knew how stressful weddings were even though, partly because of Veronica, she'd spent most of hers in 1939. But at least in Sarah's case she'd known exactly where John was the day before the wedding. It must be torture for Veronica to have lost Edward in the middle of a war zone, just as she'd looked forward to a happy ending. And if anyone deserved a happy ending it was Veronica, after all those years she'd suffered at the hands of her mother.

Veronica looked up at Sarah, white tear streaks cutting through the orange of her face. 'I'm sorry for getting emotional, but I don't know what I'd do if something happened to him. And though I'm so grateful that you came, I fear that because you were sent to me, it must indicate that he is in some awful danger!' She shrieked and hid her face again.

It was no good; Sarah would have to do the right thing. And given that she was just put here, it was debatable that she'd have much choice anyway. The Spindlies must know where she was ... mustn't they? A heavy sigh built in her chest and she blew it out with a long breath. 'It will all be okay, Veronica. Come on, dry those tears and let's go and find your Edward.'

Memories of last year's trip to the Sheffield Blitz of 1940 played in Sarah's mind as she and Veronica walked through the decimated streets of Southampton. Not for the first time, Sarah wondered how people had lived through this war and carried on with their lives without counselling, or any real recognition of the trauma they'd suffered. Huge craters and rubble piled high everywhere made walking in a straight line impossible, and jagged remains of houses lined the streets like the teeth of some giant monster hidden below the surface.

The thing that touched Sarah the most was the way that

the insides of some houses were revealed to all when only the outer wall had collapsed. On general display were a lifetime's personal knick-knacks, clothes strewn across floors, family portraits smashed and blackened by smoke, and, in one case, a table still laid for breakfast complete with toast in its rack.

After about ten minutes Sarah began to get an intense tickle in her nose and shot off a round of ridiculously loud sneezes. Veronica echoed them within seconds. 'Gosh, must be the dust still in our lungs from that cellar, a–tishoo!'

'Bit of a delayed reaction though isn't atishooo! it?' In fact Sarah couldn't remember ever sneezing so violently in her life. She sat on a half-ruined garden wall and dug around in her pocket for a hanky. Luckily she found one just as the loudest sneeze yet shot from her nose. 'Shooooo!'

'Mind you, atishoooo!, I did get the sneezes when I went back to 1912,' Veronica said, blowing her nose on her tear dampened hanky. 'It turned out that was my clue to who I had to save. I'd rather have hiccups any day like we had in 1979, wouldn't you?'

Sarah managed to stop mid-sneeze. 'Well, even though this has never been one of my clue signs, I would bet my bottom dollar that your Edward is in the immediate vicinity.'

No sooner the words were out of Sarah's mouth than the tickle went out of her nose. Judging by the look of relief on Veronica's face the same had happened to her. Then they heard a reedy little voice nearby say, 'It's all right, mister, I can see a couple of ladies through this hole here, we'll be out in a jiffy! Help! Help, ladies, over here!'

Sarah and Veronica scrambled over the ruined wall and into the garden of a bombed out house. The roof and entire first floor had gone, but the downstairs remained pretty much intact save a huge hole where the door used to be. Peering through this the two women could see a ruin of a kitchen and an old iron bedstead, through the bars of which was stuck the leg of a girl around about seven years old, and a man in a similar predicament but stuck in a crater in the concrete floor and pinned under bits of ceiling and fallen struts.

'Edward!' Veronica yelled and ran inside the house.

'Be careful, Veronica, it's not safe in here!' Edward yelled back, raising his hand in a stop signal.

Sarah's nose told her immediately why it wasn't safe as she stepped through the door. The unmistakable whiff of gas was coming from somewhere under the rubble. The slightest spark from scraping metal or an ember floating in could send them sky-high. Edward's warning fell on deaf ears as Veronica knelt by his side and showered his dusty cherub-like face with kisses.

The little girl smiled at Sarah and said, 'Can you help us? We have been stuck here for ages. I came looking for my cat, Bobby, and then some of the ceiling came down – the bed head along with it.' She nodded across at Edward. 'The mister here heard me yell and came in, but then a bit more of the ceiling landed on him.'

Edward nodded. 'She came back home unbeknownst to her parents. They're getting minor cuts and bruises sorted out at a First Aid station down the road it seems. Barbara here slipped out without their knowledge and came back home. I would have easily got her out if the ceiling hadn't decided to fall just at the wrong damned moment.'

The fact that neither of them seemed to be seriously injured was the only saving grace in the whole episode, Sarah realised. But if they didn't get them out soon they could all be seriously hurt or worse. 'Right, time is of the essence. Veronica, help me with this bedstead.' Obviously worried about her fiancé, Veronica gave him one final peck on the cheek and scuttled over to where Sarah was pulling at the mangled brass construction.

It wasn't that heavy, but Barbara's leg was twisted through it at a strange angle and therefore it had been impossible for the seven-year-old to extract herself. In a matter of moments she was free, however, and apart from a few abrasions and a nasty looking bruise she was unhurt. 'Thanks, ladies. You want me to help you with Mr Edward?' Barbara grinned and pulled up her socks.

'No, Barbara. Run along back to your mum and dad, they must be worried sick about you,' Sarah said.

Veronica assumed her haughty teacher's persona. 'Yes, go straight back now, no more looking for silly cats, young lady!'

Right on cue a long-haired tabby poked a head around the hole in the wall and gave a pitiful yowl. 'Bobby!' Barbara scooped up the cat and smothered him with kisses, though the cat looked less than pleased at this and tried to wriggle free. 'Stop that right now. I'm taking you with me and there's nothing you can do about it!' She raised a hand to them all. 'Thank you everyone, toodle-oo!' Barbara turned and hurried away down the street.

'Now for you, my darling.' Veronica and Sarah went back over to Edward and pulled at a wooden strut but it only moved a few inches. The length of the struts were across the crater leaving Edward just enough room to get his head through the hole. Once it was free it would be easy for him to climb out.

'What you need is a lever. There are lots of bits of wood around.' Gas wafted across the room again and a look of panic flitted across his kind brown eyes. 'But be quick, lasses, or better still, go and find help.'

'Leave you now? I should cocoa,' Veronica said, and shoved a table leg under a strut. A few heaves and it rolled away, allowing Edward to wriggle his shoulders free. Sarah followed Veronica's example and within minutes Edward pulled himself out and dusted himself down.

Veronica threw her arms around him and began the kiss shower again. Sarah grabbed her arm. 'Time for that later, miss. Let's get out of here.'

They ran as fast as they could but when they reached the end of the street an explosion brought them all to their knees. Edward was the first to recover and he stood up and looked back the way they'd come. His voice was tremulous as he said, 'You got me out not a moment too soon.'

Sarah helped Veronica up and followed Edward's gaze. The two women leaned against each other for support when they realised that the new pile of rubble at the end of the street was the house they had recently run from.

Sarah opened her eyes and looked at the unfamiliar surroundings of Veronica Ratchet's no nonsense, no frills bedroom. A cup of fresh tea sat on the bedside table, obviously placed there by a thoughtful Veronica. She thumped the pillow. So she was still here then, damn it. No amount of begging, pleading or cajoling to the powers that be had made any difference last night when Sarah and Veronica had arrived back in her cold little cottage by the sea.

Josiah Needler, Veronica's Time Needle, hadn't made an appearance and, of course, there was no email facility in 1941. Even if there had been, it was John who did the contacting, Sarah wasn't privy to that sort of information. Well, she had been just the once when she begged the powers to spare John after the 1928 debacle. Josiah normally contacted the Spindlies by telegram, but Veronica had no idea where he lived or how to get in touch with him. In the end Sarah had resorted to pleading out loud and shouting at the ceiling, but to no avail.

Once Edward had been fussed over, fed and settled to bed in his house next door – Sarah had been passed off as a colleague of Veronica's from a previous school who'd just been in the shelter by chance – both women had talked until late about the whole unusual episode of that day and generally had a good catch up. 'I wonder if little Barbara was the key in all this? Like you, I can't see the powers allowing you to request my help just to save Edward, lovely as he is,' Sarah mused and sipped her cocoa.

'It's possible. But I expect that's something we might never know. Just don't ask too many questions, Sarah, you might get squashed flat!' Veronica laughed and helped herself to a biscuit. Noting Sarah's glum expression she added, 'Oh, my dear, I know you wanted to go home back to your John, and you're concerned about being in the war with your babies, but if you're still here tomorrow you can come to my wedding!'

'Lovely. I spent most of mine with you, so let's not break a tradition, eh?' Sarah immediately regretted her grumpy response when she saw the excitement die in Veronica's eyes.

'Ah, yes. I am being selfish and have been a bit of a nuisance, haven't I?' A flush crept along Veronica's neck and she put the half-eaten biscuit to one side.

Sarah took her hand across the table and treated Veronica to a dazzling smile. 'It wasn't your fault and forgive me for being so grumpy. If I'm here I'd be honoured to come to your wedding.'

Sarah got out of bed and found Veronica in her dressing gown downstairs looking dejectedly into the hall mirror.

'What's up? I thought you'd be full of the joys of spring this morning.'

'Oh, Sarah, I'm so plain. I always knew it as my mother told me I was often enough. But just for once I'd like to look if not pretty, then a bit attractive at least.'

'Your mother was a liar and a selfish old bat. You have a good honest face.' Sarah crossed her fingers behind her back before she added, 'And when I have finished with you, you will look like a film star!' Though that might be a bit of an exaggeration. The pale blue wedding outfit, a typical 1940s two-piece, that Veronica had showed her last night was lovely and with a bit of work on her hair and make-up, Edward would be drooling.

Two hours, a head full of rollers and a straightening iron borrowed from Edward's sister, later and Veronica Ratchet stood in front of the mirror again transformed. Her hair smooth for the first time ever was set into a passable Bette Davis *Dark Victory* style as requested by Veronica, her eyebrows were carefully plucked and pencilled, a touch of blue eyeshadow accentuated the colour of her outfit, and a peach lipstick plumped out her lips and finished the look.

'Oh, Sarah.' Veronica's eyes filled with tears. 'I can't believe what you have done with me. Thank you, thank you so much.'

'Edward will be counting the minutes until the wedding night when he claps eyes on you, that's for sure.' Sarah grinned and handed Veronica a tissue.

To her surprise Veronica blushed scarlet and raised a shaking hand to her lips. 'Would you believe it, I am terrified about that part of it all. Before Edward I ... have never even thought about a man in that way. Mother said that apart from necessary procreation, the sex act was disgusting and evil. She only endured it for the sake of my father and afterwards told me she scrubbed herself down there.' She leaned against the wall and ran her fingers over the sparkly conch brooch that Edward had given her. 'The trouble is, when I realised I loved Edward, I have been thinking that I might want to do it. He makes me feel so divine, especially when I let him kiss me on the mouth. Is that wicked?'

If bloody Hettie Ratchet wasn't burning in hell then she damned well ought to be. Poor Veronica, almost forty-one and never had sex. Sarah shook her head. 'It's not wicked, and it's not an "act", it's natural. Making love with the man you love is the best thing in the world. You have nothing to be ashamed of. When he takes you in his arms tonight relax and enjoy it. Just put everything your mother ever told you out of your head and don't allow it back, okay? You look beautiful, Veronica, beautiful and very much in love.'

Sarah didn't have to cross her fingers that time but she did had to swallow a lump of emotion as big as a planet blocking her airways when a tearful Veronica gave her a huge hug. 'I am so please you're here with me, Sarah. I so wish we lived in the same time period because I'll miss you when you're gone.'

The small group of friends and family threw confetti at the happy couple posed for photographs on the registry office steps. Edward looked the perfect partner to Veronica as he stood beside her in his charcoal-grey suit and slicked back sandy hair. His green eyes gazed adoringly into his wife's dark ones and when they kissed for the photographer Sarah was pleased to see not a hint of a blush on Veronica's face.

A few minutes later as folk gathered to go to the local pub for a sandwich and a sherry, a tingle in Sarah's fingertips and a roll of nausea in her tummy had never felt so welcome. *Please let this mean I'm out of here.* She caught Veronica's eye and beckoned her round the corner of the registry office. 'I think I'm off home in a few moments, at last, but I want you to know that I wished we lived in the same time too.' Sarah gave Veronica a fierce hug. 'I have become very fond of you and I have reason to believe that you have a great stitching career ahead.'

'Oh, Sarah, do you think we'll ever meet again?' Veronica dabbed a corner of her hanky delicately against her eyes so not to smudge her make-up.

'Who knows? One day, perhaps.' She gave Veronica's hand a quick squeeze and then dropped it just in case

Veronica hitched a ride back with her again. 'Now, goodbye and good luck – go to that lovely husband of yours.'

Veronica gave her the sweetest smile and turned away. It wasn't a moment too soon as Sarah felt herself floating up towards the rooftops and prayed that she would be delivered safely home this time.

# Chapter Twenty-One

Damn it, his head hurt. John leaned against the wall of what looked through his blurred vision to be a tunnel or underpass or something and tried to clear it. There had of course been a huge barrier to his jaunt back in time. He'd felt as if he were running at a gigantic rubber band stretched across his forehead. It was like that last time he'd gone back in time without permission, but the headache seemed worse now. John hoped it wouldn't last long. If it did, he wouldn't be able to function. And then God knows what might happen to Sarah and the babies.

A few moments later, miraculously, the pain drained away and he could look around at his surroundings. Yep, a tunnel. Hope leapt into his heart as he realised what kind of tunnel. It was the entrance which led from the players' changing rooms at football stadiums to the pitch beyond.

John ran a few steps to the top of the slope and looked at the gigantic pitch and the twin towers just visible beyond. Wembley Stadium. Unexpectedly a pang of sadness surfaced as this old design had been consigned to history in John's time. But then a pang of excitement replaced it as he imagined what the players must have felt walking up here to the roar of the crowd and into the bright sunshine of World Cup Final day.

It was lucky he'd arrived in Wembley Stadium itself and not somewhere outside it. He wouldn't have to faff about trying to find a way in and wasting more time. *Yeah, John, but now what?* a cynical little voice piped up in his head. He had no answer. And the more he thought about it, the more unlikely it was that Sarah would be here in the stadium on World Cup Final day, or any day. Back in the sixties women would have played an even lesser role in such proceedings than they did in the present. Perhaps she was a tea lady or something and had to save a fellow colleague – a cleaner perhaps? Did they even have tea ladies for the footballers?

A gruff voice halted his ponderings. 'Oi, what you doin' 'ere? 'Ow did you get past security?'

John turned to see a small stocky man in a tracksuit marching up the slope towards him. He wore a frown across a low forehead that wouldn't have looked out of place on a Neanderthal and close-set beady eyes fixed a glare on John's.

What on earth would he say to that? He was buggered if he knew but he'd have to think of something quick – the little man was rolling up his sleeves and snorting down his nose like an escaped bull.

'Well, who are ya? You've got one second before I call the police and 'ave you booted out.'

That was the straw John needed to clutch at and he felt inside his jacket pocket. Good job he'd had the foresight to get changed into smart trousers, a shirt and jacket before he left.

If he'd been standing there in grubby overalls he'd have had no chance. Pulling his wallet out, he flicked it open in front of the little man's eyes. There was a picture of John on his driving licence in the clear wallet pocket which he flashed too quickly for the man to read and then put it away.

He leaned down to the man and whispered, 'Keep yer voice down, buddy. I'm undercover, okay. Making sure all is as it should be. This is a match where you might get a terrorist trying to ruin it, it being old rivals so to speak.' John tapped the side of his nose.

Amazingly the little man's frown disappeared and he patted John on the arm. 'I see, glad to 'ear it. And, my goodness that identity card looks newfangled, glad our taxes are being used wisely.' He gave a chortle which sounded a bit like a rusty gate and then turned to go.

'So, who are *you* then?' John folded his arms and peered down his nose at the little man.

'Oh, no need to worry about me. I'm the kit man.' He preened and puffed out his chest. 'I just got this promotion a few months ago and today's the proudest in me career. I done loads o' matches afore but 'ave never done a World Cup.'

'Congratulations on getting such a responsible job. But tell me,' John cringed at how odd his next question would sound but there was no other way to broach it, 'Is there someone who works here, or might be here for some reason, called Sarah?'

'A Sarah who works 'ere? No. I don't know no Sarah. Is she the terrorist?' Kit man's eyes lit up with excitement.

'No, don't worry.' John gave a dismissive nod. 'Right then, kit man, you'd better get about your business. I'll have a snoop around and see what I can see.'

The man raised a finger to his temple in a salute. 'Give me a shout if you need anythin'. I'll just be in the changin' room down yonder.'

John blew out a long slow breath as he watched him jog down the slope and disappear through some doors at the end. No Sarah, but at least the kit man believed the cop story. *That was expertly done, Mr Needler, if I do say so myself.* He allowed himself a chuckle and then set off in search of Sarah.

Half an hour later he felt far from happy. There was no Sarah in sight. In fact he'd seen no women at all. The only people he'd found were police which he'd managed to dodge and other official looking folk in tracksuits. The crowds hadn't started trickling in yet, but he'd overheard an official saying that it wouldn't be long now.

Outside the changing room John ran his hands through his hair and turned in a tight circle. Where in the world was she? A little roll of his stomach told him what he'd suspected for a while. Like his Dad had warned him – she probably wasn't here at all. Just then, kit man popped his head out the door, waved his hand and then beckoned him in.

'Want a cuppa?' He held a flask up to John.

But John was lost in the moment, gave a low whistle and gazed around the room. 'Wow, so here is where it all began, eh?' Very shortly eleven men would walk out of here and make football history.

'Where what began?' Kit man poured a cup of milky tea into a plastic cup and offered it to John.

John declined it. 'Er, I meant this is where it will all begin … you know England's victory.'

Kit man's face beamed with pride. 'Oh, yes. No doubt about that.'

His mission looked to have failed unless kit man suddenly produced Sarah, so John allowed himself a few moments to wander around looking at the famous red shirts hanging up around the place like icons to the glorious game. One shirt in particular drew him and he walked over to it and gently traced the number ten on the back. Geoff Hurst's, the main goal scorer.

John stood back and smiled, then he looked down at the football boots on the bench under it. He picked a boot up and weighed it, imagining its owner in an hour or so scoring a hat-trick and the crowd going wild. Hmm, they looked to be his size … could he? No, what was he thinking of? He had to get back to the future and try and figure out where Sarah was. Though whether he'd break through the barrier a second time was doubtful.

'Mr Hurst's they are.' Kit man nodded.

'Yeah, I know. He'll do well today. I can feel it in my waters.' As John bent to put them back he noticed a kink in one of the laces. And on closer inspection there seemed to be a tiny hole in it too. 'I don't like the look of this.' He frowned and held it out to kit man. 'If this snaps during the match it could ruin everything.'

Kit man looked and scowled. 'A blind man would be glad to see it. They sometimes 'ave little defects, still as strong as anythin'.'

John couldn't believe his ears, was this man mad? He assumed his 'I am an undercover cop' authority. 'I would be happier with a new pair of boots or at the very least, laces for Mr Hurst.'

'No need they are fine. 'Sides, not a good idea to play a match with brand new boots –plays havoc with yer corns,' kit man muttered, poking the boot with the toe of his.

'New laces then. If you don't do as I ask, I will make sure that you lose that promotion you're so proud of. Now get it sorted.'

Kit man harrumphed and stomped off to a locker on the other side of the changing room. From his pocket he pulled a bunch of keys and jabbed them into the keyhole one after the other as if he were trying to poke the eyes out of his worst enemy. Because he was so ham-fisted, he got the correct key in but it wouldn't turn. He rolled his eyes at John but a hint of a smirk played at the corners of his mouth. 'Stuck. Mr Hurst will just have to manage.'

John suspected he'd done that on purpose and strode over to take a look. He twisted the key but it was indeed firmly stuck. Damn it. Now what? If he didn't get that open and find new laces the whole England World Cup win might be at stake. Hardly a life saving matter, but John had the gut feeling that this was something he had to see through. And like Sarah's, his gut feelings were rarely wrong.

'Nothin' we can do, officer. Now 'ow about a nice cup of—'

'I don't want tea. I want this bloody thing open!' John growled, and pulled at the key with all his strength. The edge of the locker door buckled a bit then stayed put.

'Now that's damaged it right and proper, I don't think—'

'No, you don't, do you? Just stick your finger in that gap and pull the door while I pull the key.'

It soon became clear that kit man's pudgy fingers couldn't get a sufficient grip so John took over and with all the strength he had yanked the door back and forth until it was wide enough to get a hand in. John peered into the locker but couldn't see anything in the dark interior. 'Right, over to you.' John stepped back and wiped the back of his hand across his forehead. 'I can't see and have no idea what shelf the laces are on.'

Kit man sighed, shot in a hand and pulled it out complete with a bunch of laces. 'Okay, do you want to inspect these?' He cocked his head at John and pursed his lips.

'I do as a matter of fact.' John undid the bunch and selected a perfect pair. He then supervised the re-lacing of the boot, much to kit man's chagrin.

'That's sorted then at last, eh?' Kit man placed the boot down next to its mate and stuck his chin out as if to challenge any further action by John.

'Yeah. You thought it was all over. It is now.' John couldn't help but parody the famous saying associated with this historic match and grinned hugely at the frowning kit man.

Once more out in the tunnel, he closed his eyes and sent a silent request to return home. An unexpected task was done, but his main quest was still awaiting his urgent attention. *Please let that one be just as easy.* He shook his head. Now why did he have a feeling that it wouldn't be?

# Chapter Twenty-Two

One moment Sarah was looking at the clouds in a 1940s sky, the next she was standing in her kitchen looking at the dumbstruck faces of Gwen and Harry. Harry blanched and sat down at the table like a sack of spuds and Gwen ran forward and clasped her arms around Sarah as if she'd never let her go.

'Oh, my poor love, thank God!' Then she released her and inspected her face closely. 'Are you all right, in one piece?'

Sarah had to check too before she answered, as she felt an ache in every limb and was thoroughly exhausted. Probably the stress of the whole bloody trip. 'Yes, I seem to be.' Sarah patted her mum's hand and joined Harry at the table before she fell over.

Harry took a deep breath. 'Where's our John?'

Sarah's heart rate picked up a pace and a thousand butterflies took flight in her stomach. 'I was just about to ask you that question.'

Gwen's hand fluttered to her mouth. 'But he went looking for you, love.'

'Oh God, no. When? How long have I been gone?' The butterflies fought their way into her throat.

Harry ran his fingers through his salt and pepper curls. 'You've been gone a few hours or so. He went back to the World Cup day – Wembley 1966, first.' He held up his hand at Sarah's startled expression. 'Don't even go there. Suffice to say it was the wrong call. While he was there, I managed to glean from the powers that you had in fact gone to Topeka 1966 and was in the vicinity of Washburn University. They knew no more than that as they are still having a hell of a job sorting everything out.'

Gwen joined them and took Sarah's hand across the table. 'When John came back here we looked on the Internet and found out that it was one of the worst tornados to hit America and that Washburn took a direct hit. But all the folks who managed to get in the basement survived.'

'We found that out of the four hundred people who were on campus, only fifteen were seriously hurt. It was a damned good job that the students had left for the summer.' Harry sighed. 'Or there'd have been a hell of a lot of casualties.'

Gwen pointed at the laptop on the table with a trembling finger. 'It said that eight hundred houses were destroyed, hundreds injured, and sixteen died. Cars were tossed like toys, chunks of stone flew through the air and slammed into buildings like missiles, and afterwards, there was not a tree nor building standing for miles.'

Sarah's mind was in turmoil. They obviously didn't know about her extra detour to 1941 and neither did the powers it seemed. It wasn't unusual for minutes or hours to have passed in one time period and days gone by in another, so they hadn't really worried that she'd been missing for nearly twenty-four-hours. There seemed little point in going over all that now and it would probably only cause more worry to Gwen, so she just said, 'I just got back from Washburn ... I was safe in the basement. Please don't tell me John ...' Sarah clamped her hand over her mouth to stop herself from screaming. The looks on Gwen and Harry's faces told her all she needed to know.

'He wouldn't be dissuaded.' Harry's voice trembled and he swallowed hard. 'Said he had to get to you and the babies, even though the powers warned him to stay put and that they were working on getting you back any moment. John just didn't trust a word they said, so ...'

A moan escaped her clamped hand and Sarah rose shakily to her feet. 'I have to go back. I know that place better than he does and—'

'You will do no such thing!' Gwen cried. 'For all we know he could be on his way back and you could pass each other again.'

'Now he knows I am supposed to be there, he wouldn't come back without me, you *know* that,' Sarah said, surprised that her voice had suddenly become calm. The look in Harry's eyes told her she was right.

'But he'll do his nut if you put yourself and the babies back in harm's way!' Gwen yelled and slapped her hand on the table. The fear in her eyes shone through standing tears. 'At least you're safe now. Let's just wait and s—'

'And you'd just wait and see if you were me, huh?' Sarah pushed her chair from the table. Gwen did the goldfish act and then closed her mouth. 'Exactly – there's nothing to say.'

'Well, I have something,' Harry said. 'Your mum's right and no matter how much I love my son and no matter how much you want to help, you might end up making things worse, lass.'

Sarah knew they might be right. She also knew that John had risked his life to save her for the second time, and now her dearest love needed her help. Just 'waiting and seeing' wasn't an option. Oddly she felt strangely ready – strong even. Perhaps witnessing the everyday bravery that people endured during the war had galvanised her. Besides, she had the help of an extra Needle and Stitch in her belly. She stroked her little bump and smiled. Then she walked to the door flinging over her shoulder, 'I have to go, but I will be back with John. I promise.'

Gwen wailed and clung to Harry's arm. 'Nooo! Stop her, Harry!'

But even as Harry sprang up and set off in pursuit, Sarah said aloud, in a soft firm voice, 'Powers, take me back to Washburn, now. You owe me big time.' And then she felt as if the whole room was floating, rising, growing fainter, but Sarah stayed put. She watched the shocked faces of Gwen and Harry grow smaller and fall away as the scene disappeared sideways as though socked from her line of vision by a giant fist. And to greet her return into her new line of vision whirled the giant and brutal fist of a tornado, thumping flat the landscape – unrelenting in its terrifying power.

It was much closer than she'd seen it last time and coming fast in the green sickly evening sky. The rumble of the approaching train she'd heard when she'd been in the basement, now sounded like six of them piling into the back of each other, with the squealing of brakes and a roar of thunder thrown in for good measure. A tremor ran from her feet and through her body. She had never been so terrified. Standing in the same spot as she'd found herself before, give or take, Sarah turned from the tornado and set her face against the driving rain. The howling gale pulled at her hair and clothes like a demon as she made for the basement, but she made steady progress.

Once under the cover of the entrance, Sarah set off for the stairs as quickly as she dare, given the fact that Artie had taken a tumble on their hard shiny surface. But three steps down she heard a gut wrenching crump of metal impacting on metal come from outside. It was so loud that she imagined a plane had crashed from the sky.

Racing back up again, she saw not a plane, but a truck, concertinaed into a wall of the campus a few hundred yards away as if it was made out of cardboard, and the trunk of a tree whizzed past her only about twenty feet away. Sarah stifled a scream. *Jeez, I'm out of here – please let John be safe in the basement … because if he's outside …*

As she turned round, she heard a man's voice yell, 'RAH!' before it was snatched away by the wind. *Damn it! Someone was outside the entrance.* She took a step back and strained her ears and then there it was again, and closer, but it wasn't RAH! he was shouting. With her heart thumping in her ears she ran outside grabbing onto the handrail at the entrance and narrowed her eyes against the whipping wind. 'SARAH!'

Oh my lord! There he was, the most beautiful man in the world, soaked to the skin, his blue shirt clinging to the contours of his body, his dark curls more like ringlets in the downpour, flying out around his head as he searched up and down the driveway, unaware he was just a few feet away from her.

'JOHN, JOHN OVER HERE,' she yelled fit to bust a lung, waved her arms crazily and nearly lost her balance against the buffeting. 'THE BASEMENT IS THIS WAY, QUICKLY!'

John shoved his wet hair back from his forehead, looked over at her and then gave her the most heart-stopping smile. He raised a hand and set off at a run, tucking his body low and powering his long legs against the wind's barrier. But just as he was within reach, a forked tree branch hurtled past and took his feet from under him. Seconds later, the branch was followed by a larger stump which pinned his left leg firmly to the ground.

*What was this, nightmarish déjà vu?* Screaming fit to rival the storm Sarah ran towards him but John held his hand up. 'Get inside, Sarah!' He pointed in the direction of the tornado. 'That evil bastard's moving too fast. There's no time!' John put both hands around his leg and pulled, but the stump was too heavy.

'NO!' Sarah yelled, her tears drowned by the lashing rain. 'I won't leave you—'

'YOU WILL! FOR THE SAKE OF THE CHILDREN, GET INSIDE!'

Sarah turned and fled but she had no intention of leaving him to his fate. It was the bombed out house scenario all over again! Though she stumbled and tripped a few times she made the rest of the stairs in what felt like nanoseconds and burst into the basement.

Artie looked up and hurried over. 'Where'd you go, Sarah?'

'Never mind that now, you gotta help me. My husband's just outside and trapped under a log!' Sarah grabbed his arm and dragged him to the door.

'You'd do better to stay put, Professor.' The tall farmer from the painting stepped between them. 'By the screechin' of that hell cat I'd say we only have a few minutes afore it's atop us!'

Artie nodded and then stepped around him, his handsome face grimly determined. 'This woman saved my life, Mr Atherton. I aim to do my best to save her husband's.'

Sarah's heart was so full she had no words to express her gratitude as she ran after Artie back up the stairs, his long loping strides showing that his ankle was not as bad as she'd thought, or that adrenaline was keeping the pain at bay. Just as he reached the entrance he turned to face her.

'You stay here, Sarah. No sense in you risking your life too.'

'But—' Sarah began, and then fell silent. John's hurt and anger that day when she'd come back from 1955 was still fresh in her mind. This was not the time to put her superhero cloak on. This was the time to wait, watch and pray that Artie would rescue John and that all of them would return to the safety of the basement.

She dug her nails into her arm to stop herself from running outside as she watched Artie crouch down and strain to lift the stump, every sinew in his neck standing, his blue eyes popping into bold relief against his red face.

John was trying to do his best to help, twisting his body and trying to lever the stump with his other leg, but the damned thing rose a few inches and then the strength in Artie's arms gave out. Artie wiped sweat from his brow and yelled, 'On the count of three you pull with all your might while I lift, okay?'

John nodded and gritted his teeth. Artie counted down and pulled, his knuckles white, his biceps bulging and John wriggled and levered, but Artie's arms shook under the strain and he blew a snort of frustration down his nose and lowered the log again.

John shook his head and Sarah's last vestiges of hope were snatched away on the wind when she heard him yell, 'Go now, man! Save yourself, you did your best!'

She saw Artie shake his head and take another grip on the wood, his face focused and calm. Something about that expression made Sarah feel calm too, and in her heart, hope returned hesitantly – a splash of watercolour on paper, soaking and spreading with every strain of Artie's arms, until it created a vibrant painting, demanding the attention of every eye.

Though Sarah could see the exhaustion etched on his face, a last herculean effort from somewhere deep within brought a roar of triumph from Artie's lips and then ... John was free! In one fluid movement Artie knelt and tossed John over his shoulder as if he was a child and then powered them both towards Sarah.

Once safely in the basement Sarah knelt next to John and smothered him with kisses, just like Veronica had done to Edward yesterday, until he held up both hands.

'Okay, okay that's enough,' he said laughing.

Artie grinned down at them and wiped the sweat from his face with his forearm.

Sarah launched herself at him too and squeezed him hard. 'Thank you so much, Artie. I can't begin to tell you how grateful I am.'

'Hey, you saved me first remember ...' Artie's words were lost in the ear-splitting roar as the ground trembled and walls shook under the fist of the tornado. Sarah flung herself down next to John and she felt as if her breath were being pulled from her body and her ears popped under the pressure. They held each other tightly as the twister did its worst. And after a few minutes that felt like hours, they heard it wreaking havoc a little further off and then further still, until they felt safe to stand up and look around them.

People were praying, laughing, embracing; the joy in the room was almost palpable. John looked into her eyes; his deep olive ones crinkling at the corners as his signature smile lit the room. 'I love you so much, Mrs Needler. Thank God you listened to me for once and took a day off from heroics.'

Sarah hugged him and put her head on his chest so he wouldn't see her deepening colour. There would be time enough to tell him later on about 1941 and that she'd been safe back at home but then had come back to save him. 'I love you too, Mr Needler, and I always listen to you, darling,' she said with a sigh.

John pointed over to where Artie was talking to Dexter. 'That man is a true hero – and his name, Artie? That's some coincidence.'

Sarah explained who he was and John's mouth dropped open. 'Wow! So what he did for me out there demonstrates our theory that past and present are all inexorably linked. There actually is a strong, tightly woven cord of human essence keeping time balanced and enabling progress to the future,' he said, his face full of wonder. 'Artie's heroic act of humanity today strengthened that cord and cemented the bonds of history. You saved Artie's grandfather and his grandson saved me.'

Sarah traced her fingers along his stubbly chin and kissed him tenderly. 'He saved me too, John, because without you, my life would be over.'

Outside, the place was unrecognisable. Large parts of the grand old university were reduced to rubble, nearly all the trees gone, cars were upside down or piled on top of each other as if placed by a giant hand, sparking wires waved in the wind, and the matchwood debris of flattened buildings littered the landscape in every direction. So destroyed was this part of Topeka, Sarah felt as if she'd just arrived in a war zone after a direct hit and could in fact be back in 1940s Southampton again. Then the warmth of John's hand on her shoulder seeped through the chill of her bones and she turned into him.

'Let's see if the powers will get us back now. I expect they'll be bloody furious with me.' John sighed into her hair.

Sarah looked up at him and snorted. 'Furious? I'm furious with *them*! They had better not punish you, given that they can't seem to get any part of their job right at the moment!'

Still holding each other a few moments later they appeared in front of their parents back in the kitchen.

If Gwen and Harry had looked dumbstruck last time Sarah had come back, this time they looked as if they'd been struck by the tornado. Harry's hair was stuck up due to the continuous raking of his fingers and his eyes were red and puffy. Gwen's hair looked like she'd had a lightning rod pass through it and her eyes were barely visible through the smeared mascara which extended across most of her face.

Even though the pair had clearly been to hell and back, Sarah burst out laughing and couldn't stop. 'You ... look a real ... fright, Mum,' she managed to say between guffaws. She knew this reaction was mostly due to hysteria and relief, rather than their appearance, but the more her mother frowned and look indignant, the more she laughed.

Harry looked at John and wiped at his eyes. 'I see she's just as daft as ever, then, lad?'

John grinned and pulled Sarah to him. 'Aye, Dad, and I wouldn't have her any other way.'

# Chapter Twenty-Three

It was the kind of morning silence that only a white-out could bring, the kind of silence that makes a person think that they have had cotton wool shoved into their ears by mysterious cotton wool shovers in the middle of the night. John stretched out in the warm bed, yawned and smiled at that very surreal thought so early in the morning. Would these said shovers be pixie-like in appearance or more trollish? He'd like to think pixie-like, carrying little wicker baskets on their backs full of cotton wool balls. 'Daft as a brush, lad,' his dad would have said if he could hear his son's thoughts right now.

Certainly daft, but more ecstatically happy John decided, turning on his side to watch the rise and fall of his wife's chest as she slept. At last here they were safe together again, and this time they could rest assured that that would be an end to it unless Sarah opted to travel again. Just to do normal things like go shopping, walking or, if the cotton wool shovers had done their job properly, sledging, would be such a welcome change from being whisked back to various danger zones around time.

John hopped out of bed and twitched back the curtain – yesss, they had done their job and John felt his stomach flip with excitement. Suddenly he was six again, gazing out over the white blankets the hills were rather fetchingly sporting against the navy dawn sky, and the Christmas cake look of their circular decking iced with snow. A robin alighted on the fence and cocked his head at him and John half expected the red Coca-Cola lorry to trundle up the road in the distance, complete with fairy lights and the *Holidays Are Coming* theme tune.

'Sarah, wake up, come and look. It's snowed over night.

Isn't that great?' he called over his shoulder. A grunt and a sigh was all he received in response as Sarah snuggled back further under the duvet. John waited a few more moments and then slid back into bed a wicked tickle of glee in his belly. Carefully positioning his feet he placed them gently on the back of his wife's thighs and buttocks.

'Ow!' Sarah sprang into a half-sitting position, her eyes still bleary with sleep, the duvet clasped to her chest. 'What the bloody hell are you doing?' she yelled, pushing his arms away as he tried to cuddle her. 'Your feet are freezing!'

'That's because it's covered with snow out there. Come on, let's go sledging!'

The alarm clock rocked on its feet under the force of Sarah's clumsy pawing and she drew it close to her eyes. 'But … but it's only eight-fifteen … it must be still dark out there.' She put the clock back, yawned and snuggled down again. 'And it's Sunday … go back to sleep, sweetheart.'

'Sleep? We can sleep later this afternoon – but now, dear heart, is the time for an adventure.' John grinned and unrolled Sarah from the duvet. 'And it's nearly Christmas!'

This time Sarah was properly grumpy and she snatched the duvet back around her. She glared at him and pouted. With her frowny face and her tousled hair haloed in the lamplight John thought she looked a little like a disgruntled pixie. Perhaps she was moonlighting as a cotton wool shover and keeping it a secret. He chuckled and tried to pull her to him but to no avail. She pushed him away and sat up.

'One, let me remind you that it is only ten days since our last "adventure", one that I do not wish to repeat as long as I live. Even though it was really lovely to see Veronica again, that was a shock I could have done without.' She counted on her fingers. 'Two, let me tell you, I am all adventured out for the foreseeable, three, I am *not* going bloody sledging at this hour, and lastly, it is not nearly Christmas, it's weeks away.'

'Two.' John grinned wondering if staying in bed with the grumpy Sarah might actually be preferable to sledging. Even when she was angry she looked like sex on a stick.

'Two, what?'

'Weeks until Christmas.' John's libido won over the snow covered wonderland waiting outside. Yup, the tingle in his groin suggested that Sarah's duvet covered wonderland was definitely preferable. He snuggled down and stretched out his hand to her.

She took it and settled down under his arm her silky hair caressing his chest. 'So it is … I had no idea it was so close. I haven't even thought about Christmas shopping or anything.'

'Well, that's hardly surprising given everything we've been through lately, is it?'

'No, I guess not. I think I was just preoccupied with trying to get back to normal and so relieved on the one hand that the powers decided to leave us alone, especially after the 1941 trip that they seemed to know nothing about until a few days later, but on the other, not quite believing it, you know?'

'Well, you said yourself that they owed us big time. And they more or less said that's the reason that I didn't get punished. And the wider world owes you. Remember that little girl, Barbara, you helped to rescue went on to do pioneering work in recognising and treating mental trauma. You're always saying you can't understand how people during the war managed to cope. Well, at least Barbara could draw on those experiences in her work to help others.'

'Hmm. That's true, but I still don't get how saving Edward helped, apart from helping Veronica on a personal level obviously.' Sarah traced a finger down John's cheek thoughtfully. 'And let me tell you, if they *had* punished you after everything that's happened I would have personally hunted them down and killed them, powerful spindles or no,' Sarah muttered and kissed his chest.

John laughed and kissed the top of her head. 'I actually believe you would have, Mrs Needler.'

'You'd better believe it.' She grinned up at him and traced a circle on his chest then stroked her fingers across his stomach. The idea of sledging was melting under the heat of her hand as it moved ever downward.

'If you keep doing that, I won't be responsible for my actions.' John drew his hand down over Sarah's arm and over the swell of her hip.

'Well, thank goodness for that.' She sighed as her fingers encircled him and her tongue flicked his ear.

'I will let you have your wicked way on one condition.' John rolled Sarah onto her back, brushed his lips over her breasts and then looked into her sky-blue eyes burning sapphire-deep with passion.

'What condition?' she muttered and moved her hips against him.

'That we have breakfast in bed after and then we go sledging?'

'That's two conditions, I don't know if I can agree …' Sarah's words trailed off as John kissed her tummy and then moved his head lower.

'Your sausage is bigger than mine.' Sarah pouted as she held hers aloft on a fork.

'That's what all the guys say to me.' John grinned, taking a bite out of his and reached round behind him to plump the pillows. He still didn't feel comfy though and shuffled his legs and the breakfast tray. 'Why is it that the idea of breakfast in bed always sounds better than the reality?'

'Is that a rhetorical question? You always say the same thing, my love, and stop shuffling or the tea will go all over the place.'

John sighed and stopped shuffling. Did he always say that? He guessed he did. He also guessed that his wife knew his little foibles inside out but hadn't said no to breakfast in bed, even though she knew he'd not be comfy. And that was because he'd really wanted it and would have been grumpy if she'd refused. So the deal was, she was prepared to put up with his chuntering just to try and make him happy.

It wasn't a huge thing, but John realised that this is what *real* love was all about. Little acts of caring, selflessness made up the whole. Grand gestures of flowers and champagne, meals at expensive restaurants had their place, but moments like this, moments that mostly got overlooked were the most important. John looked at his wife munching contentedly and tried to capture that image – this moment, in his heart like a snapshot of love that he could pick out, look at and remember how he felt right now in years to come. Moments and memories made a marriage, kept it strong.

John laid his fork down and put his hand on hers. 'I love you, Sarah.'

Still chewing and with a dab of ketchup at the side of her mouth she furrowed her brow. 'I love you too, sweetheart, but why so serious?'

'Love is a serious matter, young woman, and don't you forget it.' John smiled, wiped the ketchup away and then continued with his breakfast. No point telling her what he was feeling. It wouldn't come out right and then it would all just feel a bit flat. He decided to keep it to himself, treasure it. Another thought occurred that it was because he was often pants at sharing his feelings. But all guys were, weren't they? Perhaps he should try and tell her after all. It would be good practice for teaching their boy; he wanted both his children to be able to express themselves openly and without embarrassment.

Sarah took a slurp of tea. 'Talking of serious matters, I wonder what Artie's genius great-grandson is up to right at this moment?'

John's moment of openness had passed, but there would be another time. He'd make sure of it. 'Well, as you know, the powers said that Artie the fourth is a ground-breaking medical scientist. Probably working on a cure for uncomfortable breakfasting in bed, I shouldn't wonder.'

Sarah laughed. 'Yeah, you could write and ask him to do that for you. He probably has a window in his busy schedule.' After another sip of tea she stared thoughtfully at a bit of toast in her hand. 'I wonder if we really could write to him, you know, say how grateful we are for all his hard work and that he's a credit to his dad who was another hero ... you know rescuing you, and his great-grandfather being a brilliant senator and ...' A sigh finished the sentence.

John took another mouthful and shuffled again. 'You just realised the fatal flaw in the plan, huh?'

'Hmm, he would wonder who we are and how come we just wrote to him out of the blue and—'

'And a trillion more important things, like how come we seem to be authorities on the deeds of his family and acting like some weird overseas fan club. Not to say what the powers would do if they found out that we had made contact with actual people we have been involved with in the past.'

A roll of her eyes and a shake of the head greeted his comments. 'Oh, so there's a rule about that too, huh? Why am I not surprised?'

John just managed to swallow his mouthful of tea before he spit it out. Had his wife gone potty? 'Blimey, Sarah, I don't know if there's a rule, but if there isn't, there should be. You know full well that any information about the future should never be divulged when you are on a mission. How do you think getting in touch with people and saying, hey how are you? I'm Sarah. I rescued your great-grandfather in the 1870s, pleased to meet you, would go down, eh?'

'Don't be stupid, it wouldn't be as blatant as that, you're

just exaggerating the whole idea,' Sarah snapped, pushing her tray away and flopping back on the pillow.

'Er, I don't think it's me who is being stupid, hon. Any contact at all would be very dangerous and *very* irresponsible.' He looked at Sarah who immediately closed her eyes against his stern expression.

'Yes, but it would just be a letter. It wouldn't say stuff about me rescuing both Arties, would it? And I genuinely *would* like to thank a guy who developed pioneering drugs to treat HIV, wouldn't you?'

'Of course, but it's impossible. This emotional link to the 1874 Artie has to be cut now, love.' He made his voice gentle as she opened her eyes and blinked away moisture. 'The powers said it was because of him ... Artie ... that you missed him, that you were drawn back to Topeka and his grandson. And look what a fantastic job you did there, even though you weren't even supposed to *be* there. You saved him and then he went on to marry and have a son – one of the pioneers of HIV.' He traced the back of his hand along her jawline. 'Think of all the thousands of lives you indirectly saved because of that. That should be enough for anyone, you, Super Stitch, included.' He shot her a wide smile. 'That's it and that's all, as you are fond of saying. You have to let go now, you're having your own babies in the spring.'

Sarah nodded and gave him a little smile. 'I know. And I can't wait, it's just that I find it hard to send that little blond-haired guy out of my heart. I so loved being his mother, even if I wasn't really his mother if you understand me?' She swallowed and kissed his palm.

'Of course I understand. You don't need to send him away, just have him put in a safe place like precious memories.' A beat, a deep breath. 'It's little moments and memories that are so important, don't you think? Kind of what love is all about.'

'Oh, John. That's so true.' Sarah's voice caught as she slipped her arms around his neck and hugged him to her.

*Not bad for your first try.* John closed his eyes and contentedly settled his head on her chest.

# Chapter Twenty-Four

Family meals had begun to pepper the calendar on a regular basis Sarah noted as she returned from school on the last day of term. Christmas was less than a week away and she and John were due to go round to her mum's that evening. Ella, Jason and Angelica would be there, and, of course, Harry. Harry and Gwen seemed inseparable at the moment, and although Sarah had had misgivings at first, she couldn't be happier that her mum had found someone to be happy with too.

A boisterous flutter in her tummy as she bent over to unzip her boots halted her in her tracks. That was definitely more like a kick this time. Sarah leaned against the banister at the foot of the stairs and ran the flat of her hand over her ever growing bump. She was immediately rewarded with another flutter underneath it. Little fingers of happiness twirled tendrils of love around her heart and she chuckled to herself. *Two new lives growing inside me, how cool is that?*

The first time she'd felt them was the day they'd gone sledging and tumbled off into the powdery snow. She and John had lain on their backs, a tangle of arms and legs, their guffaws of laughter echoing around the countryside, and then a flutter had Sarah up and silent. Another, and she'd turned to John looking up at her, his face chilled red, his eyes green as new shoots in spring against the white landscape.

'What's up?' he'd asked, concerned as he watched her run her hands over her tummy.

'Nothing. Everything's grand. I think I just felt our babies!'

John had jumped up and tried to feel them too, but they had decided that two flutters were enough for the time being.

Though Sarah was disappointed John couldn't feel them, a little part of her wanted to keep the experience just for herself. Perhaps it was selfish, but she loved the idea that she was a mother. A woman had a special bond with her children and just for that moment she wanted it to be exclusive.

John had felt them quite a few times after that day, and he had been as over the moon as had she been, but for that very first time when the babes had said, 'Hey, Mum we're here,' and remembering how her heart had swelled with joy, well, she wouldn't have changed that for the world.

Normally four o'clock and almost dark would have made Sarah sigh. Winter was deffo not her most favourite time of year, but this year was different. She pulled the curtains and switched on the fairy lights on the tree they had put up at the weekend. The scent of pine resin filled the room and she hugged herself, a big soppy grin on her face as she watched the lights twinkle on and off. This time of year was much more exciting when you were expecting, in a lovely home *and* with the man of your dreams. There had been one Christmas after Neil had left her that she had barely functioned. If it hadn't been for Gwen she shuddered to think what would have happened.

Still, that was all behind her now and 'forward' was the only button she need press in her life. Christmas would be perfect this year, she just knew it. A white Christmas had been predicted and unbeknownst to John, Lucy and her husband were due to come over from France. They had managed to get some friends from a nearby stable to feed and care for the horses for ten whole days, so John would be chuffed to little mint balls. Sarah thought that Harry might spring it on him at the meal later. He'd said to her the other day that he had a little something up his sleeve for that evening.

'There must be *something* I can bring, or do to help on Christmas morning, Mum,' Sarah said, popping an olive into her mouth. In Gwen's warm and homely kitchen Sarah and Ella perched on the breakfast stools handing their mother this or that and chatting for England. The atmosphere was charged with excitement, the smell of mulled wine, Christmas spices, holly wreaths and surrounded with love. Sarah felt just like she had in the run up to Christmas when she'd been growing up.

Gwen frowned at her question. 'No, I told you. You are to put your feet up. Me and Ella will do it all.'

Ella rolled her eyes and put the back of her hand to her forehead theatrically. 'Oh, why is it always me, poor Cinders, who never goes to the ball?'

'You suggesting I'm an ugly sister?' Sarah playfully poked her sister in the arm. 'And seriously, Mum, I'm pregnant, not ill.'

Gwen pointed a wooden spoon at her. 'You need your rest after all that time-tra—' Gwen flushed and covered her mistake with a cough. 'All that time you spend teaching and pregnant with twins, for goodness sake.'

'Okay, don't get your noodle in a knot,' Ella said, thankfully oblivious of the faux pas. 'I am only too happy to wait on my favourite sister hand and foot.'

While Ella busied herself making garlic bread, Sarah rolled her eyes at her mother and shook her head.

Gwen shrugged and whispered in her ear as she passed. 'I know. But I covered it well, didn't I?'

Though there was nothing more Sarah would like than to tell Ella all about time-travelling, she knew it was out of the question. The Spindlies had already allowed Gwen to keep her memory; one more person would be one step beyond. It just felt wrong keeping a person she'd always confided in out of the loop, especially now her mum knew. But it couldn't be helped. It was what it was.

Could she pack in one more forkful of her mum's incredible

lasagne? Sarah was answered by a burp rumbling. Nope. That would be just too piggy ... but that garlic bread?

Her ruminations were interrupted by the sudden scraping of a chair and the tinkle of a spoon tapped on a glass. She looked to the end of the table where Harry had risen to his feet, his face flushed and his blue eyes twinkling with excitement. This must be the moment where he tells John that Lucy was coming over soon. She looked at John sitting opposite and winked at his puzzled expression.

'Okay, everyone. Now that we have eaten our fill of this wonderful woman's glorious banquet,' he inclined his head towards Gwen and smiled adoringly, 'I have one or two announcements to make.'

A glance from Ella was tipped in Sarah's direction and Sarah nodded to confirm the unspoken question. Ella knew about Lucy's imminent arrival, however, Sarah herself was puzzled by the mention of 'one or two' announcements.

Harry raised a finger and hurriedly checked a text message on his phone. Then he shot them a huge grin and said, 'I am happy to tell you all that my daughter Lucy and her husband are joining us for Christmas!'

John's face lit up brighter than the Christmas lights. 'Really, Dad? That's fantastic! When are they arriving?'

Harry raised his finger again and scuttled out of the room. He returned a few moments later followed by a beautiful, tall, willowy woman with chocolate curls and a smile to rival John's. She had sparkling green eyes too though hers had hazel shots. And behind her she led a very tall, raven-haired, angular-featured man with faded blue eyes and enough designer stubble to sand down a small coffee table. In similar dark tailored trousers, smart shirts and causal jackets, they looked like they'd just stepped out of a magazine and most around the table were gobsmacked, including Sarah.

John's gob was un-smacked however and he launched

himself at Lucy like an over-excited puppy. 'Lucy! Why didn't you let me know?' He smothered her in a huge bear hug. 'How long are you here for? We have so much to catch up on!'

Lucy laughed. 'I didn't let you know because Dad wanted it to be a surprise. And we are here until the day after Boxing Day.'

'Bonsoir everyone. I am looking forward to getting to know you all,' her husband said, his French accent deep and rich, his smile put two dimples in the stubble.

Sarah and Ella exchanged glances. Ella put her hand to the side of her face to shield her mouthed; *Oh my God, he's gorgeous* from everyone but Sarah and then pretended to fan herself with her napkin. Sarah giggled and Jason frowned at his wife, obviously suspicious of what she was up to, but not quite sure.

'Oh, my manners,' Lucy said, pecking her husband on the cheek. 'I haven't introduced you. Everyone, this is Corbin.'

Corbin grinned and nodded at them each in turn as Harry introduced them.

As Sarah was introduced, Lucy clapped her hands and breathed, 'Oh, you are even prettier in real life than in the wedding photos, Sarah.' Lucy pulled a face. 'So sorry we couldn't make that, but as you know, I had the damned shingles.'

'Thanks for the compliment. You too. And it was such a shame that you missed it.' Sarah returned Lucy's warm smile. 'Can't wait to get to know you now, though.'

Extra chairs were produced for Lucy and Corbin and the conversation resumed in earnest mostly with questions to the couple and lots of 'oohs' and 'ahs' from Ella at almost everything Corbin said. She kept winking at Sarah and giggling. Sarah told her she was incorrigible, but such good fun nevertheless.

A little while later, after Gwen's scrumptious home-made

sticky toffee pudding and cream, Harry brought out two buckets of champagne on ice and placed them on the table.

John commented to Lucy jokingly that he never got this treatment when he came round to visit. 'Prodigal daughters, eh?'

'Ah, lad, this is not *just* for our Lucy. I did say I had one or *two* announcements earlier. And this is number two,' Harry said, tapping his glass again. He held his hand out to Gwen, who clasped it and stood up next to him as he continued, 'It gives me great pleasure to announce ...' Gwen flushed and looked about twenty-five as she looked into his eyes. Harry swallowed and gave her the sweetest smile Sarah could ever remember seeing. She caught her mum's eye and her tummy did a forward roll ... she knew what was coming. 'To announce that I have asked Gwen to marry me and she has accepted.'

For a snap shot, slow-motion moment, Sarah looked on while Ella let out a whoop and danced her mum round in a circle, Lucy and John hugged each other and Lucy, tears flowing down her cheeks, hugged Harry and the rest gathered, stood and clapped ... but Sarah's heart was full of thoughts of her dad. Why did he have to die? Why was life so cruel? He should have been here this Christmas awaiting the spring birth of his grandchildren, just like Gwen.

Suddenly she was aware of Ella at her side whispering in her ear, 'I know what you're thinking, but Dad would have wanted this for Mum. Accepting Harry doesn't mean betrayal, trust me, I've thought it out *and* I'm your big sister. I know these things.'

Sarah choked down a torrent of tears and hugged Ella. Then over her shoulder she noticed two anxious sapphire-blue eyes fixed on hers. A smile and a few steps led her into her mum's embrace. 'So happy for you, Mum. You couldn't have picked a better guy.' Sarah realised that she meant every word.

'Apart from your dad, eh?' Gwen's eyes spilled over and Sarah couldn't speak. 'I *do* know what you and Ella are feeling. I'm feeling it too. There was no finer man than your dad and I wish life hadn't handed me these cards. But it did, and thank God my Harry is an ace in the pack.'

Sarah nodded and they both looked at Harry pretending to guzzle a whole bottle of champagne down amid hoots of laughter.

Gwen shook her head and chuckled. 'Even though he is a right daft chuff at times.'

The 'right daft chuff' beckoned Sarah and John over an hour or so later and ushered them out of the room. 'Follow me, you two, I found summat out this afternoon but haven't had a chance to get you on your own 'til now.'

Once in Gwen's bedroom he shut the door behind them and sat on the bed. 'Sit down then.' He gestured to the sofa in the corner.

'What's this all about, Dad? I'm not sure I could take another surprise today,' John said, sitting down next to Sarah.

'Me either,' Sarah said. 'Mum's not expecting, is she?'

'Yep, she is. How did you guess?' Harry laughed out loud and then lowered his voice. 'No, it's about 1966.'

'England won, 4-2, we know, Dad.'

'Oh, very funny. No, it's about the reason you went there. You thought you just went by mistake instead of to Topeka and tried to make the best of it with the bootlace thing, but the powers reckon it was more than that. Sarah was scheduled to do the Wembley job at a later date.' Harry looked at Sarah and scratched his head. 'But buggered if I know how a lass could have even got into the changing rooms.'

Sarah tutted. 'That'd be right. Should Sarah be dealt a nice easy-peasy job like that, sorting bootlaces, or instead

229

flung into one of the worst tornado's America has had?' She put her finger on her chin and rolled her eyes to the ceiling. 'Hmm … methinks some spindly little article has it in for me.'

John snorted. 'And *scheduled* is rather a defunct term isn't it, with everything they've got wrong lately.'

Harry folded his arms and sighed. 'It wouldn't have been that easy, Sarah, as I said. A woman *would* have found it difficult to get in there … but I'll grant you it was a better job than Topeka, love. So, do you want to know about it all or not?'

'We're all ears.' Sarah nodded and was immediately rewarded with an image of Veronica. Poor old Ratchet, who she'd only seen married a short while ago, would be long dead now … and that thought saddened Sarah. It would have been good to have got to know her better. After they had parted on the bridge that day there was a real sense of friendship between them and that was strengthened the day they went looking for Edward and then the next day when she'd acted as impromptu maid of honour at their wedding. Ah yes, Veronica had blossomed into a real good egg, as she would have said.

'You listening, Miss far-away stare?' Harry's voice snapped her out of her ponderings and she saluted him and pretended to sit to attention. 'Right, well, I got an email this morning to tell me that had John not sorted Geoff Hurst's laces they would have most likely broken and England would have lost.'

'How come they didn't email me?' John frowned. 'And a loss for England would have been disappointing and I love football as much as the next man, but it was hardly a matter of bloody life and death, was it?'

'I think they emailed me as a courtesy to you and Sarah. They had wanted to leave you well out of the business for a while as a reward for all the high jinks they'd put you through.' Harry rubbed his nose and looked down it at them with a superior glint in his eye. It was clear that he was pleased to be the only one in the know after his retirement from 'the business' a good four years previously.

'It's about time they were a bit more sensitive,' John grumped, putting his arm round Sarah and pulling her to him. 'I mean, how on earth would we have coped if I had been off doing my regular needling job alongside all this?'

'Indeed,' Harry resumed. 'And it *was* a matter of life and death, actually. Not in the way you think – the score and all, but to one bloke in the crowd that day, an England win changed his life beyond all recognition. He was a hopeless drunk and his wife and baby son were on the verge of leaving him, but he wouldn't or couldn't show any signs of changing. But on that day in 1966, that England win and the euphoria surrounding it, for some reason made the difference – made him see the light. He gave up the booze and everyone lived happily ever after with roses round the door and so forth.'

'That's fantastic, Harry. But life and death? There's normally a bit more to it than that,' Sarah said, knowing full well there was probably more, but couldn't help teasing him. He was such a one for dragging out the point. Any minute now she guessed he'd start on about 'he knew a woman who'.

'Blimey, what an impatient wife you have there, John.' Harry sniffed and gave her a withering look. 'I was coming to that, Sarah. So anyway the baby son grows up to be a volunteer in Africa and spearheads one of the first successful conservation and irrigation programmes. Just think how many lives those bootlaces actually saved?' He smiled at John with pride shining in his eyes.

'Wow, that's fantastic. Do you know, I think I might go over to stitching rather than needling. Want to swap, love?'

'No. And as far as I'm concerned my time-travelling

boots are well and truly hanging in the locker room forever.' Sarah noted a glance of disbelief pass between John and his dad but decided not to comment. They could think what they liked, she'd had enough and who could blame her? Bloody Spindly Ones had blamed her twins for the upset. Even if they were causing it, the Spindlies should have been able to sort it. Nope that was it and that was all. Sarah could hold her head high; she'd done her bit and then some.

Just then Lucy popped her head around the door. 'Oh, *there* you are! I was hoping for a bit of a chat with Sarah.'

'Thank goodness, I can't wait to see the back of these two.' Sarah chuckled and gave John a shove off the sofa.

'Huh, I know when I'm not wanted.' John grinned. He pecked Lucy on the cheek as he passed and followed his dad out of the room.

Lucy sat down next to Sarah and gave her a small hug. 'Welcome to the family sister-in-law. Shall I say I've heard so much about you, and then you say only good I hope? Or shall we just have a good old natter?'

Sarah laughed. She had warmed to Lucy as soon as she'd seen her which was rare for her. It normally took a while to weigh folk up, but Lucy's personality and kind nature came across right from the off. 'A good old natter, I think. So tell me, what was John like when he was little?'

The hour they spent chatting flashed by so fast that Sarah thought it couldn't have been more than twenty minutes. She'd found out that John was the best brother in the universe and that he'd always been there for his younger sister, that Lucy had known all about the 'travelling malarkey' as she called it but hadn't felt in the least tempted to try it.

'Three weirdoes in the family was enough for anyone. It wasn't easy having both parents and a brother in the business.' She was the one who anchored them all to reality she'd said.

Lucy had even confided in Sarah how worried about Corbin she was at times. In the two years they had been married she had been incredibly happy and adored the man, but sometimes he tended to go off for hours without telling her, sometimes in the middle of the night and the shingles she'd had at the time of Sarah and John's wedding was in fact a cover. Corbin had gone missing the day before and hadn't returned until the evening of the next day. Corbin apparently needed time alone to think now and then.

Unsure of what to say as Lucy tossed her head and tried to hide the fact that she was close to tears by pointing at Gwen's chintz curtains and commenting that they were charmingly old-fashioned, Sarah had just patted her hand and said, 'Anyone with eyes can see he adores you. Some people do need time to think ... I guess.'

'But why can't he phone to say that? The first time it happened I was a mess, you know, wondering where he was? I phoned round his friends – even the hospitals in the end.' Lucy shook her head. 'I just hope "time to think" doesn't actually mean "time to shag somebody else".'

Of course at first Sarah had been thinking exactly that. She was sure that women flung themselves at Corbin on a regular basis, but in the end a gut feeling told her that he wasn't a cheat. But his 'time to think' didn't feel right either.

'Hey, I'm sure it doesn't, Lucy. He is obviously a lovely caring man who just needs time on his own to contemplate the universe or something.' Sarah shot her a big grin.

'Or something.' Lucy attempted a smile in return.

When Gwen came to find them to announce cake was being served, Sarah was reluctant to go. She had really enjoyed Lucy's company and wished that she didn't live so far away.

Lucy put her thoughts into words as they walked to the kitchen arm in arm. 'I am so glad we have managed to have a good chat. My brother picked very well – the best.' She smiled and squeezed Sarah's arm. 'And France is hardly the other side of the world. You must come and see us.'

'We so will. And you are the best sister-in-law a girl could hope for, too. Will you be over to see the babies when they come in May?'

'Try and stop us.' Lucy twinkled. 'I have already bought clothes, toys, rattles, a separate house to put it all in, yadda, yadda …'

'So are you okay about your mum and my dad, then? I haven't had a chance to ask you,' John whispered as they walked down the path to their car at the end of the evening amidst a chorus of 'see ya soons' and 'nighty nights' from Harry, Gwen, Lucy and Corbin waving from the front door.

'Yeah. I had a wobble but now I am totally cool with it.' Sarah waved back and then got into the passenger seat.

John jumped in next to her and raised his eyebrows. 'Totally?'

'Totally.'

'Thank goodness for that.' John smiled and kissed the tip of her nose. 'I had a similar moment after dinner when I thought of Mum. But in the end there's nothing we can do to bring either of them back, so we have to make the best of it. And I reckon that your mum is one of the best.'

'Yes, ditto your dad. And Lucy is so lovely! No wonder you missed her.' Sarah gave a final wave as John pulled away from the kerb.

'I'm so glad you two hit it off. I haven't really had much chance to catch up tonight but they are here for a while, so plenty of time. Corbin seems nice, don't you think? I met him at their wedding, of course, but then they went off to the Bahamas that evening on honeymoon so I haven't spoken to him much.'

Keeping her voice light as she didn't want to betray Lucy's confidence regarding her concerns about her husband,

Sarah said, 'Yes. I think he seems really nice, and *very* good looking.' She grinned at John's affronted expression.

'Oi, watch it, madam. Just because he's tall, dark, handsome and French doesn't mean that he's more gorgeous than me. You have a prize guy right here beside you,' John joked, but Sarah could tell he was perhaps a tiny bit jealous.

'Oh, I *know* that, believe me. Nobody could hold a candle to you, my darling.'

'And I am so glad he makes my sister happy. She looked on cloud nine, didn't she?'

'She did indeed,' Sarah said. But a heavy feeling settled in her chest when she remembered Lucy's tears and she worried about exactly what Corbin was up to when he went off 'to think'.

# Chapter Twenty-Five

Barringtons had more baby clothes than you could shake a stick at according to Ella. Why anyone would want to go into a department store armed with a stick and shake it at items of small people's clothing was beyond Sarah, but she'd agreed to meet her sister there for coffee and a browse.

Four days before Christmas and anyone would think it was the last few hours of Christmas Eve. The traffic leading to the shopping mall crawled along inch by inch and Sarah drummed her fingers on the wheel and looked at her watch for the third time. Twenty minutes to cover a mile. Why had she allowed Ella to persuade her to come? Instead of this madness she could be at home right now with her feet up watching *It's a Wonderful Life* and stuffing her face with mince pies and perhaps even a teeny-weeny sherry.

Throughout the pregnancy Sarah had craved her red wine, but had resisted valiantly. But a sherry wouldn't be so bad, would it? Just a very miniscule one that you could hardly see with the naked eye? She decided that, yes, it would be fine and she'd have one as soon as she got back. Sarah rolled her eyes at the procession of cars in front. *If* she ever got back.

If the traffic on the way to the mall had been bad, the traffic of bodies inside was even worse. Through fake snow, past giant Santas and Rudolphs festooned with a trillion fairy lights, people rushed hither and thither, misery hanging on some faces, anxiety on others, various packages shoved under arms, carrier bags clutched in death-grips. And all the while in the background, a continuous barrage of Christmas songs assaulted their ears and pummelled their brains into mush.

'If I hear Andy Williams telling me "it's the most wonderful time of the year" once more, I swear I'll scream,' Sarah hissed in Ella's ear as they fought their way past elbows and harassed faces from the till past the end of the coffee queue and into the seating area.

'Me, too,' Ella groaned, sliding their tray onto the last available table in the place, jammed up against the wall. 'Why does everyone look so bloody miserable?'

'Because,' Sarah shrugged her coat off and squeezed into a seat, 'they have been stuck in traffic for three days to get to a place they don't want to be, to buy stuff they can't afford, have no idea if their purchases will fill their loved one's hearts with delight or revulsion, and are all wishing they were at home with their damned feet up.'

'Ooh, get you, Mrs Bah-Humbug.' Ella pulled her tongue out at Sarah and took a sip of her cappuccino.

'I am allowed to be bah-humbuggish. I'm pregnant, tired and hungry.' Hot mince pie and cream steamed in the dish on the table and she attacked it with her spoon as if it had personally affronted her in some way. 'Oh dats budder,' she managed between mouthfuls.

'Dad's butter? What are you on about?' Ella chortled and tucked into her own and a contented silence punctuated only by a few slurps and mms fell over the table for a few moments. 'So did you get chance to find out more about the unfeasibly sexy Corbin when you chatted with Lucy the other day?'

'Yep. I found out that he *is* unfeasibly sexy. He has to make love with Lucy four times a day or he gets grouchy.' Sarah burped and took a swig of coffee. 'She never says no because he's such a good lover she can't resist him, even when she's knackered.'

Ella's eyes grew round and she practically dribbled onto

the table. 'Oh my God, really?'

Sometimes Ella was so gullible. 'No, you daft mare. The conversation didn't include their sex life – strange that, considering I have known her for all of an hour or so.'

'Oh, but he is SO hot. I would do it four times a day if I were his wife ... five maybe,' Ella mumbled into her cup.

'Well, you aren't his wife, you're Jason's. And behave!' Sarah laughed.

'A woman can dream, can't she?'

Pie finished, Sarah felt a small flutter of hello from one of the babies which reminded her of a few questions she'd been going to ask Ella. Last year when she'd gone back to 1874 Kansas she'd had to pretend that she knew all about childbirth because the 1874 Sarah had been a mother to Artie and was helping Martha, Sarah's sister, to give birth without pain relief a month early on the dirt floor in the middle of nowhere. She had managed somehow, with help from her memory of a *Casualty* episode where a woman had given birth on a train after it had crashed, but it had been tough and Martha had really gone through it.

How Martha's mother had given birth to twelve in those conditions she'd never know. Tragically the woman *had* died giving birth to the twelfth, but Sarah imagined that if she'd had to do it, she'd have trouble having even one without the latest pain relief or medical help. Even with all the help and twenty-first century medical technology that would be available to her with the twins, she was secretly pooping her pants. Martha's red-face streaked with dirt, eyes bright with pain and veins straining in her neck kept surfacing every time she thought of it, so she just pushed the whole idea out of her mind.

'Penny for 'em?' Ella had finished her pie too and was looking at her curiously.

'Er ... nothing really.' Sarah thought that she'd sound like a wimp if she spoke her fears out loud. She had thought she'd just ask Ella a few questions about childbirth in a bright and breezy type of way, but was scared that panic in her voice would reveal her fears.

'Come on, it's me you're talking to.'

'Okay ... I was just a bit curious about the actual birth thing. The ante-natal classes are helpful but I thought you might have a better idea having had Angelica not that long ago.' Good. Her voice sounded normal.

'You were wondering if it is hell on wheels and you're pooping your pants, right?'

Hmm, Ella saw straight through her. 'Yeah. And about pooping ... I knew a woman who ...' Then she stopped because she was scared that she was turning into Harry.

Ella raised her hands and said in a New York accent. 'That's the least of your worries, hon. By the end of it you will be begging them to kill you.' She laughed out loud at Sarah's horrified expression. 'Just joking, you'll be fine. I had gas and air and pethidine. It hurt like hell at the time, fifteen hours in total, but my baby was so worth it. And it's true what they say; you can't remember it after a while.'

Fifteen hours of pain isn't what Sarah really wanted to hear but she was grateful her sister was being honest. And *she* was having twins, so it would be 'no picnic' as Gwen had said the other day.

'Right ... and the poo thing? It doesn't bother me so much about the midwife seeing, it's—'

'John seeing? Yep, I can understand that. I was lucky enough to feel sick the whole day so didn't eat much – no poo ... unless Jason was just telling me what I wanted to hear. But if you do, you do. He'll just have to be brave and look the other way.' Ella grinned, an evil twinkle in her eye.

After another struggle through the crowded mall they emerged into the car park with armfuls of packages, parcels and misery writ large on their faces.

'Thank God that's over. Why on earth did I let you persuade me to come out here today?' Ella quipped and ducked Sarah's scutch across the head. 'At least I have all these gawgeous baby clothes to drool over when I get home. I think I might be getting a tad clucky.'

'Just think about the fifteen hours,' Sarah said in the New York accent. 'That'll cool your jets, honey-pie.'

The two parted company and then Sarah sat in the snail race for another hour, a journey that normally would have taken half that. By the time she swung the car into her driveway she was contemplating a vat of sherry – only in her dreams, of course. Then she saw Lucy and Corbin's car parked at the side of the cottage. Her heart sank. Of course she'd like to see more of them, but right now she just wanted to relax.

Still, she thought as she stepped over the threshold, at least she might get to find out more about what made Corbin tick.

'Oh, there you are!' John said, throwing his hands up. 'Lucy and Corbin are just off. I tried to ring you a few times but kept getting voicemail.'

'Really?' Sarah scrabbled around in her handbag for her mobile and found that she had somehow managed to switch the damned thing off. 'Oh, what a shame to have missed you. Mind you, even if the phone had been on I couldn't have just popped back home as the traffic is nightmarish.'

'Not to worry, love,' Lucy said, stepping forward and giving her a peck on the cheek. 'We just dropped by unannounced to ask if you had any idea about what Gwen would like for Christmas. We don't know her well enough to just have a stab.'

'A stab? How very violent. You English are so, how you say, "eccentrict" about the terms you use.' Corbin grinned and flashed his dimply stubble at Sarah.

'I guess it is. I'd never thought about it before and it's eccentric – no T.' Sarah smiled back, thinking that Ella would have probably melted into a puddle by now if she was here.

'We *had* thought some nice perfume, but of course we don't know her favourite and Dad is hopeless at that kind of thing.'

Lucy slipped her arm around Corbin as he leaned up against the kitchen sink and he looked down at her adoringly. Sarah could see it was genuine and most of the rest of the fifteen minutes or so they were all chatting together, he rarely looked at anyone else.

Just as they were about to go, John drew Lucy to one side and said in a stage whisper, 'I need to borrow you a minute, top secret Christmas stuff.' He winked at Sarah and ushered his sister into the living room.

'Alone at last,' Corbin said and chuckled to himself. Although he was obviously joking, Sarah gave her nervous laugh, felt a flush creeping up her neck and pretended to pick something off her fluffy pink jumper … now in serious competition with her face. Not the fluffy bit, well at least she hoped not. It was her own fault she was embarrassed, saying those daft things about him to Ella.

'So, let's get to know each other a little, Sarah. Tell me, do you like your job?' Corbin stroked his chin, his bright blue eyes searching hers. It was a perfectly reasonable opener if a little stilted, but somehow there seemed to be an underlying question that made her feel uncomfortable.

'I do, yes. I'm glad I reduced my hours though, it can be very stressful.' She shifted in her seat and for some reason best known to her jumpy fingers flicked the edge of a Christmas card on the table. It collapsed and would have skittered onto the floor if Corbin hadn't shot out a strong capable hand to catch it.

'Stressful? Yes, I can definitely relate to that. But, oh so rewarding too.' He nodded and gave her a wide smile. Then he leaned forward and frowned slightly. 'You seem a little stressed now, no? A good job I was here to, er, *save* your lovely card.'

Save the card, an odd word to use. It would hardly have shattered into a million pieces would it, for goodness sake?

'I'm not stressed, Corbin, just a bit tired.' Sarah cringed at the high-pitched tone of denial someone had obviously slipped into her voice when she wasn't looking.

He looked less than convinced and remained silent. He then continued to remain silent and just stare at her across the table as if he was having some telepathic connection with her brain. If he was, she knew nothing about the conversation. What the hell was wrong with him? After a few more moments of the silent treatment, the tick of the kitchen clock became deafening and she could stand it no longer. Either she excused herself and scuttled off, or she grew some balls.

'You said you can relate to the stresses and rewards of teaching, Corbin. Do you have experience of it?' She levelled a calm look somewhere over his left shoulder – looking into his eyes was very disconcerting, he seemed to have this knack of making her feel as if he knew something she didn't. She sniffed and leaned back in her chair.

A slow smile curled his lips and her eyes were pulled back to his. The hairs on the back of her neck began to rise as he leaned forward again and said in a near whisper, 'Teaching, Sarah? I didn't think—'

'Righty-ho, let's leave these two folk to the rest of their afternoon, Corby.' Lucy breezed in and patted her husband on the shoulder.

He pushed his chair back and raised a hand in farewell to John and Sarah.

Damn it. Why had Lucy picked that moment? Sarah would never know what he'd been about to say now.

'See you both soon. Have a lovely rest, Sarah. Don't get stressed about the job.'

John frowned at her and put his head on one side. Sarah dismissed his concern with a quick shake of her own. 'I'm not stressed at the moment. Corbin must have missed something in translation.'

Corbin ignored that and followed his wife out of the door. He stopped halfway down the path, pulled a rolled up newspaper from his back pocket, ran back and placed it in Sarah's hand. 'Sorry, I was flicking through your paper earlier and stuffed it in my jeans by mistake. Lots of interesting articles. Au revoir!'

A nice cup of coffee and yet another mince pie later, Sarah was feeling more like herself. John was in the kitchen making a hearty stew for dinner, and *White Christmas* was on the box. You couldn't get much better than that, eh? It was a damned sight better than fighting your way through the shopping mall, endless traffic and then having strange conversations with enigmatic French guys.

Sarah was in full flow singing along to the *Sisters* song and then yet another commercial break advertising last minute bargains loud enough to explode her eardrums broke the mood of 1950s Hollywood. Why did the adverts always have to be so loud? Did the promoters think people were deaf, stupid or both? Sarah knew one thing; the obvious increase in volume to grab the viewer's attention did just the opposite in her book. She grabbed the remote and punched mute.

'Want a cuppa, love?' John shouted from the kitchen.

'Oh, yes p—' Sarah's words stuck in her throat as the title and opening paragraph of an article caught her eye in the paper that Corbin had handed her. With trembling fingers she picked it up from the cushion next to her and read:

## The Oldest Woman in Britain Celebrates
## her 113th Birthday

Ex-schoolteacher, Mrs Veronica Thomas (nee Ratchet), last week proved that not all teachers tend to die earlier than those in other professions. She believes that the secret of her longevity is a lively interest in history, the world around her and to help others when she can. 'I think that the survival of humanity depends upon the love of our fellow man and woman and a healthy respect for the past and the sacrifices people have made over the ages for others. If one doesn't remember the lessons of the past with clarity, how can one progress with any kind of confidence to the future?' Mrs Thomas commented yesterday. It is clear that her great age has certainly not dulled her sharp mind or muted her articulate speech – a fantastic role model for young and old alike.

Underneath the copy was a photograph of an old lady propped up in bed surrounded by nursing staff that were smiling and raising glasses of champagne to the camera. The old lady had a long angular face, haystack white hair, and amongst a face of many wrinkles, a faded mole and two lively dark eyes. A ghost of a smile played over her lips as one of the staff held a glass of champagne to them.

'Did you say yes please?' John stepped through the door holding the kettle, then stopped when he saw the shock on her face. 'You okay, love?'

With a heart tattooing a tom-tom in her chest, all Sarah could do was to point at the article and do the goldfish act.

John handed her the kettle and picked up the paper. After a few seconds his mouth dropped open too. 'Bloody Norah, she's still alive!'

'I know, I can't believe it.' Sarah's hand fluttered to her head where an idea thrust itself forward. 'Where is that nursing home, John?'

'Southampton. Looks like she stayed in her home town all these years.'

'Right, well it's not *that* far away. Tomorrow's Sunday, I could get a train and—'

John lowered the paper and frowned at her. 'Hang on. There is no way, I mean absolutely *no way* you are visiting her tomorrow.'

'I think you'll find I am.' Sarah folded her arms and stuck out her chin.

John waggled his finger in front of her face. 'Er, hello. It's just before Christmas, snow is forecast so you might get stuck there, it IS that far away ... *and* you are pregnant!'

'As if I have forgotten any of that, John. Look, it will be fine. I'm not asking you to come, I can go on my own.' Sarah stood, put her arms around his neck and gazed earnestly into his eyes. 'Don't you see that I have to go? It's a sign that Corbin handed me the paper folded to that page. If he hadn't, I wouldn't have seen it. You know I don't read papers much.'

John sighed. 'But what if you get snowed in? You'll miss Christmas and everything.'

'I won't. I can feel it in me water.' Sarah smiled. She couldn't, of course, but she knew she had to go, something almost physical was pulling her to Veronica.

John looked at her for a while, a far away expression on his face as if weighing up the pros and cons, then he said, 'Well, if you are determined to go, I'm determined to take you. We'll drive down tomorrow morning and be back by tomorrow night, probably a seven hour round trip – take it or leave it.'

'I'll take it!' she squealed, jumping up and down, her heart full of excitement. 'My God, I never thought I'd set eyes on the old trout ever again, and now I'll see her tomorrow. It's like a bloody miracle!'

'It'll be a bloody miracle if we get there and back without any problems,' John grouched. 'But it is pretty marvellous, I have to admit.'

'Oh, John, did I ever tell you that you are the—'

'Bestest husband in the whole wide world? Yes, yes you did.' He grinned and kissed her.

# Chapter Twenty-Six

It wouldn't hurt to check the oil again. Just like the tyres, the water and the lights, the oil was about to get the once over ... for the third time. Some might call him anal. He would call himself sensible. Better safe than sorry on long journeys, especially at this time of year. Holding the dipstick up to the light, John was satisfied that everything was as it should be. He still didn't like the idea of haring off to Southampton, but Sarah's mind was made and there was no point trying to talk her round.

The bonnet slammed down for the last time and he walked out of the garage before he could open it again to do more checks. Now that really would be anal. Hugging himself against the cold he looked out over the landscape. Just past eight in the morning the hills and vales were just revealing their curves to him like some timid lover on a hot date. The moon was still up and the cobalt sky seemed reluctant to shuffle off to Bedfordshire, even though it was being valiantly shoved over by the silver-grey of a winter dawn.

Tipping back his head he looked up at the scatter of fading stars and sniffed the air. Though John said so himself, he was a genius at assessing the weather ... nope. He sniffed again, his built in snow detector was showing negative. That didn't mean it wouldn't snow today, just not in the next few hours. A memory crept over the dry stone wall and took him unawares – his mum shoving him out the door one summer morning with an umbrella in one hand and a bathing costume in the other. 'Right, which one do I take on holiday, my little weather man?' she'd asked, then laughed as he held up the brolly. 'Typical!'

Christmas, summer holidays, weddings, all had a Mum

shaped hole in them. John missed her all year round, but at special times, family times, memories of her weighed bittersweet in his heart. When Harry had announced that Gwen had accepted his hand the other night, he of course was happy for him, but just like Sarah, he wished it could have been different. He hadn't let on to her how much it had hurt because he wanted her to be happy, but it had and it did. Gwen was a fine woman, none finer, but she wasn't Mum and never would be. One day he was sure it would become easier, but today, as his mum stood laughing at him holding that brolly out on the lawn in that long ago summer, her head of auburn curls tipped back, her freckled face turned up to the sun, the pain was as real and as raw as the day she'd died.

The smell of toast replaced the pungent winter crispness in his nostrils and he blew a kiss to the heavens, shook off the past and went into the cottage. Inside, Sarah still in her dressing gown was running around the kitchen like an insect with a colourful behind, buttering toast, pouring tea, fishing out boiled eggs from the pan and generally flapping in the usual Sarah kind of way.

'Car's ready, no more than twenty minutes and we must get off.' John calculated that his brisk manner would send her into more of a flap, and he needed a chuckle.

'Twenty minutes?' Sarah spun round and glared at him. 'We haven't had breakfast yet and I'm running late having not slept a wink all night wondering what Veronica might say at us just turning up unannounced. It might be too much for her.' Sarah licked butter from her fingers. 'I mean she *is* one hundred and thirteen years old.'

'Calm down, woman, we don't want the twins born just yet … and I could stretch the time of departure to half an hour.' John laughed and tucked into his egg.

'So, do you think it might be too much for her?' Sarah sat opposite and took a bite of toast.

'You kidding? Old Ratchet sounds brighter than a brass button if that quote in the paper is anything to go by. She'll be over the moon to see us ... well, you.'

Sarah had said last night that it might be a good idea if John was just to pop his head round to pay his respects but then leave Sarah and Veronica alone.

'Are you all right about not staying, love?' Sarah said, putting her hand on his. 'It's just that she was always a bit scared of you, I think. You know you *were* the one in touch with the scary powers and in charge of sending her back to a war zone.'

He was totally fine about it, but for some reason he was in a very devilish mood today. 'To tell you the truth, hon, I do feel a bit left out of it all. I mean there I'll be stuck in a dingy cafe or something after driving all that way and there you'll be having a whale of a time reminiscing about the exciting adventures of 1979 and 1941.' He pouted and knitted his eyebrows together. His face refused to stay in that position however as she looked at him aghast.

'Bloody hell, John, I thought you were serious for the moment,' Sarah growled and threw a crust at him. This turned his smirk into a burst of laughter.

'Yes, I gathered that when your face looked as if somebody had stuck something up your ar—'

'Okay, enough of your tomfoolery, we have to be off. Don't you think you need to check the oil again while I'm getting dressed? You can't be too careful, you know.' Sarah licked her finger, drew it down the air and flounced off.

Thirty miles to go. John looked at the clock on the dashboard. 12:40, not bad going if he did say so himself. He glanced at Sarah dozing next to him and felt a sudden rush of panic. Whenever they had been in contact with old Ratchet, things had gone wrong. What if something awful happened today? What if Ratchet was about to croak and grabbed Sarah's arm as she did so? That would be one trip that he wouldn't be able to rescue his wife from. A shiver ran down his back. There was no way Sarah was holding the old bat's hand today and he'd make sure she promised him.

Then he sighed and told himself not to be so daft. It was just his protective side coming out, it was normal to feel like that about Sarah; particularly now she was having their babies. She'd be fine. The Spindly Ones had okayed the meeting last night, apparently they weren't worried that Veronica would alarm anyone if she let slip that she'd been visited by a time-traveller, because who would believe the ramblings of someone of her age anyway?

And they surely wouldn't let anything untoward happen to Sarah, not now, not after everything else.

Sarah opened her eyes and gave him a little smile. Yep. They were going to have a brilliant Christmas. He had a great present for her. Lucy had helped him book a pampering spa weekend for them both in the New Year – just the thing for pregnant women and their partners apparently. They had all their family around them, the twins would be here in a few months or so, and Sarah had hung up her stitching shoes. At first he had been a little sad when she'd told him of that decision, but he totally understood why. And now he was pleased that she had. They would feel more like a normal family – well, normalish, as he would still be needling – and they would all live happily ever after with roses around the door and so forth as his dad would say.

'Nearly there?' Sarah yawned and stretched her arms above her head.

'GPS says half an hour, and I agree.'

'Thanks for doing this, John.' She ran her fingers over the dark hairs on his forearm. 'I know you didn't want to.'

'Nope, but I guess it will be okay. But you must promise

it will be two hours, tops, and then we must get back. My nose tells me we will have snow before the night is out.'

'Yes, sir, Cap'n. We can't afford to ignore a snout with such clout.' Sarah giggled.

'You saying I have a big nose?'

'Nope, just a sensitive one ... like its owner.'

'Hmm. And, Sarah.' He swallowed. He wasn't going to say anything but he couldn't help it. 'You won't hold on to her hand or hug her for long, will you? Because last time—'

'Oh, please. I hardly think she'll be taken on a mission at her age, John.' Sarah rolled her eyes.

'Neither do I, but just be careful, eh?' John just received a withering look in response. But he couldn't shake the sense of foreboding he had about the meeting.

In the end John decided he'd stay in the car outside the imposing red brick Victorian building, once a merchant's house, now The Harbour View Residential Home. He couldn't see the point in going in really and both of them popping up out of the blue might just confuse Veronica. It would also lengthen their stay and that was not a good idea.

As Sarah walked towards the reception she guessed that the truth was he just didn't want to see Veronica as she had been part of all the 'Cross Stitch malarkey' that had caused so much trouble for them. But Sarah had seen another side to her, grew to like her and in the end Veronica had been caught up in the whole thing just as much as she herself. The powers were to blame, nobody else.

'I'm here to see Mrs Veronica Thomas,' Sarah told the receptionist, putting on her most dazzling smile reserved for such occasions. She expected that there might be a problem getting in to see Veronica, waltzing in just like that, but they hadn't phoned to make an appointment yesterday as that might well have set the cat amongst the pigeons. Veronica could have been thrown into shock and told the staff that Sarah was a Stitch and all about her, and then they would have thought she had been tipped over the edge by a visit and consequently decide that it might be for the best not to let Sarah come.

The receptionist smiled back. 'Are you a relative? We don't have a record of anyone coming today.'

'Not really. But I am her oldest friend's great-granddaughter. Her dying wish was that I visit Veronica every Christmas until she herself ... you know.' Sarah pointed to the ceiling and sighed.

'Ah, right, okay. I'll just pop along and ask if she'll see you. She has been feeling a bit tired lately, not surprising at her age. Who shall I say is calling?'

Sarah watched the receptionist bustle down the corridor and open a door. A few seconds later a shriek accompanied the woman's hurried exit and she beckoned Sarah forward. 'I've never seen her so excited! She can't wait to see you,' she said as Sarah dashed over.

Once inside the receptionist closed the door behind her and Sarah looked over to the bed in the middle of the bright and airy room. Veronica, dressed in a yellow flannelette nightdress scattered with blue butterflies, held her trembling hand out to Sarah, a huge smile banishing the weight of ages from her face. Sarah stepped forward and took her hand which felt paper dry and as light as down. Then she sat on the bed and hugged her gently, feeling Veronica's frail form shaking with excitement. If John could see her he'd have a coronary.

'Well, if it isn't Sarah Needler. You took your time, madam.' Veronica grinned holding Sarah at arm's length. 'I expected you last week for my birthday!' Her voice was more or less the same, but quavery and it had lost the imperious tone.

Sarah shook her head. 'You haven't changed much, still

demanding, eh? And I wouldn't have been here at all if I hadn't managed to see an article about you in the paper.'

'I know. I'm a bit cross with my grandson for not just telling you outright, but he thought you might just be too freaked out by it all – you being in the family way. So he left it to chance.'

Perhaps she had become confused after all, Sarah decided. She wasn't making much sense, but then what did she expect? At least she seemed to recognise her. 'You have a grandson? That's nice.' Sarah hoped she didn't sound too patronising.

'Yes, and he's lovely, don't you agree? All the staff here were practically falling over themselves when he came for my birthday – just indecent.'

'I'm sure he must be lovely, has to be with a gran like you, eh?'

'What do you mean, "must be"?' Veronica's sharp dark eyes twinkled mischievously. 'You met him the other day. Lucy's a perfect match for him, don't you think? She came with him for my birthday.'

Everything Veronica said suddenly made sense. But that was crazy, surely. 'Corbin, Corbin is your—'

'At last you get it!' Veronica laughed. 'He is indeed my grandson. He's the age that a great-grandson would be for those folk who have babies at a more orthodox age, but I started a bit late. Edward and I had our first child, Malcolm, when I was forty-four and a daughter, Evelyn, when I was almost forty-six! We took a while, but we did it! Thanks to your little pep talk, I soon got over my worries about sex and so trying was such fun!'

'My goodness, that's fantastic!' Sarah said, hardly able to get her head around the whole thing.

'It was. We had been trying for ages and at one point thought it would never happen, but great things come to those who wait. Evelyn married a French man and moved to

Calais. Of course her dad and I were sad to see her go, but she was so happy and we saw her quite often. And you'll never guess what?' Veronica leaned forward and fixed her eyes on Sarah's. 'The guy she married, Corbin's dad, was called Marcel Aiguille ... Aigulle is French for needle.'

The hairs on Sarah's forearms prickled and her heart thumped up the scale. Surely Veronica wasn't saying ... that was impossible ... wasn't it? Veronica watched the penny hesitantly drop in Sarah's brain. 'You mean ...?'

'Yes, Marcel was a Needler, and Corbin took after his dad! He has been doing it for about twelve years, since he was eighteen. Very good he is too. Lucy's in the dark about it. The powers told Corbin early on in their relationship about her mum, dad and brother, plus the fact that she wanted nothing to do with stitching and all. So he decided not to tell her. She was always saying to him that she wanted a down to earth man and so on.'

Sarah was listening to Veronica's words but they weren't sinking in, just lining up along the quicksand that had become logical reason in her consciousness.

'But in the end, surrounded by so many bloomin' time folk, I think she might find out and come round to the idea after all.' Veronica cocked her head to one side. 'Shame you've packed it up, my dear.'

A few words sank beneath the surface, and then a few more. 'So *that's* what Corbin is up to when he goes missing,' Sarah said breathlessly.

'Yes. The reason they missed your wedding was because Corbin went back to the time of the Russian Revolution to rescue a Stitch and got stuck with the mad monk Rasputin! He put some kind of mesmerising spell on him and he couldn't function as a Needle. Luckily the spell wore off and he was back the day after. A right pickle and no mistake.'

'But ... but it seems too fantastic to believe. Another

Needle in the family *and* he's your grandson ...' Sarah's words ran out and she began to feel quite faint.

'You okay, Sarah?'

Sarah grasped the edge of the quilt and shook her head, no.

'Here, sniff these.' Veronica thrust a small round brown bottle at her face.

Sarah was aware of a peppery coal-tarey smell almost singeing her nasal hairs, and a moment later she was back to normal. 'Bloody hell, Veronica. What the hell was that?'

'No finer thing than Smelling Salts to clear the senses. Here, do you want them? I have lots more that I once whipped from an apothecary in the 1850s. Don't make stuff like that any more.'

Sarah held up her hand. 'Er, no thanks, they are probably lethal and unsafe for public consumption ... especially pregnant public.' She gave Veronica a withering look.

'You always did fuss too much.' Veronica chuckled and gave Sarah a warm smile. 'It is so great to see you after all this time, my dear.'

Sarah smiled back. 'You, too. And I mean if that were not enough, you go and spring the Corbin thing. It just seems too much of a coincidence, doesn't it? Lucy, daughter and sister of a Needle and a Mum who was a Stitch, marrying a Needle who just happens to be your grandson? Do you think the Spindly Ones had a hand in it ... and if they did, why?'

'I wondered that. But in the end I have to say I really don't know. Stranger things have happened in life, as we both know with our mad existences. And might I say I thought you were brilliant in 1955.' Veronica's eyes were full of respect. 'But you could say that there is no such thing as coincidence ... that "reality is an elaborate fabric of interlinking and overlapping experiences, the pattern of which we can only glimpse in small sections".'

'Blimey, Veronica, did you make that up?'

'No, my favourite author, Dean Koontz, did. He wrote to me a few times, you know.'

Sarah's mind boggled further and then an idea hit her like a lightning bolt. 'So apart from saving little Barbara when I came to help you find Edward in 1941, it wasn't a personal favour after all, was it? If I hadn't helped you get him out of that house with the gas leak, that would have been the end. So if you hadn't married him, you wouldn't have had Evelyn and she wouldn't have married a Needle and wouldn't have had Corbin. Therefore loads of lives wouldn't have been saved in the future!'

Veronica nodded and smiled. 'I can only imagine that's the top and bottom of it, Sarah. Whatever the truth, I'm glad that our two families are linked. It gives me great comfort to know that you will be part of my grandchild and great-grandchildren's lives, even if I can't be.'

Sarah decided she was glad about that too, but one or two trillion questions buzzed round her head like wasps at a picnic. 'How come you know so much about my life – the 1955 trip, the wedding and all?'

'Well, the latter is down to Corbin. He has visited me a few times and until recently, before I started feeling my age, I used to go over to stay with my daughter. Corbin and I email lots too.'

'You know how to email, at a hundred and thirteen?' Sarah blurted. Her own mother had taken ages to get the hang of it.

Veronica narrowed her eyes and puffed out her chest – the old Ratchet was back for a moment or two. 'Yes, why not? Don't be so ready to write off us older folk.'

'I'm not. Just really bloody impressed!' Sarah laughed. Older folk – she doubted there were other older folk in the country.

A satisfied nod of the head and a smile returned Ratchet

to Veronica. She looked at Sarah sidelong and smoothed out her quilt with long ivory fingers. 'Of course the Spindlies keep me informed of most things nowadays too. I email and ask them about how Corbin's doing and you and John, of course. By the way, ask him to pop his head round before you leave. I *have* overcome my fear of him, you know.'

Sarah could tell by the knowing twinkle in her eye that she realised exactly why John had chosen to stay away today. That both alarmed and astounded her. 'How in the name of all that is holy, to quote you when we first met, did you know?'

'That's not all. I have been expecting you for a while, just got it out by a few days. I *know* lots of things. Must be a combination of my great age and stitching, perhaps I have developed an extra sense? The Spindlies agreed to tell me things because they have decided that I have earned my metaphorical stitching medal. I was doing it right up to the grand old age of seventy. I now realise I was but a lass.' She gave a wheezy chuckle. 'Anyway, they more or less forced me to retire, but I have my finger on the pulse still.'

'You certainly seem to have, yes,' Sarah said, bewildered at the amount of crazy information whirling around her brain.

'Right, Corbin said that I wasn't to get you too frazzled.' Veronica patted Sarah's bump. 'Not with you in your condition ... so let's talk of the old days, eh?'

'The old days for you, only a short while ago for me. That in itself is just mad, isn't it?' Sarah marvelled.

The receptionist, Pam, brought tea and biscuits and for the next hour they reminisced about how they met, Gerry and the 1979 trip, the 1941 trip, and laughed awkwardly about the way Veronica had inadvertently been part of ruining Sarah's wedding, and then almost came to blows with Wesley when she'd managed to get into Sarah's school. Now, of course, Veronica was truly mortified at her behaviour. She apparently had learned a lot about positive relationships in the classroom since then.

'However, I do still think teachers need to be a bit more assertive than they are. Children need to know who the grown up is, you know?' she said, sticking her chin out.

Then the talk turned to Veronica's marriage and life with Edward and her long and esteemed stitching career. Sarah discovered that Edward had never known about it, apparently he wouldn't have coped.

'Edward was a down to earth meat and potatoes man. Luckily I never got into a pickle like poor Corbin, and Teddy spent most of his time at work or at the allotment, so he never wondered where I'd popped off to.'

'But weren't you ever missing overnight?' Sarah wondered.

'Yes, of course. But he was increasingly deaf as he got older and once his head touched the pillow he was out like the proverbial. I didn't return to it until after the kids were in their early teens, so no worries about them waking and finding me gone at unusual times.'

Sarah helped herself to another chocolate biscuit. 'That was lucky then. I won't have that worry as my two will be in "the business" so they tell me.'

'Yes, so I hear. How marvellous! That was why your travelling went tits up and why we ended up crossing paths in the first place, wasn't it?'

An explosion of laughter burst from Sarah's lips and half the biscuit ended up back on the plate. 'I never expected you to just come out with that phrase, even though you found it so funny before,' Sarah spluttered.

Veronica squawked 'You'd be surprised how I have mellowed over the years. I have been known to say bugger sometimes!'

'You little tinker.' Sarah grinned. 'But tell me, didn't Evelyn ever wonder what Marcel was up to? And Corbin?'

'No. Marcel was a travelling salesman – a perfect job to fit with "the business". And Corbin was already at university and away from home when he started. I had wanted to confide in her but she's very much like her dad in temperament and there seemed little point in upsetting her. The powers weren't too keen either, of course.'

All too soon Veronica became visibly tired and John texted Sarah to tell her time was up. She asked him to pop his head round, which he duly did and was rewarded with a huge warm hug and kiss from the previously prudish Miss Ratchet.

'Might I say you are looking remarkably well for a woman of your years?' John flattered.

'You might indeed. And may I say what a pleasure it is to be hugged by a fine virile specimen such as yourself?' Veronica chuckled wickedly and Sarah hid a smirk at John's red face.

'Two minutes, Sarah. I want to beat the snow, okay?' John patted Veronica's hand and left them alone to say their final goodbyes.

'Sarah, open that drawer in the bedside cabinet, would you?' Veronica asked, dabbing tears away from her eyes with a lace hanky. 'Gawd look at me, I promised myself I wouldn't get all wussy.'

In the drawer Sarah found a small box shaped package wrapped in red shiny Christmas paper and an envelope addressed to her. She held them up to Veronica questioningly. 'These?'

'Yes. You aren't to open them until Christmas day. Make sure you open the gift before the letter. And don't ring to thank me or anything. You'll understand why when you read the letter. I'm not very good at saying things that mean a lot to me, face to face.'

It was clear by the tremor in her voice that she was barely

259

holding it together and Sarah felt a huge lump of emotion rise and lodge in her own throat.

'Thank you, Veronica. I came here in such a rush that I didn't think to bring anything for—'

Veronica flapped her hanky. 'Don't be ridiculous, woman. You just being here was worth all the presents in the world. Thank you *so* much for coming and I wish you every happiness for the future, my dear.'

Sarah sat on the bed and hugged her again. Her heart was so full it left no room for any words she might have wanted to say.

'Now go to that lovely husband of yours. I don't want you getting stuck in the snow.'

Sarah stood and walked to the door. She opened it and then gave Veronica a little smile and a wave. Old Horse Face, Ratchet Features and other names Sarah had given to her when she'd been a fierce old crow at the beginning, had become Veronica, a compassionate and worthy Stitch whose lively spirit was now waving back at her from behind the eyes of a frail old lady.

'Bye, Veronica. It's been grand meeting up again,' Sarah managed.

'That it has, my dear. Now run along.'

Sarah waved once more and closed the door behind her.

# Chapter Twenty-Seven

John drew curtains back on a perfect white Christmas morning. Well, it should have been perfect but Sarah seemed intent on ruining it. Since their return from Southampton two days ago, the snow had come down heavily – along with Sarah's mood. She hadn't been herself at all. She mooched about, kept shaking the gift box from Veronica, holding the letter up to the light, and yesterday had asked him if he thought she should open it early. When he said she should stick by Veronica's wishes, she'd sighed and scrunched up her face.

Though he had been thankful that Veronica hadn't whisked Sarah away to beyond the grave when they'd visited, his sense of foreboding about the meeting hadn't been wrong. Old Ratchet's incredible revelations had really put the damned cat amongst the pigeons. Once he was over the shock of it all, he and Sarah had batted back and forth an argument about the pros and cons of getting Corbin to tell Lucy about 'the business' and he had been dead against it. Sarah hadn't been, and desperately wanted Lucy to be put out of her misery. Of course he wanted his sister to be happy, but John wanted nothing to do with sticking his nose in her private affairs. It was their business, not his and Sarah's.

The sun broke through a cloud and cast a wintery sparkle over the snow-clad hills. The Murray's farm three fields away stood out red against the white and smoke puffed from it's chimney into a sky growing ever bluer. A pair of robins hopped along the fence fluffing their feathers and in the distance church bells began to peal Christmas greetings to the village. It was real traditional Christmas card scene, one that lifted the heart and invigorated the spirit, but his wife wasn't here to share it.

261

Upon waking, John had stretched his hand but found that her side of the bed was already cold. He let the curtain fall back into place and set out to see what she was up to. A heavy sigh left him as he walked downstairs. Why couldn't things have just gone on nicely without all this upset? They had both been looking so forward to this Christmas and now ...

'Merry Christmas, my darling!' Sarah, wreathed in smiles, held her arms open to him as she sat by the fire next to the Christmas tree.

John stood by the door pleasantly surprised, but a little puzzled, at her transformation in mood. She jumped up, gave a little shiver and wrapped her dressing gown more closely around her. 'Come on, open your presents. I have managed three cups of tea waiting for you, my lazy bones.'

John stepped forward and into her embrace. 'Why, what time is it?'

'Eight-thirty. I have been up since six, but then I always was over-excited at Christmas.' She gave him a big kiss and hugged him again.

'You certainly seem a lot more cheerful than you have been for the last few days.' John sat on the sofa and rubbed his eyes.

'I am. And that's because I have sorted my head out – thanks to Veronica's brilliant present and letter.' She looked at him and grinned. 'Mind you, it's a good job you weren't up when I opened it. I cried buckets.'

Oh great, what the hell had the old witch given her? 'Right ... good, I think.'

'It is good, honestly nothing to worry about. Here read the letter while I make you a lovely breakfast.' She handed it to him on her way out. Then she popped her head back round the door. 'And we have to be at Mum's for one-ish, so I think we should get Lucy and Corbin round before that ... oh and look at what's in the box before you read the letter. It's on the arm of the chair.'

Getting Corbin and Lucy round? They never agreed to that. What the hell was Sarah on? Still, at least she was a cheerful little soul at the moment. John sighed, grabbed the box and shook out the letter. Taking the box in his fingers he slowly prized up the lid. It was a brown leather box, battered with age and he worried that the flimsy hinge might snap. Nestled against a black velvet cushion was the beautiful diamante conch brooch that Veronica had worn when they had first met her, the brooch that Sarah had adored, the one that Edward had given to his sweetheart before the war, the one Sarah had told him Veronica had worn on her wedding day. Wow, no wonder Sarah had cried. It must have been a wrench for Veronica to give something as precious as that away.

John put it on the cushion next to him and opened out the letter.

*Dearest Sarah,*

*By now you will have opened the gift box and I can just picture your face. I don't have to ask you if you like the brooch. I remember how much you admired it that day in my cold little cottage by the sea, way back in 1939. My goodness, that was such a long, long time ago. I had thought of giving it to Evelyn, but somehow it didn't feel right and she's got lots of my other things. It just felt fitting somehow that you should be its new owner. I hope you will wear it now and then?*

*So, as you know, I'm not much cop with the emotion bit face to face so here is what I need to say:*

*Without you I would never have become a Stitch – you were my inspiration and mentor. And that day in that 1979 Bristol park when you told me about the holes in time, threads of humanity and answered all*

*my questions, you really opened up my mind, made me
take stock of what was important to life ... to our very
existence. As you probably guessed, for all my bluster, I
was a bit of a wuss underneath, but from that day on, I
changed irrevocably.*

*I have been privileged to know you, Sarah, both as
a woman and a formidable Stitch, so thank you, thank
you so much.*

John noted that the paper was still damp at the end of
that sentence and he could see why. The old trout really
knew how to tug at the heart strings.

*Talking of stitching, I hope you will reconsider. It
would be a great loss to the world and I think your
future happiness if you never went on a mission
again. Without giving too much insider information
away, I feel that Lucy might need your support and
encouragement if she ever does decide to go for it. I
think she could be as good as me ... and nearly as good
as you in time – no pun intended! Perhaps that's the
reason our families are linked – we have lots more lives
to save in the future. Your two babies, as you know, will
become a Needle and Stitch, and eventually, one day,
you will become the matriarch and Chief Stitch of the
whole clan! I am sure that would appeal to your Super
Stitch mentality. ☺*

*Anyway, my dear, I'm signing off now. We won't meet
again, but my spirit will live on through Corbin and
Lucy's children. I am ready to go to my Edward now –
have been ready for a while actually. LOL. Hey, get me
using slang stuff. I'm down with the kids!*
*Much love,*

*Veronica xxx*

Sarah bounced back in before John had time to clear his thoughts. 'Isn't it beautiful?' She ran her fingers over the brooch.

'It is, and the letter, too.'

'It really is, and I'm so grateful to her for helping me to make a decision about stitching.'

John felt his heart sink. 'I thought you had already made it. You aren't going to.'

'Yes, but I could tell by the look that passed between you and your dad the other week that you didn't believe me.'

John hadn't at first, but as he'd reflected the other day on the drive to Southampton, he was really pleased about it. Now though, a nice 'normal' family life was teetering on the edge of a brooch and a letter, soon to topple into an abyss of 'madness and mayhem forthcoming' by the looks of it.

'Yeah, but do we really want all that worry and stuff that goes with time trips, now we have the babies coming?' John stretched his hand out and pulled her onto his knee.

'I won't do it for a good few years after the twins, sweetheart, and then only now and again. But Veronica's words have made me realise how much I would miss it if I packed it in forever.'

Before John could respond the phone rang and Sarah rushed off to answer it. A few minutes later she came back, another big smile on her face. 'Right you, open your present from me and then jump in the shower. That was Lucy to wish us Merry Christmas, and I asked her and Corbin to pop over at about eleven for a sherry.'

John groaned and rubbed his hands vigorously over his face. Something he tended to do when he was frustrated. Sarah always commented that he looked like a hamster shoving nuts into its cheeks. 'Bloody hell, Sarah. We didn't agree to tell Lucy. Let's just keep out of it. Just because Ratchet wants her to go into the business doesn't mean that—'

Sarah kneeled in front of him on the carpet. 'Look, I promise I won't try and convince her of anything – won't even mention her stitching in the future.' Sarah licked her little finger and crossed her heart. 'I just think we should persuade Corbin to tell her. Trust me, he will be so pleased that he doesn't have to hide it any more and she will be delighted that he's not up to any shenanigans.'

'But if Corbin wanted to tell her he would have already, wouldn't he?'

Sarah pulled a face and ruffled his hair. 'No, silly. He's worried that she would go crazy, perhaps even leave him if he did. Veronica mentioned that Lucy always wanted a down to earth life after her unorthodox upbringing. Normality, you know?'

'Oh, yes, I know,' John muttered.

'So, we're agreed, yes?'

'You're agreed. I am keeping well out of it.' He watched Sarah's face fall, and felt a bit like the bad guy, but this had to be said. 'Seems to me that you want to be the centre of attention, Sarah. Veronica had you covered with the Chief Stitch thing.'

To his surprise, Sarah nodded. 'And she borrowed your Super Stitch term, too, yes I know. I hold my hands up to it, I guess. But I truly believe that Lucy needs to hear the truth and I would love you to be behind me on this.'

John lifted his hands high in despair. Seems his sense of foreboding was justified the other day. Veronica had certainly chucked a few spanners in the works. 'Okay, you win. But that's exactly where I am going to be … very much behind you. If this blows up in your face then you have only yourself to blame.'

The conch brooch looked just perfect twinkling on the green velvet top Sarah had matched with the black leggings she'd bought when she'd been out with Ella. Turning sideways she smoothed the top down over her bump and felt a surge of happiness – it had definitely grown since yesterday. It was all going to be fine. Christmas was here at last and it had snowed. John loved his present – a hot air balloon ride – and she loved the spa day gift from him too. Gwen was cooking up a master feast and John had agreed, albeit it reluctantly, to her plan. He would come round when it all went swimmingly.

Sarah put a little dab of perfume, a present from Gwen, on her wrist. She was convinced that it all *would* go swimmingly. She could feel it in her gut and her gut was rarely wrong.

Lucy and Corbin brought the breath of winter in on their coats and as she closed the door behind them the scent of holly from the wreath hanging on it made Sarah wrap her arms around herself with contentment. This was so exciting. John had agreed to give her a moment to discuss the situation with Corbin while he asked Lucy to help with a few canapés and sherry.

Corbin settled by the fire and gave her his signature stubbled dimpler. 'So, Sarah, how are you this fine Christmas?'

'I am very well and so it seems is your grandmother.' Sarah grinned back.

He cracked out laughing and then put his finger to his lips and pointed to the closed kitchen door. 'Mustn't let Lucy hear. So glad you went to see her. I was supposed to tell you when I was here the other day, of course, but thought the shock might be too much for you.' He nodded at her bump and ran his fingers through his raven-black hair. 'I tried to hint with talking about your "job" and "saving" the Christmas card – you know, like stitching saves lives?'

'Oh, yes.' Sarah giggled. 'I did think it was an odd choice of word.'

'And then I just stared at you while I wondered how to pass on my grandmamma's message in a non-shocking manner. You must have thought I was a, "how you say", loopy-cracker.'

*Oh, how cute. Ella will just swoon when I tell her.* 'We say crackers, or loopy, Corbin, but not generally both. I do like loopy-cracker, mind you.'

Corbin smiled. 'I see, yes. And then Lucy walked in and I couldn't think how to tell you, apart from leaving the newspaper … a little to chance, nevertheless. But chance smiled on you, no?'

'No.' Sarah nodded, then laughed. 'I mean, yes. We had a lovely time catching up, Veronica and I. Though I must say I found the whole story of you and needling hard to take. Didn't Lucy ever wonder about your surname?'

'Non. She has some French but not enough to realise that my name meant needle. Though she's getting more fluent now, having lived in France for a while, so eventually she might think it is a little odd – us sharing the same surname in English and French.'

'To be pedantic, our name is Needler, not Needle, but we are splitting hairs here.'

'Hares? You mean rabbit creatures? How cruel and what have they to do with it?'

Sarah could hear that Lucy and John were about ready to bring out the drinks so hissed, 'Never mind that now. Veronica and I think that Lucy could be a great Stitch if she was given some encouragement.'

Corbin raised his eyebrows and then shook his head slowly … no.

Sarah chose to ignore it and ploughed on. 'But in order for that to happen, I think it would be a good idea if you tell her that you are a Needle, Veronica's link and everything.'

'Absolutely not,' Corbin growled, an angry blush darkening his handsome features. 'Can you imagine the shock of it? She would feel humiliated realising that I had known all along about her family through the powers, but had decided not to tell her. She wouldn't understand. And that might be the beginning of the end for us. Do you have any idea how much I love her, how much I want to protect her from any unhappiness?' Corbin's pale-blue eyes flashed almost navy with anger.

Oh dear. This reaction had not been drawn upon Sarah's perfect storyboard strip of the day. John had warned her, but had she listened, had she? Oh, no, just steamrollered in as per usual, imagining she knew best for the whole family. Well, perhaps she did, but she had to admit that she had a good few years ahead of her in matriarch school before she could just take it for granted. Corbin had looked away into the fire, his fingers drumming on the arm of his chair.

Damn it. What to do now? After a few moments looking anxiously from Corbin to the kitchen door and listening to the laughter coming from behind it, her heart said, just tell all the truth and nothing but. Deep down the main reason she wanted to tell Lucy wasn't for any glory or family leadership, it really *was* just to make the woman happy. And if Lucy didn't want to join 'the business' it didn't really matter. Sarah calculated that her next words could change things for the better, and she didn't see another way through if she was honest.

'Listen, Corbin. If in the end you decide to keep things as they are, then I will of course respect that, but please, just listen for a moment?'

He turned from the fire and sighed. 'I'm listening.'

Sarah told him everything Lucy had said when she'd confided in her about her worries the other day. 'So, you see, it would be best for everyone if she knew. You wouldn't have to hide what you were up to and slink off any more and Lucy would feel supported by us all, whether or not she chose to stitch in the future.'

Corbin stood and threw his hands up. 'But I would never have an affair! How could she even think it?'

'What would *you* think if it was the other way around?' Sarah levelled a calm stare into his confused face.

Corbin sat down again and cupped his face in his hands. 'I just don't know ... this whole story. Grandmamma, me, you ... it is too fantastic for anyone to believe.'

'Lucy isn't anyone, is she? She's grown up with it. She's the daughter of a Needle and Stitch – her brother's a Needle, too.'

'Hmm.' He looked at her, his face clouded by worry. 'I guess the real problem is that she'll leave me. After all, I have deceived her from the beginning. I couldn't bear that.'

'I would bet the farm on her not leaving you if you tell her. But I think she might if you keep up all this cloak and dagger stuff, though. Lucy has already jumped to the wrong conclusion and will continue to jump, I reckon.'

'I didn't know that you had a farm ... and I don't have a cloak or dagger.'

'You look serious, sweetheart,' Lucy said, coming in from the kitchen with a tray of canapés.

Sarah released the tension and her amusement at Corbin's misunderstanding by allowing a torrent of hysterical giggles to escape. After she got her breath back she said, 'No, it was something I said that he took literally. Now I want a miniscule sherry. Anyone care to join me?'

# Chapter Twenty-Eight

In her best French accent Sarah whispered in John's ear, 'I was right, no?' She handed him a glass of wine, slipped her arm around his waist and leaned her head on his shoulder as he looked out from the patio windows at Lucy and Corbin. The two of them looked so much in love walking arm and arm round Gwen's garden later that afternoon.

'Aye, but remember it was touch and go before he agreed to tell her, madam. So don't get reyt cocky wi me,' John whispered back in an exaggerated Yorkshire one.

Sarah giggled and prodded his belly.

'Ow, watch out for me turkey and stuffing. I'm liable to explode.'

'Christmas pud time in a bit. You need to save the explosion for later.' Sarah groaned. The Christmas dinner had been outstanding, one of her mum's best, but the thought of pudding was one morsel too far. Thankfully the morsel of earth shattering importance had been duly passed on by Corbin to Lucy before they had arrived at Gwen's. Corbin had taken her for a drive around and told her as they were driving. He had figured that was safest as Lucy wouldn't be able to strangle him or storm off.

Sarah hadn't managed to talk to Lucy about it yet, but as they walked into her mum's, a little late, she had smiled at Sarah and mouthed 'thank you'.

The guess was that Harry had been told though, as not long after lunch, Sarah noticed him chatting in a corner to Lucy and then him walk over and clasp Corbin to his chest in a bear hug. Then the two men had left the room deep in whispered conversation. Lucy had looked as if she was going to come over and talk to Sarah after that, but she was collared by Ella. Now though, as the happy couple walked in though the patio doors, Lucy grabbed Sarah's arm. 'I want a word with you, young lady,' she muttered and manhandled her into one of the bedrooms.

Once ensconced in Gwen's en suite Lucy sat on the bath edge, face deadpan and pointed to the toilet. 'Take a pew.'

Sarah did as she was told, not entirely convinced any longer that Lucy was thankful of her interference. Perhaps she had been just putting on a show for Corbin to make him think she was happy with what she'd learned. Perhaps now Sarah was for the high jump. 'Are you okay with Corbin—'

'I ask the questions here,' Lucy snapped, her eyes narrowing.

Sarah gulped and looked at the floor. Damn it. Looked like she was in big poop. Then she felt a gentle thump on her shoulder.

'Your face!' Lucy chortled. 'So easy to wind up. Just like your daft husband.'

With her spirits rising in competition with her colour, Sarah laughed. 'You had me there! So you *are* happy with it?'

Lucy tossed her chocolate curls, her eyes bright as two precious emeralds. 'Hmm, I can't say that I am in love with the revelations. It would have been preferable for Corbin to have explained his absences by telling me he had an unhealthy obsession with night-fishing, photography or something. Anything apart from he's a bloody Needle.'

Sarah nodded sympathetically and patted Lucy's hand.

'But I am *so* relieved he's not cheating on me that the rest is bearable.' She gave Sarah a huge smile. 'And I am so thankful that you pushed him into it.'

'Phew, that's a relief. I agonised about getting him to tell you, but I was sure that it would put you out of your misery. Well, partly, you still have to put up with a family of "time folk" to quote Corbin's grandmamma.'

'What a character! I warmed to her immediately when I met her on her birthday.'

'She is, and so lovely too. I didn't use to think so though.' Sarah gave Lucy a potted history of her travels with Veronica.

'What do you make of the weird link between her, you and us? It blew my mind, I can tell you.' Lucy leaned her elbows on her knees and cupped her chin in her hands.

'I have no firm theory, but Veronica thought that our families were linked because we all had more lives to save and ...' Sarah hesitated. She had to make sure she didn't blurt out about her being Veronica's mentor and so the logical support for Lucy in the future etc. 'And we could all rely on each other to help each other out ... be in the know and so forth.'

'Hmm, I think there's more to it than that, but we shall see. Time will tell, pardon the pun.' Lucy crossed her arms and studied Sarah's face carefully, obviously searching for any telltale sign of more information under the surface.

Sarah deliberately kept her expression unreadable. Lucy had clearly learned to look carefully out of habit when talking to her big brother. A chuckle bubbled in her throat when Sarah realised she herself was employing John's ENF.

'Right, then. We'd better go back to the festivities. Did you tell your dad about it all?'

'Yep, and he will have told your mum by now. He was well chuffed that his son-in-law is a Needler. In fact, everyone here seems to be but me.'

'The people here in the know, you mean,' Sarah said, leading the way out of the room.

'Ah, yes. The only people who don't know about our bloody weirdo lives are Ella, Jason and Angelica. Is that right?' Lucy asked.

Sarah nodded.

'Lucky beggars. How nice to be oblivious of the whole madcap situation.'

'Yes. And John is a bit fed up of it all at the moment, well

273

fed up of me doing it, that is. I think he would like me to settle down and just have a normal family life.'

Lucy put her hand on Sarah's arm just before she went back into the living room. 'But I thought you *had* decided to do just that after everything you have been through recently?'

Sarah stopped and thought for a moment. 'Yes ... but Veronica made me reconsider. Her love and enthusiasm for "the business" reminded me of why I agreed to do it all in the first place. It's a bit like teaching, I guess. The rewards outweigh the misery.' She patted Lucy's hand and opened the door and gave a sudden laugh. 'Well, most of the time.'

Still under the quilt at past noon, Sarah nuzzled John's shoulder and whispered. 'Time to move your bones, baby. We can't spend all of New Year's Day in bed, can we?'

'Don't see why not. A man needs his rest after his body has been used so wantonly all morning.'

Sarah laughed and slapped his bum. 'Didn't hear you complaining.'

A grunt and a yawn was all she received in return, so she got up and allowed the shower to waken her resolve to go downstairs and do something about lunch.

Wrapped in a towel ten minutes later she went back to the bedroom to find her clothes and found instead, John, just replacing the phone on the handset. Unaware of her return, he sat on the bed, grim faced and pushed his hands through his hair.

*Oh God, what the hell had happened?* A twist in her gut prevented speech and then he saw her in the mirror.

'Oh, Sarah ... that was Corbin phoning from France. Here come and sit by me.' He patted the bed.

Sarah couldn't move. Had something happened to Lucy? She put her hand against the wall to steady herself. 'Just tell me, John.'

274

He swallowed and took a deep breath. 'It's Veronica, love. She passed away this morning at eleven o'clock.'

A wave of relief tinged with a brushstroke of sadness rushed through her. 'Thank God, I thought it was Lucy!' She went over and sat by him.

John's look of surprise was only surpassed by his babble of confusion. 'Oh, yeah, right – no, it isn't her, thank goodness. But I thought you would be devastated about Veronica.'

Sarah was silent for a few moments while she remembered her old friend, then she took his face in her hands and kissed him tenderly. 'I am saddened, yes, of course, but I kind of expected it. So really, I suppose I am happy for her. She's gone to be with her Edward and we will raise a glass of champagne or perhaps in my condition a Bucks Fizz to celebrate her life later.   I am so glad I saw her before she went.'

'I'm glad you did too.' John took one of her hands and kissed it. 'I wasn't at first because you came away wanting to stitch again, and as you know I wanted a "normalish" life. A bit like you wanted before you deigned to make your commitment to me last year,' he said with a chuckle.

'Er, it was hardly that straightforward, mate,' Sarah growled. 'There were one or two spokes that the Spindlies decided to hurl into my wheels.'

'Yeah, and I have decided that without ever stitching again you wouldn't be the Sarah I have come to know and like a bit.'

'You like me? Oh, I am so flattered.' Sarah put the back of her hand to her forehead and pretended to swoon.

'You are my wife and reason for life, dear heart.'

'Aw, how lovely.' She stood and went to find her clothes noting that John had slid back under the covers, a soppy smile on his face. Perhaps now was a good a time as any to spring her idea on him.

'John?' she said, zipping up her jeans, something which she wouldn't be able to do much longer.

'Yup?'

'You know we haven't talked much about names for the twins and when we have we can't agree?'

'Ye-s.'

'What do you think about these? I thought Esmé Veronica and Harry John.' Sarah held her breath as she watched him silently chew them over.

'Harry John for a girl, that's not working for me.'

Sarah stuck out her tongue.

'Seriously, I couldn't have picked better if I had pondered for weeks, and Dad will be thrilled.' He grinned.

'Yay! That's sorted then. Okay get showered, dressed and by then I will have lunch on the table.'

*Cold spicy chicken, garlic bread, salad and pickles ... now what's missing?* Sarah surveyed the table. *Ah yes.* Sarah rushed off to find the mayonnaise and bumped into John in the doorway.

'Steady on, anyone would think you were hungry.' He laughed.

'I *am* starving. You would hardly credit it after all the stuff we've gobbled this Christmas, especially after Mum's gigantic and too delicious dinner.'

'Yes and talking of her we have a lovely wedding to look forward to this year. In fact,' he rubbed her tummy. 'We have one or two exciting things to look forward to this year.'

'We do indeed.' Sarah nodded, side-stepped him and grabbed the mayonnaise from the fridge. 'It is going to be a great year.' She stuffed a bit of garlic bread in her mouth and sat down at the table.

'The best.' John smiled and then reached for something behind his back. 'Okay, give me a kiss, woman, and then lets demolish this lot.' He held a battered piece of mistletoe over his head and leaned forward across the table.

Sarah felt a little tickle of mischief leap up and caper around her tummy. She adopted a Harry pose – hands behind her back chin pulled to her chest and mimicked, 'Why would you want to kiss someone who refuses to give you a normal family life with roses around the door and so forth?'

John laughed and pulled her towards him. 'Normal is overrated and roses are a bugger to keep clear of greenfly.' He tossed away the mistletoe and placed his lips on hers.

As Sarah melted into him she made a wish that they would remain as happy in the future as they were in that very moment. A tall order when life had this really annoying habit of tripping you up, especially with the crazy life that they had. But she decided that with the bestest, cutest, sexiest, unselfish, and supportive husband in the whole wide world by her side, they just might manage to achieve it.

# *About the Author*

Amanda James was born in Sheffield and now lives in
Cornwall with her husband and two cats. In her spare
time, she enjoys gardening, singing and spending lots
of time with her grandchildren. She also admits to
spending far too much time chatting on Twitter and
Facebook! Amanda recently left her teaching role (teaching
history to sixth form pupils) to follow her ambition to
live her life doing what she most enjoys – writing.

Amanda is a published author of short stories and her first
novel with Choc Lit, *A Stitch in Time* was chosen as a *Top
Pick* in *RT Book Reviews* magazine in the US in July 2013.

Follow Amanda:
Blog – www.mandykjameswrites.blogspot.co.uk
Facebook – www.facebook.com/mandy.james.33
Twitter – @akjames61

# More Choc Lit

### From Amanda James

## A Stitch in Time

### Book 1 in the Time Traveller series

**A stitch in time saves nine … or does it?**

Sarah Yates is a thirty-something history teacher, divorced, disillusioned and desperate to have more excitement in her life. Making all her dreams come true seems about as likely as climbing Everest in stilettos.

Then one evening the doorbell rings and the handsome and mysterious John Needler brings more excitement than Sarah could ever have imagined. John wants Sarah to go back in time …

Sarah is whisked from the Sheffield Blitz to the suffragette movement in London to the Old American West, trying to make sure people find their happy endings. The only question is, will she ever be able to find hers?

*Prequel to Cross Stitch*

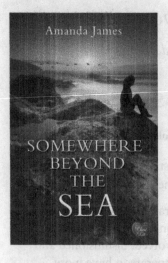

# Somewhere Beyond the Sea

**When love begins with a lie, where will it end?**

Doctor Tristan Ainsworth has returned with his family to the idyllic Cornish village close to where he grew up. The past has taught him some hard lessons, but he'll do anything to make his wife happy – so what's making her so withdrawn?

Karen Ainsworth daren't reveal her true feelings, but knows her husband has put up with her moods for too long. A chance to use her extraordinary singing voice may set her free, so why shouldn't she take it? Surely her past can't hurt her now?

As a tide of blackmail and betrayal is unleashed to threaten the foundations of their marriage, Karen and Tristan face a difficult question. Is their love strong enough to face the truth when the truth might cost them everything?

Visit www.choc-lit.com for more details including the first two chapters and reviews, or simply scan barcode using your mobile phone QR reader.

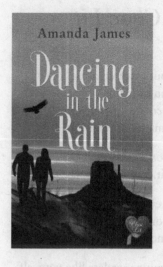

# Dancing in the Rain

**What if the responsibility for preventing a major disaster lay with you?**

Jacob Weston has felt like he doesn't belong for as long as he can remember and the strangely vivid dreams he experiences only serve to make him feel more alone ...

But when his job in research science takes him thousands of miles away from what he thought of as home, Jacob finds the mystery of his past begin to unravel. A trip to the breathtaking Monument Valley and an extraordinary encounter with a Navajo guide seem to hold the key to who Jacob really is.

After meeting the beautiful Rosenya Neboyia, Jacob feels he may have found what he'd been searching for. But with this meeting is the discovery that his dreams come with a responsibility, and that responsibility is bigger and scarier than he could have ever imagined ...

Visit www.choc-lit.com for more details, or simply scan barcode using your mobile phone QR reader.

# Introducing Choc Lit

We're an independent publisher creating
a delicious selection of fiction.
*Where heroes are like chocolate – irresistible!*
Quality stories with a romance at the heart.

*See our selection here:*
www.choc-lit.com

We'd love to hear how you enjoyed *Cross Stitch*.
Please leave a review where you purchased the novel
or visit: **www.choc-lit.com** and give your feedback.

Choc Lit novels are selected by genuine readers like yourself.
We only publish stories our Choc Lit Tasting Panel want to
see in print. Our reviews and awards speak for themselves.

**Could you be a Star Selector and join our Tasting Panel?**
Would you like to play a role in choosing which novels we
decide to publish? Do you enjoy reading romance novels?
Then you could be perfect for our Choc Lit Tasting Panel.

*Visit here for more details...*
www.choc-lit.com/join-the-choc-lit-tasting-panel

*Keep in touch:*
Sign up for our monthly newsletter Choc Lit Spread for
all the latest news and offers: www.spread.choc-lit.com.
Follow us on Twitter: @ChocLituk and Facebook: Choc Lit.

Or simply scan barcode using your mobile phone QR reader:

*Choc Lit
Spread*

*Twitter*

*Facebook*